The Island of Always

Stephen Evans

Book Layout ©2017 BookDesignTemplates.com

Cover design by Tanja Prokop of BookDesignTemplates.com

The Island of Always/ Stephen Evans —1st ed.

ISBN 978-0-9915759-7-8

The Marriage of True Minds

"He laughed to free his mind from his mind's bondage."
—James Joyce

Alteration

Minneapolis Star-Tribune

June 11

Local barrister Nicholas Ward was arrested yesterday for releasing more than 100 live lobsters into the indoor pool at the mayor's mansion in Minneapolis.

Mr. Ward, formerly a prominent environmental attorney and founding partner of the local firm Ward and Grant, allegedly persuaded 12 Minneapolis grocery stores to donate the lobsters by claiming that the crustaceans were the rightful property of endangered Hawaiian monk seals. The seals, Mr. Ward reportedly explained, are currently on the endangered species list because humans are stealing their lobsters.

At Mr. Ward's request, Department of Public Works employees filled the mayor's pool with non-chlorinated saltwater and more than 100 blocks of ice. Unnamed sources at the department confirmed that Mr. Ward convinced them the mayor was having a beach party. The ice, he claimed, represented the effects of global warming on arctic populations.

Once the lobsters were safely deposited in the mayor's pool, Mr. Ward summoned the media. During the ensuing lecture, he defended his actions by citing at length numerous obscure judicial precedents. He then made his getaway in a chauffeured stretch limousine, accompanied by a gray-and-white sheepdog puppet.

No charges have been filed, pending a psychiatric evaluation.

Impediments

Lena stepped alone onto an elevator in the Wells Fargo Building in downtown Minneapolis. For forty-four floors, visions of ambulances, fire departments, and SWAT teams danced in her head. She had been out of town for three days. That was more than enough time for disaster to strike again.

On the forty-fifth floor, Lena rushed out of the elevator and sped down the corridor. At the end of the hallway, she stopped and performed her ritual invocation, running her fingers across the raised letters of the sign:

> *Ward and Grant*
> *Attorneys at Law*

She dashed past the reception area and fled into her private office without speaking to her assistant, Sharon. Wise to the evasive tactic, Sharon quickly followed her in.

The office furniture was a cool mixture of glass and steel, with several small exceptions: on the shelves behind the desk, stuffed animals roamed a law-book jungle. Most were elephants, ranging from just a few inches in height to nearly a foot.

Lena moved behind her desk and sat, gripping the cool edge with both hands, steadying herself for the news.

"Welcome back," Sharon began.

"Just tell me," Lena replied.

"How was the conference?"

"Just tell me."

"I'm glad to see you too."

The desktop surface was one of a kind: antique Veronese crystal, six feet long, three feet wide, and one inch thick. Clear glass pillars six inches in diameter supported each corner. At sunset on high-summer evenings, the light swept through the floor-to-ceiling windows at just the right angle, refracting in the crystal edge, spectral shards blossoming across the office walls and ceiling.

Lena never kept anything on the desk.

"Just tell me."

Sharon consulted her notes for dramatic effect, violet eyes highlighted in the reflection from the desk.

"You got calls from a chauffeur, twelve grocery stores, CNN, and the mayor."

Lena paused for a moment, evaluating the news, correlating the results. At least it wasn't an ambulance or the fire department or the SWAT team. She marshaled her energy, closed her eyes, then exhaled her mantra: *WhyMe.*

"Anything business-related?"

"Harrison Cross and the Luria gang confirmed for one o'clock."

"Good. Call the grocery stores and give them my credit-card number. Get me the mayor now."

As Sharon left the room, Lena pulled a worn notebook from the credenza behind her and flipped back in search of a blank page. To a stranger, the scribbled notes would have communicated only haste and emotional duress. Not even Sharon could decipher them. But the doodles in the margins comprised a hieroglyphic record of post-marital dissolution:

Page 1: A heart with an arrow through it.

Page 10: A heart with two arrows through it.

Page 50: No heart. Lots of arrows.

Page 100: A hairy, dog-like creature.

Page 150: *AAAAAAAAHHHHHHH!!!!!!!!!!!!*

She had turned a few more pages and found a blank one, but had not yet begun to write, when the phone rang. She swung around in her chair, stared at the device on the credenza. Again and again the noise tingled in her brain like a sweet electrocution. Finally it stopped.

Sharon poked her head into the office.

"The mayor's office is on line one."

Lena donned the wireless headset like a tiara of thorns, then punched a button.

"Lena Grant for the mayor. Yes, I'll hold."

Lena could not imagine a sequence of events that connected a chauffeur, twelve grocery stores, a cable news network, and the mayor. But she knew who could.

"Hello, Mayor, it's Lena, I'm surprised to—"

Lena stopped. Her eyes widened, then narrowed.

"Where did he get that much salt? Oh. Yes, I suppose it does look bad when road salt intended for public safety ends up in the swimming pool of an elected official. I promise I will talk to him. Thank you, Mayor. I'll see you at the fund-raiser next week."

Lena had to find Nick.

She could try his cell phone. But either he didn't remember to carry it or he didn't remember how to retrieve messages or he did remember but wouldn't. Or maybe it was just her messages he ignored.

Lena paced in front of her office windows. If she looked straight down, the height still made her uneasy. If she looked out over the city, her eyes were inevitably drawn to the southwestern part of Minneapolis, where Lake of the Isles lay hidden behind neighborhood hills. The lake also made her uneasy. The area had become Nick's favorite haunt. When she had to find him, it was always her first stop.

If Nick wasn't at the lake, holding vigil with the squirrels or marshaling the geese or communing with the Norway pines or whatever it was he did there, she could try his condo about two blocks away. She had bought the place for him after the divorce, hoping he would enjoy having a home near the lake. She had liked the feel of the place, the streaky light morning and afternoon, the old whitewashed stucco walls and the burnished wooden floor. It seemed healthy, and that was what he needed, she thought. But the neighbors informed her that he mostly used the apartment for storage. What he had to store she didn't want to know.

If he wasn't at the condo, then the bank on Lake Street would be her next stop. Nick ventured into the branch at unpredictable intervals, withdrawing large amounts of cash that apparently lasted him for months.

She had opened the account after the divorce, when she had borrowed enough to buy out Nick's share of the law firm. Nick had more or less absconded from life during that period, so Lena and Nick's sister, Grace, a real estate broker who lived in Phoenix, were also listed on the account, just in case. Lena visited the bank every once in a while to educate a new branch manager about Nick. When she had last checked, there had still been a quarter of a million dollars in the account.

Sharon interrupted the planning for Lena's expedition.

"You have a call."

"I'm not here," Lena pleaded. "Unless it's an ambulance. Or the fire department. Or the SWAT team."

Sharon paused to get it right.

"It's your ex-sister-in-law."

Lena retrieved the headset, walked back to her desk, flipped open the well-doodled notebook.

"Hi, Grace. We're meeting with—what?"

As she listened, Lena once more silently reenacted her personal psychodrama:

AAAAAAAAHHHHHHH!!!!!!!!!!!!!

"Where is he?"

She wrote: "GVPI 9021" and sighed

"Okay. I've got it. I'll be in touch."

Lena once again ripped off the headset and sent it flying into space. Then she donned her sunglasses, snared her briefcase (hefting it to make sure it possessed the proper density), and strode briskly into the office corridor. Sharon was playing a noisy game on her computer.

"You know, this Luria game is fun."

For a few seconds, Lena was caught up watching the game. A knight in rusty armor struggled alone across a treacherous moat while battling demon slime rats with a glowing lance to reach a haunted castle where a legendary treasure was concealed.

It all seemed vaguely familiar.

"I'm going to hell," Lena announced.

Sharon didn't lift her head from the screen.

"I'll forward your messages."

*   *   *

Lena's Carmon Red Porsche convertible flared into the parking lot of the Golden Valley Psychiatric Institute, halting just before impaling the "Visitors Only" sign. She thrust the car door too wide, grabbed her briefcase, and hugged it to her breast like an umpire's chest guard.

She closed her eyes and took two long breaths.

When she opened them again, her focus drifted up to the top floor of the nine-story white building, then down the long row of barred windows.

Lena marched up the daisy-lined path and through the revolving glass doors. She entered the reception area in fullback mode, swinging her aluminum briefcase when necessary like a mirrored wrecking ball. The receptionist greeted her with "Please sign" but didn't quite get the "in" out before Lena was in the elevator.

*   *   *

On the ninth floor, an attendant sat reading a comic book, his orange-sneakered feet contrasting with the tiny white desk on which they rested. As Lena approached, he jammed the book into the pocket of his white lab coat and stood, apparently aiming for cool but willing to settle for official. Lena guessed he'd been on the job only a few weeks.

She stared expectantly at the attendant. Under her implacable yet marginally amused gaze, he fiddled with his bright orange Tweety Bird tie, reminding her of a beagle bravely wagging its tail at the veterinarian. After deciding that nothing was likely to happen in the near future without some form of communication, Lena gave in.

"Nicholas Ward."

"Oscar," replied Oscar.

Lena had a daily threshold of vexation beyond which any additional exasperation began to seem funny. In the face of enormous irritation, she would sometimes begin to giggle uncontrollably. She had already passed the vexation threshold but was successfully suppressing the nervous response, which made her face turn brittle and her eyes squint slightly. Oscar began to puddle under her stare. Lena came to his rescue.

"I'm here to see Nick Ward. He's in room 9021."

"And you are?" Oscar asked.

"Busier than you."

"That's a broad category."

Lena's smile burst through but was quickly withdrawn.

"Follow me," Oscar said, more question than command.

He unlocked the double steel doors, and she followed him through and down a long white corridor in which only the numbers differentiated one room from another.

"Why is everything white?" Lena asked.

"Don't know. Maybe it shows the clean better," Oscar replied.

"I think people would prefer some color."

"This place has been here for a hundred years. Maybe back then they didn't think of patients as people."

Lena glanced at the comic book hanging out of his pocket. The cover was torn in half, and the staples holding the pages together were gone.

"I didn't mean to interrupt your reading," she said.

Oscar reached down and drew out the rumpled book.

"Doctor Strange has just entered the mystical dimension and is battling his archnemesis Baron Mordo with the All-Seeing Eye of Agamotto."

"That one looks like someone slept on it," Lena noted.

"A comic book in mint condition is an offense against the multiverse. I only collect damaged comics with torn covers and missing pages."

"Me too," Lena replied.

Oscar gently turned a few pages.

"There's no telling what you can learn from comics."

"No telling," Lena agreed.

Oscar halted at a door at the end of the corridor and raised up on tiptoe to look in the window. Then he unlocked the door, braced his weight on the handles, and, lifting his feet, rode the door open.

Quickly filling the open passage, Lena scanned the tiny enclosure. The room was small and rectangular. A neatly made single bed lined the wall to the left. A tiny dull-white table and upright wooden chair stood against the right wall, leaving a small space in front of the barred shatterproof window. There was no mirror, no decoration, no place for personal items.

At first Lena didn't see the puppet sitting on the bed, braced upright by a pillow, almost invisible on the bland bed coverings. When she had first seen him years before, twenty-four inches of soft fake fur had gleamed white amid patches of gray. Now he reminded her of a disheveled furry Buddha, his gray coat matted, wisps of ash-colored hair spilling over his forehead. Well, it happened to everyone else, she thought, why not him?

Finally she looked at Nick. As usual, she had the odd sensation that she was seeing him for the first time, as if she had never met him before. He was always taller than she remembered. And thinner, she thought. He always looked thinner. Of course the straitjacket he was wearing emphasized his lanky frame, rough cloth tapering from broad shoulders to slim waist, reminding her of a human cyclone, as though at any minute he might sweep the room into chaos. She noted the effect, wondering how she could re-create it in her own wardrobe.

Nick wheeled his entire taut body around in baby steps.

"Quick! Hide!" he warned the reclining moppet.

Lena was not amused.

"Take it off," Lena ordered. Oscar jumped.

"Excuse me?"

"The jacket," she said. "Take it off."

Oscar started to peel off his lab coat. Lena, patience not quite working into a smile, explained: "Not yours. His."

Oscar glanced at Nick and assumed a worried expression. Lena guessed that removing straitjackets was beyond his charter.

"Restraints are hospital policy with new patients who are potentially violent," Oscar contended.

Lena swung her briefcase in a blurry arc into the steel door. An ominous thud reverberated down the white-tiled hall.

"The question is not," Lena informed Oscar without taking her eyes from Nick, "whether *he* is going to hurt *me*."

Oscar walked quickly over to Nick and removed the straitjacket. Then he took off his own coat just in case.

Nick tilted his head, a look no one but Lena could decode. She flashed her dark lashes in mock Morse code response.

"You want me to stay just in case?" Oscar asked with concern.

"That won't be necessary," Lena assured him.

"Actually, I was talking to him."

Lena turned to Oscar with renewed appreciation, which he appeared to interpret (correctly) as a mild threat.

"I'll leave now," Oscar added quickly.

Lena smiled her approval. Oscar mouthed the word *Sorry* to Nick as he closed the door.

Lena laid her briefcase on the small table and sat on the bed. She waited without speaking.

Lena always waited for Nick to speak first. It was her only way of knowing which Nick she would be dealing with. She had come to think of his pantheon of moods as different people, in the tactical rather than psychosocial sense. She had in her mind isolated twelve different Nicks, all undeniably Nickish though she could never quite determine what core element linked them all together. Like a shattered mirror that retained in the shards the final image before the catastrophe, bits and pieces of Nick flashed out but the whole was chaos.

"Well," said Nick finally, "look what the sharks dragged in."

She sighed internally with relief, hoping she recognized ironic, slightly acrimonious ex-husband Nick. She could at least talk with him, maybe even convince him of the trouble he was in.

"I told you I'd always be there for you," Lena responded.

"Yeah, but then you threw me out."

"I meant I'd be there for you as long as you weren't there for me."

Nick rubbed his arms and wrists to restore the circulation.

"What are you doing here?" he asked.

"Your sister called me."

"Grace from Grace."

"I'm defending you."

Nick picked up the puppet and held him close.

"And me without my belt and shoelaces," he lamented.

"Want mine?"

"Always the humanitarian. Say hi to Sancho," Nick said, holding the puppet out to her.

"Hello, Sancho," Lena said with more genuine sweetness than she intended. "We need to get him cleaned up. He's gotten a little dingy."

"Manufacturer's instructions: Clean with a mild soap and damp cloth. Do not dry clean—the fumes make him sneeze. Do not microwave—he is not zucchini. Do not blow dry—he looks like he just stuck his head out of a speeding car."

Lena readjusted the atmosphere by opening her briefcase and shielding herself with papers.

"Nick, you do understand how serious this is?"

"You're just after my money."

"I have money."

"Can you lend me some?"

Lena stepped back.

"Why do I do this?" she asked Sancho.

"I'm magnetic," Nick explained. "Exotic. Quixotic!"

Lena stuffed the papers back in her briefcase.

"And what do those words have in common?"

Nick pondered, then ventured: "-ic?"

"Exactly."

Lena knocked loudly on the door.

"Let me out," she pleaded.

"Practice makes perfect," Nick explained to Sancho.

Lena swung around. Nick ducked.

"Why did you dump lobsters in the mayor's pool?" she asked, curiosity overcoming her urge to flee.

"Two reasons," Nick replied, morphing into the persona Lena had nicknamed the Thin Man, the detective elucidating the modus operandi in the final reel. The persona had often been an advantage in a law partner, but was a disadvantage in a husband, and extremely frustrating in an ex.

"No politician will condemn animals to death on national television."

"National television?"

"Lobsters in the mayor's pool make for exceptional video. I have CNN on speed dial."

"Why lobsters?" Lena asked.

"They were depressed. The blank antennae. The listless mandibles. The lack of interest in everyday scuttling."

Lena sighed.

"Do you want to see the secret sign of the International Brotherhood of Crustaceans?" he asked.

Without waiting for an answer, he placed his fist to his forehead, extended his index and middle fingers, and wiggled them.

Lena ran a hand through her Porsche-blown hair.

"What is the mayor supposed to do with a hundred lobsters?" she asked, certain she did not want to know the answer, or at least not Nick's answer.

"One hundred and forty-four," Nick corrected. "I have it all taken care of. I donated two hundred and fifty thousand dollars to the Marine Education Center at the Minnesota Zoo to fund a lobster exhibit. The mayor will reap loads of publicity at the opening. We just need to send lots of ice in the meantime."

Lena's eyes flared. That was all of the money he had. All of which she had borrowed to pay him. All of which she had struggled to finally pay off only a few months before.

"Nick! Are you nuts?"

"Hmmm. Let's examine the evidence," he said, picking up the straitjacket.

"No. I mean. You can't afford that! What are you going to do? This is a very bad plan."

Nick looked at her and smiled.

"I don't make plans. I have visions."

Lena paused, struggling to catch up.

"Why ice?"

"Lobsters prefer a water temperature of forty to forty-five degrees Fahrenheit."

"But."

"If only you had seen the facets of relief, even hope, reflected in their grateful eyestalks."

Lena shook her head.

"Nick. How do you expect to live?"

He paused. She hated when he paused because it gave her time to hope. Then he started singing.

"E come vivo? Vivo!"

Lena growled inwardly. His familiar mélange of mysterious amusement and ironic compassion always forced her into momentary doubt, no matter how certain she was that she was right. Yet she smiled in spite of herself that he remembered her favorite opera.

"Tu sol comandi, amor," she replied.

Oscar swung open the door.

"It's good to see you again," Nick whispered as Lena brushed by him. A breathtaking plummet into heartsickness stopped her, turned her slowly back to him.

"It's good to see you too, Nick. But you have to understand. I can't do this anymore."

Nick glanced past her at Oscar.

"Actually, I was talking to him."

*   *   *

Lena and Oscar walked in silence down the hospital corridor, until Oscar finally asked: "So what's the deal with him?"

"What do you mean?"

"Is he dangerous?"

"Are you planning to marry him?"

"No."

"Then you're safe."

They began to walk again, the only sound Lena's heels tip-clacking down the spotted white linoleum that had been all the rage in asylum corridors fifty years earlier.

"Who is his doctor?" Lena asked.

"Richardson. Second floor. Good guy."

"Thanks."

"So what's wrong with him?"

Lena paused, replaying as she did each night the years of turbulence to see if the possibility of a conclusion could be found. Finally she dangled a set of keys before Oscar's eyes.

"You figure that out, you can have my Porsche."

"Deal," Oscar agreed.

∗   ∗   ∗

The congenial comfort of the second floor contrasted with the forced courtesy of the first and the blank efficiency of the ninth. Lena wandered down the unpretentious hallway for a few moments before locating the office of Dr. Henry Richardson. She knocked on the door and entered.

A heavyset man of medium height sat, eyes closed, behind an uncluttered desk. Music was playing. Piano. Chopin. A nocturne.

"Dr. Richardson?"

"Yes?" replied the man, not moving or even opening his eyes. His hands were lightly clasped, as if he were meditating or praying or making a pronouncement from the bench.

"My name is Lena Grant. I'm an attorney representing Nicholas Ward. He is being held here."

The doctor opened his eyes and focused on her for the first time.

"Mr. Ward has been admitted," the doctor corrected her. "I spoke to his sister yesterday."

Lena glanced around at the furnishings. Something was missing, something she expected to see but didn't. She couldn't put her finger on what it might be.

"Grace called me."

"Please sit down," said the doctor, indicating two chairs in front of his desk. Lena sat in one of them. The doctor came around the desk and sat in the other.

"He was brought in last night," the doctor continued. "Someone at the precinct knew him—"

"He's an attorney also," Lena stated. "I mean he was."

"We administered one hundred milligrams of Thorazine, which kept him sedated most of the night."

"Thorazine?"

"An antipsychotic drug. We administer Thorazine to inhibit delusions or hallucinations. Right now he seems relatively functional, so we are giving him lithium for mood stabilization."

"He wouldn't hurt anyone," she stated.

"He may not intend to hurt anyone," the doctor corrected her.

Lena sat back and took a moment to absorb the information.

"Have you known him long?" the doctor asked.

"He was one of my professors in law school. And we were partners in a law firm."

"I see."

"And we were married."

The doctor looked up, moved back around to the other side of the desk, and began taking notes.

"How long ago was the divorce?"

"Almost two years ago."

"Any kids?"

"No. We. No."

"May I ask why you got divorced?"

"Why? I mean, why are you asking why?"

"Don't worry. I don't date lawyers," the doctor assured her.

"You're smart."

"Yes, I am. Is there any family history of mental illness?"

"He drove me crazy. Does that count?"

The doctor smiled. Lena shook her head.

"No," she continued. "Not that I know of. I mean. No. Doctor, are you telling me that there's something seriously wrong with him?"

Dr. Richardson got up, walked back around the desk, and sat again in the chair next to Lena.

"Do you mind?" he asked, pulling out a cigar. Lena shook her head. "It's against the law and hospital rules. But sometimes ..."

She nodded, but his need for it made her nervous. He clipped one end of the cigar, lit the other, inhaled, and blew the smoke away from her. Then he extinguished it and chewed the smoldering cylinder.

"You know what a delusion is?" he asked.

"I told you I was married," Lena replied.

The doctor's smile flashed again, then faded quickly.

"From a psychiatric perspective, a delusion is a false belief that the patient maintains in spite of substantial contrary evidence. While it's too soon yet for a definitive diagnosis, I believe Mr. Ward has what we would call delusional disorder."

"Is that serious?"

"It can be. The neural activity, or brain function, in these cases is extraordinary. The French philosopher René Descartes once said: 'I think, therefore I am.' In a sense, your ex-husband thinks too much, so he isn't who he is."

Lena felt her heart beat rapidly as the fears that had grown slowly over the last few years coalesced inside her.

"Can it be treated?"

"Treatment can be effective in some cases. A combination of medication and therapy."

"You don't sound too encouraging"

The doctor relit the cigar, took another puff, and then put it out again.

"As I said, it's too soon. But there are unusual symptoms in your husband's case. The puppet, for instance. It's not uncommon for delusional patients to see an inanimate object as human, though this anthropomorphic behavior can take many forms.

"In most cases, when you challenge a delusion, the patient will be insistent, even to the point of violence. The unusual aspect of Mr. Ward's illness is that when you challenge his delusions, he readily acknowledges that they are fantasy. Yet out in the world, he behaves as though they were real. That's a conundrum."

Lena made a professional effort to smile. The result was brittle and unconvincing.

"Did the divorce cause this?" she asked.

The doctor's expression smoothed over.

"No. The biochemical and genetic mechanisms of the disorder would already have been in place. Most likely the illness would have manifested in time regardless. Did the stress of the divorce affect the progress of the disorder? Possibly. The resulting disruption could have precipitated the initial episode. But that does not mean that you were at fault."

"Doctor, I'm a lawyer. My business is identifying who's at fault. I know where the blame goes."

Dr. Richardson saluted her.

"I'm going to start sending my patients to you."

Lena sat up straight.

"There are no books here," she stated.

The doctor smiled.

"No books," he agreed.

"I expected books. Shelves and shelves of books. Is there a reason that you don't have books?"

"Yes," he said, adding nothing more.

"Okay. Well. I'm glad there's a reason."

The doctor leaned back in his chair.

"It must be nice to be in a job where you win once in a while," he said. "The best I ever seem to do is tie."

"The only victory in life is being a good loser," Lena replied.

"Who said that?"

"Somebody dead."

*　　*　　*

Preston Winter's desk always reminded Lena of a Bavarian castle. Case files stacked around the perimeter formed uneven battlements. A coffee-stain moat spread across the faded gray rug, evidence of sieges past. Lena entered the office without knocking and sat by the northwest turret.

"I hate paperwork," Preston said.

"Then you picked the right job," Lena responded. "Assistant state's attorneys never do paperwork."

Preston emitted a quasi-amused blurt.

"You're early," he said. "I thought we were meeting at the gym."

"I have a problem."

Preston peered at her.

"You divorced him."

"This is serious."

Preston leaned forward.

"Is he dead?" he asked.

"Don't."

"Sorry. Injured?"

Lena folded her arms, at the same time defending and enhancing her breasts, a masterwork of effective communication she had perfected in junior high.

"He's in Golden Valley," she continued.

"Psychiatric Institute," Preston completed. "And the problem is—what?"

Lena leaned in, slipped off his glasses, and held his eyes with hers.

"I need a favor."

Preston jumped up, almost tumbling Lena into the northeast spire, and gathered a stack of papers.

"I have a meeting."

Lena beat him to the door.

"It's Nick," she pleaded.

"Exactly," he answered harshly. "It's Nick. Stay out of it."

Preston brushed past her.

"I told him," Lena announced.

Preston froze in the doorway but didn't turn back.

"What did you tell him?"

"I told him," Lena said slowly, pulling him back to her, "that this is the last time. After this he's out of my life for good."

Preston sighed.

"I'll do what I can," he said.

"See you at the gym," she said. "Dinner afterward?"

"What are friends for?"

✳   ✳   ✳

Sharon was standing outside the conference room doorway, holding a folder.

"Harrison Cross and his entourage are inside," she said.

Lena's eyes brightened. Eager to confront an adversary on whom she could profitably focus her frustration, she accepted the folder, constructed a smile, and strolled confidently into the room.

The decor in the conference room was casual but professional. Even the toy giraffe that poked its head through the silk tree in the corner wore thick horn-rimmed glasses.

Lena sat on the near side of the table. Across from her, a team of four attorneys conferred with quiet confidence. Sharon took her usual seat beside Lena.

Lena carefully laid the folder down on the conference table, then covered it with her hand. From across the polished mahogany divide, eight suspicious eyes peered down at the folder as the smug atmosphere cracked just a bit.

"I apologize for the delay," Lena began pleasantly.

"Ms. Grant, we have a flight to catch."

"Certainly, Mr. Cross. This won't take long," Lena reassured him.

Lena mentally reviewed Sharon's research on the man who sat across from her. Harrison Cross had been lead internal counsel for Luria Corporation since its formation in the early '80s. He had guided the transformation of the company into a colossus of entertainment software, pocketing not only a substantial corporate salary but also millions in stock options.

Luria's new video game, Parzival II, scheduled for a holiday release, had received record advance orders. Cross seemed quite sure that neither he nor Luria had anything to fear from a boutique firm like Ward and Grant.

"The Luria Corporation illegally appropriated software designed by my client. All we are asking for is fair compensation."

Cross leered back at Lena.

"Ms. Grant, let me stop you there. I understand that this is not your standard practice area, so let me assure you that our settlement offer of fifty thousand dollars is more than generous, considering. Surely your client could use that money for her college education."

Cross leaned back in his chair. His three cronies followed suit. Lena sensed their confidence: they were going to be able to buy their way out of this cheaply. Even if Luria had appropriated the code illegally, they reckoned the court proceedings would bankrupt the tiny opposition firm long before a final verdict was rendered.

Cross explained: "Even if you win in court, I remind you that the appeals process alone could take ten years. Is your client prepared to wait that long? Are you?"

Lena didn't answer. She stood up hesitantly and moved to the corner. She knew that Cross would presume she did so to hide the defeat in her eyes.

Lena petted the giraffe, then straightened the eyeglasses that had fallen down over its elongated snout. Facing out the window, she said: "You are correct. This is not an area in which I often practice. I agreed to meet with you because the client is my ex-husband's niece. So this a family matter. Of sorts. And my client can wait as long as necessary. But as for me ..."

Lena turned and smiled again. As she moved gracefully back to the conference table, something crystallized in her eyes. She leaned across the table and added in her most pleasant voice: "I hate waiting. Sharon?"

Sharon thrust the folder toward Cross, who stared at it but didn't move to touch it, as though he knew the folder was legal toxic waste.

"This is a motion for a temporary injunction preventing your company from selling any electronic gaming software in the United States. I plan to file this injunction in federal court today."

Cross stared hard at the folder, then responded dismissively: "You can't win."

"I don't have to win," she said with a shrug. "I just have to file."

Cross did not respond. Lena positioned her hand palm down over the folder.

"Once this motion is filed, the market will conclude that your software might not be on the shelves at Christmas. Your stock price will fall to its knees like a two-dollar whore," she continued. "And I will make sure you get fucked."

On the opposite side of the conference table, babble erupted from four alarmed faces.

Lena sat down next to Sharon.

"After the emergency stockholders' meeting, I predict that the new board of directors will settle generously with my client and terminate each of you for gross incompetence."

For a moment, there was no sound, though Lena imagined the flutter of evaporating stock options. Then Cross said: "That's stock manipulation."

"I'm just defending the innocent."

"Is this supposed to intimidate me?"

"Now, you could sue," Lena reminded him. "However, the appeals process alone could take ten years."

Lena set her watch on the table. Eight anxious eyes followed the leisurely yet jubilant progression of the second hand:

One.

Two.

Three.

Four.

Five.

Six.

Seven.

Eight.

Nine.

Lena observed the lawyers pass Three in anger, Five in denial, Seven in bargaining, and Nine in a fusion of acceptance and financial exhaustion. Lena released them.

"Are you prepared to wait that long?" she added with concern.

Cross hid behind his legal pad.

"What do you want?" he blurted out finally.

"Two point five million plus future royalties."

He winced.

"We'll have to talk to our board of directors."

"Talk fast," Lena said.

The Luria cohorts filed out of the room, arguing with one another while texting discrete messages to their brokers. Sharon closed the door behind them and turned to Lena.

"I've never heard you use that kind of language before."

"It's a matter of fairness," Lena replied. "We have a responsibility to communicate in a way they will understand."

Sharon nodded.

"You know, it was sort of a mixed metaphor."

"Well, it's not my standard practice area."

Lena offered the mysterious folder to Sharon.

"What's really in this?" Sharon asked.

Lena balanced the folder carefully in her hand.

"My guess is two million plus."

Sharon accepted the precious repository.

"Is this my bonus?"

Lena's smile didn't fade until she was midway into her office, when she saw the waiting stack of messages. The elephants saluted her with upraised trunks.

*   *   *

Lena lay on her back with her legs splayed wide. The fact that she was doing this in public was slightly embarrassing, abnormally irritating, and numbingly familiar.

She stared at the gym ceiling, forcing the weights up over and over while pondering Greek mythology. The names Sisyphus and Tantalus hovered in her sweat-induced haze. She couldn't remember which was which. And this annoyed her.

One of them was always thirsty, bound in a lake from which he couldn't drink. The other was always weary, condemned to push a boulder up a mountain forever; when he got almost to the top, it would roll down again. It occurred to her that if the one on the mountain freed the one in the lake, they could roll the boulder up together, then go down and get a drink.

Men, she thought. Never knew when to ask for help.

Lena closed her eyes and listened to the noises around her. Grunting, groaning, sighing, and puffing merged into a purgatory of uneasy flesh. And then she saw that it was not just in this room, but all through the city, the country, the world, every activity performed day in day out was just a variant of lying on your back with your legs spread wide, mindlessly pumping up and down. Then the ultimate solution flashed into her mind: Juice.

My blood sugar must be low, she thought.

Suddenly Preston Winter's face loomed over her.

"Hello, Pressssston," she grunted as she pressed the bar as high as she could.

Preston grunted in response, which made her laugh and almost lose control of the bar. He was standing at her head, looking down at her, which her visual orientation converted into hanging from the ceiling.

"Get down from there," she said crossly.

"The mayor?"

She had never looked at his face upside down before. Somehow the hemispheric perfection that anointed his football-hero looks in the everyday world was not sustained when that world was topsy-turvy. His eyebrows were crooked. Or was that because he was frowning?

"Preston?"

"The mayor!"

Lena reached up and centered his face over hers. It was bad enough that he was hanging from the ceiling, but did he have to be a bobblehead too?

"It's my case now. I hope you're happy," he said.

Lena grabbed his hand.

"Drop the charges. We'll agree to counseling and community service."

"He's nuts," Preston muttered. Lena wriggled out from under the bar and sat up.

"I can't let him go to jail."

Preston moved in front of her and sat on the bench, edging her thighs outward, his back to her. Lena slid her arms around him, easily encircling his chest, and sighed.

Preston covered her sweaty arms with his and inhaled deeply, pressing his polyester-plated back into the spandex-delimited cushion of her chest, interrupting her sigh with his own.

"Counseling and community service. And he stays on medication. The arraignment is tomorrow."

She kissed his neck.

"Thank you. I'll tell him tonight."

She rested her head against his shoulder.

"This is a nightmare," she said.

Preston twisted around.

"He is a nightmare. You need to wake up."

*　　*　　*

Lena and Oscar stood outside the door to Nick's hospital room, rapt in a silence that hovered just this side of distress. Inside the room, Nick was marching around the tiny space with Sancho on his arm.

Down and back.

Over the bed.

Up the chair.

Across the table.

It was better than a treadmill, Lena decided.

Given the specific choreography of leaps and gyrations, Lena guessed that they were parading to Nick's favorite: *The Liberty Bell March* by John Philip Sousa. He knew by heart each piccolo trill and trumpet flourish. Actual music was superfluous, apparently, since the only sound in the room was the patter of Nick's bare feet.

Oscar moved close to Lena.

"They're good."

"Practice makes perfect," Lena sighed.

Oscar opened the door. Nick crashed down on the bed as if playing fantasy musical chairs.

"At ease, soldier," Lena said as she stepped warily through the opening.

"Your husband is a very lucky man," Nick announced proudly.

"I don't have a husband."

"Then he's a very lucky man," Oscar muttered.

Lena turned to Oscar, able to summon irritation but not anger.

"I heard that," she said.

Nick looked around her, smiling at Oscar.

"She did, too," Nick confirmed. "Don't ask me how."

Oscar shoved his hands in the pockets of his white coat.

"I meant that he's a very lucky man ever to have had the remarkable good fortune of ..."

"Leave now," Lena said.

"While you can," Nick added.

Lena waited until the door closed and then walked to the window. It was late, only a few cars left in the parking lot. Her car was visible from the window. She wondered if Nick had seen her arrive, whether the marching was for her benefit.

She had seen him march before. Once, after a few glasses of champagne, she had even marched with him. It had been exhilarating. "Okay, here's the deal," she announced.

"How is Preston?" he asked.

"Preston is fine. The deal is they drop the charges without prejudice, which means—"

"I know what it means."

"Which means, if you violate the terms of the agreement, they can reinstate the charges. In return, in addition to general good behavior, you agree to medication, counseling—"

"Who do they want me to counsel?"

"And community service."

"Who do they want me to service?"

Lena glared.

Nick shrugged. "And if I refuse?"

"Then they'll order a psychiatric evaluation."

Sancho shuddered.

"They'll have a hearing."

A bigger shudder.

"And then they'll make a determination as to whether you are committed to a psychiatric ward or go to prison."

Sancho hid his head in Nick's shoulder.

"Can I think about it?" Nick asked. Lena ignored the request.

"The arraignment is tomorrow. No puppets."

Sancho looked around at her.

"He prefers 'Imaginary American,'" Nick explained.

Lena nodded apologetically and turned to leave. Then she felt a furry nudge on her shoulder. She turned back and found Sancho close enough to tickle her nose. Sancho's face moved aside to reveal Nick's unusually somber and genuine expression, like a souvenir of a lost adventure.

"We just wanted to say thanks," he said.

Her heart flashed. Lena had tamed her sadness, given it a home, taught it tricks (roll over, fetch, play dead), and made sure it would never run away. But occasionally it bounced up and surprised her.

"Amazing," she commented after a few seconds of intense interpretive effort convinced her that he was sincere. "You learned a new word."

As she reached for the door, Oscar swept it open from the outside.

"Everybody's learning," she said. "See you in court."

She did not look back.

*   *   *

Lena walked confidently into the hearing room. Her arrangement with Preston was approved. The paperwork was in perfect order. Nothing can go wrong, she thought—but nevertheless something would. She didn't know what, but she knew why.

The courtroom was small, with the judge's chambers directly behind the large wooden panel flanking the bench. To the right was the jury box (which was empty), to the left was the room where defendants were held before trial. About five feet in front of the bench were two long tables, one for the defense and one for the prosecution. A short wooden railing divided the court from the small gallery.

Nick was already sitting at the defendant's table playing tic-tac-toe with Sancho. His restraints had been removed. Oscar was in the first row of the gallery, draped over the railing, alternately observing the game and reading an Iron Man comic book that might once have been the insole of someone's shoe.

Lena laid her briefcase on the table and stood looking down at the game.

"I said no puppets," Lena reminded Nick.

"Puppets? Where?" Nick asked as he and Sancho scanned the room.

Oscar leaned forward.

"Good luck in court today," he said.

"You should say, 'Break a leg,'" Nick replied.

"That's for the theater."

"Wherever I go, it's always theater."

Lena growled.

"People always tell me I look like Brad Pitt," Oscar said.

Both Nick and Lena swiveled to look at him.

"It's the eyes," Oscar explained.

Preston Winter entered the courtroom and took his place at the prosecutor's table. Nick and Sancho regarded him closely. Preston returned the dual stare for a few seconds, then shook his head at the pair. Sancho hid behind Lena, occasionally peeking around to see if Preston was watching, then ducking quickly out of sight.

Lena, still standing, faced Nick, laid her hand lightly on his shoulder, then dug her fingernails into his back as hard as she could.

"Cut it. Out," she commanded under a smile.

She sat down next to Nick at the table, spreading out her documents, noting peripherally that Nick was wearing his cherished dark-blue suit with the nearly invisible pinstripe that complemented the dark scarlet of her outfit. Suddenly and unexpectedly, she was engulfed by successive tidal waves of déjà vu and nostalgia and panic.

When they had decided to work together, Lena had not known what to expect, or how the dual aspect of their partnership would work. What she had not anticipated was the sense of transcendence, of gaining a context. She had learned to treasure that. And to mourn its loss.

Sitting next to Nick again alarmed Lena. She had not been in a courtroom with him since their last trial together as partners. He had neither contested nor acknowledged the divorce, except to sign the papers.

Lena ransacked her litigation case for an extra copy of the plea agreement and handed it to Nick.

"You might want to glance at this," she said and noticed that the document was trembling in her hand.

Nick smiled and settled down.

"Sure," he said and began to peruse the agreement.

The bailiff stood.

"All rise."

The judge walked briskly in and sat.

"Sit sit sit," she said.

Lena had never met Judge Anne Ritchfield, though they had attended some of the same political functions. Ritchfield was a rarity, a judge who had never practiced law. She had started as a psychiatric social worker, gotten her Ph.D. in clinical psychology at Emory University, and then attended law school at the University of St. Thomas while working as a child advocate. She had been appointed to a seat on the family court for Hennepin County, then elected to a seat on the Fourth Judicial District court for the State of Minnesota. She knew Preston well. Nick was unknown to her.

The judge scanned the courtroom quickly and gestured for the bailiff to approach.

"There is a stuffed animal on the defendant's table."

"Yes, Your Honor. I tried to take him away, but Mr. Ward claimed he's a material witness."

"And you just left it at that?"

"Yes, Your Honor."

The judge leaned over the bench and whispered: "What's the pool up to?"

The bailiff stuttered: "Uh. I. Twenty bucks."

"What was your guess?"

"That you'd confiscate it in under a minute."

"You lose. Call the case."

The bailiff paid the court reporter twenty dollars and declared: "State versus Nicholas Ward."

To which Nick replied, holding up the puppet: "Et al."

The judge ignored Nick. Lena glared at him, then stood.

"Elena Grant for the defense, Your Honor."

"Preston Winter for the state," Preston said, also standing.

Nick stood as well.

"Your Honor," he said, "if it please the court, we cite *Tahoe-Sierra Preservation Council, Inc., et al. v. Tahoe Regional Planning Agency et al.,* in which the court held that a regulation temporarily denying an owner all use of her property might not constitute a taking if the denial is part of the state's authority to enact safety regulations."

"What are you doing?" Lena interrupted.

"We have a responsibility to communicate in a way they will understand," Nick explained.

"Would you just let me do my job?"

Nick sat back down.

"Thank you, Mr. Ward," said the judge, "for that cogent yet completely irrelevant piece of information. I understand there is an agreement here," she continued, shuffling through documents.

"Yes, Your Honor," Preston and Lena said together, then smiled at each other.

The judge picked up the plea document and read for a few seconds.

"This agreement specifies one hundred sixty hours of community service."

"That is correct, Your Honor," Preston agreed.

"Plus mandatory counseling."

"That's also correct."

The judge flipped a page and threw Lena a quizzical glance.

"You're his ex-wife?"

"Yes, Your Honor."

"And his ex-law partner?"

"Yes."

Nick stood.

"Your Honor, the defense is willing to stipulate that counsel is ex-rated."

"Nick, sit down and shut up!" Lena ordered.

Nick sat.

"Counselor, what is going on?" the judge said.

"I'm representing the defendant. Today. Only," Lena explained. "Today only."

"Sounds like a sale at K-Mart," Nick whispered to Sancho, and then Nick stood again.

"Your Honor," he said, "may I have a minute to confer with counsel?"

"Does the state object?" the judge asked.

"Yes, but go ahead," Preston said in a sulk.

"Make it fast, Mr. Ward."

Nick turned to Lena and got down on one knee.

"I imagine that I will love you for as long as we both shall live."

"Don't even think—" was all Lena got out before Nick stood, bent her back over the table, and kissed her, the rest trapped behind clenched lips as shock, panic, memory, and hormones fused with oxygen depletion.

"Thank you, Your Honor. No more questions," Nick announced, releasing Lena and sitting down just in time to avoid her flailing elbow.

The judge hefted the gavel as though contemplating whether to use it or toss it.

"Ms. Grant," she ordered in her sternest voice, "please control the defendant."

"Your Honor," said Lena, "that's not a case, it's a career."

Nick stood again.

"Your Honor, for the record, I'd just like to point out that technically I am not the defendant, since I have not yet been arraigned on the charges."

"Thank you, Mr. Ward," said the judge. "And I would like to point out that technically I am the one who decides whether you will be a defendant."

Nick considered.

"Your point is better than mine."

He sat down again. Lena muttered to him:

"What are you—"

Again Nick stood.

"However, since I am still an officer of the court, I feel it's my responsibility to point out that there is no provision in this agreement for supervision."

Lena and Preston exchanged expressions of chagrin. Nick was right. The judge glared at Preston.

"Is that correct, Mr. Winter?"

"No, Your Honor. I mean, yes, Your Honor, that is correct."

"Is the state ready to accept responsibility for the unsupervised actions of this def—of the accused?"

Preston glanced at Lena as if to say: "You owe me."

"Yes, Your Honor."

The judge nodded, then shook her head.

"Well, this is an election year, and you are braver than I am. Is there a responsible party who can take charge of the accused and oversee the counseling and community service?"

Preston and Lena both spoke at once: "Your Honor."

Then Preston continued: "I really don't think supervision will be necessary in this case."

"Well, I do. Is there a responsible party or not?"

"Your Honor, the defendant is—"

Lena glared at Nick, searching frantically for options that would keep him out of a psych ward or a jail.

Then she saw it.

She had seen it so often before. Yet the moment of recognition still captivated her.

Events simplified.

Intentions clarified.

And out of the frantic chaotic mystery, the hidden objective was achieved.

In the courtroom, she had seen it time and again. Always it was magical when Nick's rambling antics stood revealed—too late to act but not too late to appreciate—as reality unfolded at his command, the World According to Nick. All that was left to her, to anyone, was to play the destined part.

Lena stood and announced: "I'll do it."

"No fucking way!" Preston shouted.

"Counselor!" the judge admonished.

Lena looked back at Preston, shrugging while asking for sympathy she knew she would not get.

"Your Honor, there isn't anyone else," she explained. "No local relatives. No human friends."

She turned back to Nick.

"I'm all he has."

His innocent eyes infuriated her.

"And he knows it."

The judge turned her attention to Lena.

"Ms. Grant, are you sure you know what you're doing?"

"Yes, Your Honor. But I'm going to do it anyway."

The judge nodded.

"Very well," she said. "He's all yours. Amend the order and I'll sign it. Next case."

Lena ran to Preston, trying to explain. Nick, impassive, watched them argue on the other side of the courtroom. Oscar walked up behind Nick and picked up the puppet.

"Speaking of breaking a leg, I think she's going to break yours."

Preston cut off his conversation with Lena and stomped over to Nick.

"If you even breathe on her improperly, I will make it my life's mission to put you away permanently."

Lena flashed up to him. The words snapped out with chilling precision: "Wait. Till. I. Get. You. Home."

She whirled away and marched out of the courtroom.

Hand in hand with Sancho, Nick followed her through the polished swinging doors.

Time's Fool

She graduated from Princeton with a B.A. in developmental neurolinguistics. Her undergraduate thesis examined the effect of the Dick and Jane series of children's readers on the ventromedial prefrontal cortex. In the summer after graduation, she rigorously researched potential life strategies:

- ✓ Who she should be?
- ✓ What she should do?
- ✓ When she should begin?
- ✓ Where she should live?
- ✓ How she should start?

In the process, she identified five cities in which she might want to reside and continue her education:

- ✓ Boston
- ✓ Seattle
- ✓ San Francisco
- ✓ Chicago
- ✓ Washington

Accordingly, she set forth on a mission. After spending several days in each city, she compiled a dossier, rating each according to the following factors:

- ✓ Professional

✓ Educational

✓ Cultural

✓ Historical

✓ Social

Eventually she settled on Minneapolis, though it wasn't on the original list and she had never been there. But she had a feeling about it, which was intensified by the fact that she hadn't liked one thing or another about each of the other cities she had actually visited. And the fifty-mile-long Grand Rounds bike path around the city was a definite plus. Biking was one of her lifelong passions.

Several areas of graduate study intrigued her, but after lengthy and prudent consideration, she decided to study law. After researching well-known Minnesota law firms, she discovered that they hired extensively from the University of Minnesota. So, though it was very late in the summer, she applied to the law school. She was amazed when they contacted her almost immediately and told her she had been accepted for the fall term. She soon moved to a little apartment off University Avenue and began life in the Middle North.

In her first year of law school, she learned that she enjoyed studying The Law (she always thought of it that way, as if it were a mystical entity or an embodiment of elemental forces). She had imagined that The Law would be cold and arithmetic in precision. Instead she found in it a reflection of human life both as it was, and as it could be, lived.

In her second year, she discovered that she might enjoy being a lawyer. The practice of The Law as she envisioned it required strategy supported by organization, argument supported by information, art supported by compensation. Both the challenge and the complexity appealed to her.

In her third year, she enrolled in a class in environmental law because she had heard that the instructor was funny. She was mildly curious how anyone could make such a subject amusing, and slightly annoyed that anyone would try.

The instructor was an adjunct professor who taught the course at night while maintaining a solo practice during the day. He was rumored to have a legendary memory for environmental jurisprudence, able to cite word-for-word case law on both the federal and state levels.

When he first breezed into the lecture room, she puzzled casually over his looks, the lanky frame in the impeccable blue suit contrasting with the unkempt hair and muddy hiking boots. How could so many disparate components be combined in such an attractive way? she wondered.

As the term progressed, she was surprised to find that the instructor began to interest her more and more. She was well aware of the dynamic of teacher and student, had occasionally indulged in it, and found that the interest usually disappeared quickly after the indulgence. She had also known other brilliant, accomplished, and attractive men. They tended to see the world as a reflection of themselves and expected the women in their lives to be the perfect mirror. This was not a role she enjoyed.

Most of all, it was the instructor's combination of passion and humor that fascinated her. After class, he would sit in the front row of the lecture hall, usually just a few empty seats away, and talk genially about whatever legal conundrum intrigued him at the time. He inevitably started by joking about his little solo firm and his lack of interest in the business of law.

But his intellectual conviction would eventually overcome his ironic self-awareness, and his fervor for his latest cause would ignite his verbal energy. Then he would leap up on stage as if someone had pulled the strings on his marionette body, launching an argument astonishing in its complexity, insight, and elegance. It was unlike any practice of law she had imagined.

And he was unlike any man she had known. He never lectured from notes. Often she suspected that he was fabricating at least some of the tales he related in class. But she discovered that each story had some basis in reality, though often slanted to enhance the entertainment over the educational value. A lobster really did have ten thousand eyes and saw by reflection rather than refraction. The Hawaiian name of the endangered monk seal was Ilio holo I ka uaua, which really did mean "the dog that goes in rough water." And the Minnesota Department of Natural Resources did in fact sponsor a volunteer loon survey, though it was not, as he suggested, a survey of volunteer loons. Nor was the questionnaire he handed out to the class ever approved by the state.

Once he told the story of Henry David Thoreau and Mosquito Pie.

"On a journey to Minnesota in 1861," he said, "the famous author and naturalist Henry David Thoreau visited Minneapolis and cataloged many unknown species of Minnesota wildlife. Of these, the most famous by far was the St. Anthony mosquito, which, he reported in letters, was the size of a common wren.

"Early Minneapolitans hunted mosquitoes in the marshes, and mosquito pie had long been considered a local delicacy. Based on Thoreau's enthusiastic report, the pie was soon shipped worldwide, becoming as popular as beaver hats and buffalo robes in some European circles.

"In 1911 the city of Minneapolis finally dredged the marshes to encourage settlement in the area. Canals were built to allow boat passage among the lakes. And the series of parks now known as the Grand Round of Minneapolis took its modern shape.

"The loss of the wetlands, however, along with extensive overhunting to supply the relentless European demand, contributed to the extinction of the St. Anthony mosquito. And mosquito pie vanished forever from American frontier cuisine."

She was certain this time that she had detected a fabrication. But when she researched the story, she found that

Thoreau had in fact traveled to Minneapolis in 1861 in the hope that the dry plains air would cure his consumption. She could never confirm or deny the part about mosquito pie, though she had seen (and felt) large enough mosquitoes in Minnesota to lend some credence to the possibility.

To deal with the unpredictable array of his lecture topics, she established an intricate and precise organizational scheme for her notes. Each subject area was tabbed with a particular color. Animal rights was red. Air quality was blue. Water quality was green. Wildlife regulation was yellow. Miscellaneous was purple.

During class, she found herself leafing back and forth among colors as his lecture topics ranged from the mating habits of the endangered Queen Alexandra Birdwing butterfly to the effect of automobile emissions on sunsets. As the semester progressed, the lecture topics began to rotate in errant patterns that sent her flipping through her notebook pages in an unremitting determination to categorize.

One day toward the end of the term, as she was frantically juggling colors to track the bizarre minutiae of his legal scholarship, she flipped too hard and her notebook spun noisily across the lecture room floor.

Everything stopped.

She looked up.

Everyone was watching her.

She turned to him to apologize and saw the enormous grin he was incapable of hiding. Suddenly the maddening vectors of lecture topics throughout the term fell into place for her. He had done it for her. Or to her. She arched her brow and asked: "Professor. My notebook. Would you mind?"

After class, he asked her out for coffee. After coffee, he asked to take her home.

"You had this all planned," she said.

"I don't make plans," he answered. "I have Visions."

Those words slipped inside her like a key into a lock.

"What vision do you have for us?" she asked.

He closed his eyes, conjured the answer.

"For the rest of your life, you'll never doubt that no one could love you like I do."

She wrestled with the double negative.

"Is that a good thought or a bad thought?" she asked finally.

"Yes," he said. Then he kissed her.

Her eyes opened as the key turned.

*   *   *

He was better at Saturday afternoons than anyone she had ever known. A trip to the grocery store was an adventure. A matinee was a vacation. But staying home was paradise.

*   *   *

The purple-and-black graduation gown rustled in the wind outside Northrop Memorial Auditorium while the tassel dangling from the mortarboard cap swung annoyingly from side to side in front of her eyes.

"I look like a raisin with a flat head," she said.

"You do not," he said. "Raisins don't have heads."

She flipped the tassel to one side and smoothed out the ruffling folds.

"You are always such a comfort."

"I try," he said, rearranging the mortarboard.

"Don't. Leave. Not the hair."

He backed away.

"Thank you," she said, pulling out a mirror and checking the damage. "I have got to find a new brand of hairspray."

He took her hands.

"You look stunning," he said. "Don't worry. You've been through this before. And I promise not to whistle from the faculty seating area."

She glared.

"Don't even ..."

"I promised."

In the short time they had been together, she had come to learn that that word meant something to him. He seldom used it. And he never said it when he didn't mean it.

It was not exactly a guarantee, despite the best of his intentions, especially if it involved dry cleaning, a process he found both environmentally unsustainable and socially unnecessary. Though he made an exception for his signature blue suits. For someone with a prodigious, even legendary, memory for legal arcana, he had very little hold on the details of everyday life. She finally decided it had to do with his attention—not the span of it, but the extraordinary force of it.

A promise *not* to do something was more reliable, though, and he had promised not to embarrass her. She was fairly certain he would not whistle. But she would not have been surprised at a serenade.

"Be good," she said. "This is important to me. These are my future colleagues."

A look passed over his face, one she had seen once or twice before. She had thought about that look and deduced that somehow his imagination leapt over or into or through uncounted alternate futures and somehow coalesced into a vision. It was a vision he would not, possibly could not express.

But it was a future shared. She was sure of that. The thrill made her shiver. He wrapped his arms around her.

"I am so proud of you," he said.

She rested her head against his shoulder. She no longer cared whether anyone saw them together. For several months, at her request, they had carefully hidden the fact that they were seeing one another, were all but living together in his Warehouse District loft. But there was no longer any need or desire for privacy on her part. He had never cared.

"I'd better go in," she said, pushing away.

The graduation ceremony lasted an hour and forty-five minutes. The guest speaker was a former university law school graduate and current associate justice on the Minnesota Supreme Court who spoke eloquently on the responsibilities of the advocate in modern society and signed autographs after the ceremony.

Standing backstage afterward, she joked and shared congratulations with a few others among the graduating class, comparing notes on various professors and answering pointed questions about one in particular.

He rushed up to her, carrying a large package wrapped in brown paper.

"We have to go," he announced.

"What is it?" she asked.

He grabbed her hand.

"It's an emergency."

"What about the reception?" she asked, running along with him as quickly as she could in the long, encumbering gown. The cap fell somewhere behind her. "This is a rental. I have to pay for that."

"Here," he said, stopping suddenly and reaching for the zipper. "Get that thing off."

She slapped his hand away instinctively.

He laughed.

"What are you wearing under there?" he asked.

"Not enough," she answered. "I thought it might be hot in the auditorium."

"Good thinking," he answered, smiling. "Here. Put this on."

He handed her the package. The return address said Italy; she did not recognize the name of the town. She opened the wrapping paper carefully, not fully trusting his taste in graduation presents.

Inside the package was a suit, a dark burgundy silk with an almost invisible pinstripe that complemented the hue of his perpetually favorite costume.

"Try it on," he said.

She slipped into the ladies' room and changed. The fit was impossibly perfect. She had never seen such exquisite tailoring, certainly could never have afforded it herself. In the mirror, her long slender limbs and willowy frame, which she had often imagined gangly and ungraceful, now seemed dynamic, even daunting, as if she absorbed powers from the outfit itself. All she needed, she mused, was a cape.

He nodded as she emerged.

"Stunning."

"So where are you taking me?"

"Someplace you have wanted to go for years."

"Italy?"

"Better. Court."

Hand in hand, they left the building, descended two at a time the broad steps outside, and entered the waiting limo, his preferred method of transportation if he could not walk. She preferred the bicycle. Neither of them liked to drive. She had no idea how he could afford to travel by limousine, since his small practice never seemed to bring in any money that she was aware of. And neither his speaking fees nor his university salary were likely to add up to much.

As the limo pulled away, she turned to him.

"You have a court date today?"

"Yes," he answered. "The most important case I've ever had."

"You haven't mentioned it before."

"You've been busy with finals and graduation."

"So what am I doing here? You need an audience?"

He took her hand.

"I need your help."

She was puzzled.

"Since when do you need my help?"

The limo turned the corner onto Hennepin Avenue and sped past the lofty downtown buildings.

"I need you to be my co-counsel."

She was even more puzzled.

"I haven't passed the bar. I don't have a license. If anyone found out—"

"Would I let you risk everything? I just need it to look like my firm is more than a one-person shop."

She shook her head.

"It will be fine. I promise," he whispered.

"I have a bad feeling about this."

"Trust me."

The limo pulled up outside the county courtroom. She stepped out. The brilliant sunshine blinded her for a moment.

"So what is this case about?" she asked as they headed for the courtroom.

"Oh, don't worry about that. Just scowl at the other side once in a while."

"I'll pretend it's you."

He pushed through the double doors of the courtroom. She hesitated behind him, pausing a moment out of respect. In the few months they had been together, she had adopted his almost spiritual apprehension of The Law as a great imaginative human force for balance and justice. The Law as taught, The Law as intended—not the law as practiced.

The courtroom was small and almost empty. The judge was sitting behind the bench. Another man waited at a table on the left. A third man was already seated at the witness stand. Yet they were all connected, and beholden to, that greater numinous entity.

Despite her anxiety, she felt both exhilarated and confident. She knew that whatever happened in this room, she could handle it.

"You're late," the judge admonished them.

"Sorry, Your Honor. Our previous engagement ran long," he replied.

"I'd say this one was a little more important, wouldn't you?"

"Yes, Your Honor. We apologize."

"Great," she whispered as they passed through the vacant gallery and sat side by side at the empty table. "I have no license and we've already antagonized the judge."

He squeezed her hand.

"Don't worry so much."

He stood.

"Your Honor, I call my first witness."

He moved around behind her. His large right hand rested on her shoulder. Underneath the stiff fall of her hair, his thumb traced the line of her neck. He bent down to whisper in her ear.

"Watch this."

She twisted in her seat to glance up at him, then turned back quickly to watch.

He stepped out from behind the table.

She pulled over the folder on the table and began to examine the stack of papers inside for some clue as to what was going on. The papers were blank, except for row after row after row of little hearts with arrows through them.

She stood immediately.

"Your Honor," she said, "it's getting late in the day. I suggest we reconvene until tomorrow."

"It's one-thirty. We just finished lunch," the judge replied.

"Right. Sorry, Your Honor," she said.

The judge turned back to him.

"Continue."

He glanced at her, pleading silently for some clue.

"Your Honor," he said finally, "may I have a minute to confer with my co-counsel?"

"Make it fast," said the judge.

She stood quickly. He descended to one knee.

"I imagine that I will love you for as long as we both shall live."

"What are you—"

He brought her face down to his, kissing her. She thought she was pulling away but found after a few seconds that she wasn't.

"Thank you, Your Honor," he said finally. "I believe we are ready to continue."

He vaulted over the table, spilling the paper hearts all over the floor.

The judge gaveled furiously.

"Counselor!"

He turned to the judge, surprised.

"Yes, Your Honor?"

The judge glared and pointed his finger.

"I want to see counsel at the bench. Immediately!"

He stepped forward, along with the other attorney. Even the witness leaned in from the stand.

The judge aimed the gavel at her.

"That means you too, young lady."

She rose and approached, marshaling her courage. The judge glared.

"Where is your license?" the judge asked.

"Your Honor," she started, "I'm here simply as—"

"I have it!" he interrupted, removing a crumpled document from deep within the breast pocket of his suit. He unfolded and smoothed it before handing it to the judge too quickly for her to see. It looked official but she couldn't tell what it said.

The judge inspected the document carefully, then examined her over his wire-rimmed glasses.

"Very well. This seems to be in order," he grunted and then handed the paper to her.

She looked at it carefully, but could not process the information for a second, as if it were written in a language she could not translate.

It was not a license to practice law.

It was a marriage license.

Now the judge was smiling.

As was the other attorney.

And the witness.

In moving to the Midwest, she had secretly hoped she would encounter a cyclone. But she had never imagined one would take up permanent residence in her life.

She looked over at him, standing two feet away, not smiling but somehow embodying a smile. His eyes burned with that vision. And then she had a vision of her own, not of her life (though she sensed, had always sensed, that her life would be joyful but not happy) but of him, the true him, the him she could not possibly yet know but nevertheless for this one moment had access to.

And with that vision came a sign that the choice she must make had already been made, and that he knew it already, had known it, and that it was the same for him. The elemental forces had aligned. A word of resistance would alter their course. But no resistance was possible or even at that moment conceivable for either of them. He slipped a ring on her finger.

The judge began.

"Will you take this man to be your husband?"

And then she saw.

There was no bailiff.

No clerk.

No court reporter.

No gallery.

No trial.

Just a judge.

And two witnesses, not one.

She turned to him.

"In a courtroom?"

"Where else should two attorneys get married?"

He slipped a ring on her finger. The uncut ruby welled over the gold like blood. But the color matched her suit perfectly.

"I do," she said.

"Me too," he added.

*   *   *

The librarian glared at both of them as he descended to one knee. Her face sank out of sight behind a volume of the Minnesota Statutes Supplement.

"Please?" he begged.

"No," she whispered.

He shifted to the other knee.

"Please?"

"No. Be quiet."

Both knees.

"Please?"

"No."

"I want you. Only you. Forever," he declared.

"I believe you. No."

She decided to move for summary judgment.

"I love you," she continued, "in a way I never knew was possible. I am happily married to you. I love our life. I love our time together. So please don't misunderstand when I tell you that the thought of spending every day twenty-four hours a day with you is absolutely appalling."

He got up off his knees.

"I'm a brilliant lawyer," he said. "Brilliant lawyers win clients. But great lawyers win cases. You're a great lawyer. Or you will be. I know it."

"So you're saying I'm not brilliant?"

"No. Of course you're brilliant. Just. Not relatively. But. You know. Vice versa."

"Did you ask me to marry you so I would join your firm? Because that would be ..."

"Absolutely not!"

"Flattering—"

"Really?"

"In a deeply disturbing way."

He took her hand.

"Look," he said, "this is the thing. Separately we can do good things. Together we can do great things. We have an obligation to our own wonderfulness."

"Save the whales?" she asked.

"I know some very nice whales."

"Save the rainforest?"

"It's the least we can do."

She took back her hand.

"Who's going to save us?" she asked.

"Every relationship requires some sacrifice."

"Not usually human."

"Okay," she said at last, discovering she could laugh and shudder at the same time. "Partners. But let me pass the bar first please. Okay?"

"Okay."

The librarian wagged her finger, warning them both.

*   *   *

It was her third time accompanying him. Every year he flew into Florence, drove narrow roads rising through orchards and falling through vineyards to the tiny village of Collodi, where he bought five blue suits of the same superfine wool cloth, each handmade by Maestro Carlo. At the end of the day, they would have tea at the stunning seventeenth-century gardens of the Villa Garzoni, then inevitably spend an hour or two at the Parco di Pinocchio, the exquisitely designed park commemorating the adventures of the famous puppet.

She knew the small hill town well, the constricted cobblestone passage, you couldn't call it a street, ascending the mountain past immaculate terra-cotta homes. But after several hours of wandering, she finally decided she was lost, and did not care. The town was perfect: espresso served in tiny cups older than any place she'd ever been; alleys so narrow and winding you could walk for hours and be home in minutes; rainbow food in rainbow bowls under roofs that had sheltered Medicis; wine fresh as morning.

Finally, turning a corner, she peered through the afternoon glare on a shop window to find the puppet perched in the window box, the familiar gray-and-white face gazing contentedly out over the Piazza del Piccolo, keeping a watchful button eye out for straying Italian sheep (unruly but well groomed). She stooped to enter, bracing herself on the worn lintel until her eyes adjusted to the relative dark.

"Perfecto," said the maestro.

"He's not talking about the suit," he said.

She smiled at him. He descended from the tailor's block and glided toward her, one sleeve on, one sleeve off.

"Here," he said. "Tonight."

"We'll see," she answered.

*   *   *

Every day when she came home, she found Sancho somewhere new. Washing the dishes. Vacuuming the oriental carpets. Hiding in a closet (inside her raincoat). Sliding down the banister. Reading to the other stuffed animals (of which there were many). Once he even greeted her at the door sitting on top of the coat rack with roses scrunched between his padded white paws.

Soon the variations became more frequent. When she left the room, he might be on the sofa. When she came back, he would be rocking in the rocking chair. Or he would have changed the channel on the television. Or taken a bite from her candy bar.

No one else was ever around.

When the possibilities at home were exhausted, she began discovering him at the office. Hiding in a file cabinet. Sitting in her chair. Writing a letter to Santa Paws on her computer. Perusing her law books with tiny bifocals perched on his furry white muzzle.

It was the most charming coercion she had ever experienced.

*   *   *

The crystal surface of the desk glittered silver in the moonlight shining through the office windows. Six months before, they had finally moved out of his cramped yet colorful loft space in the Warehouse District and into the more professional setting in the Wells Fargo Building, which she had carefully designed and furnished.

He was a dark outline against the night. She was grateful that she could not see his face.

"I'm sorry. I have to," she said almost to herself.

"Okay."

"I'll buy out your share of the house."

"Okay."

"And the firm. I know you started it but—"

"Okay."

"I'll have someone we know draw up the papers."

"Okay."

"It's for the best."

Somehow she felt him smile.

"I don't want the best," he said. "I want you."

A litany played through her mind of every hope fulfilled and left dangling in the failure of the wrong success.

"You make me laugh," she said.

"Okay," he replied. "Okay."

An Ever-Fixèd Mark

Like the New Jerusalem of the Book of Revelation, the modern city of Minneapolis lies foursquare, split into quadrants by Highways 94 and 35. The heart of the city is the Mississippi River, which flows through the center before wending east and south all the way to the Gulf of Mexico.

Hennepin Island stands in the river at very nearly the center of Minneapolis, just upstream from the University of Minnesota, just downstream from the old Pillsbury flour mill and St. Anthony Falls. The falls were "discovered" by Father Louis Hennepin, a missionary and historian who traveled with La Salle in 1678 on his first expedition to La Nouvelle France. He named the falls after his favorite saint, the patron of monks and hermits. Father Hennepin had a history of making history with waterfalls, having been the first European to write home about Niagara.

In the middle of the nineteenth century, a four-story building was constructed near the northern end of Hennepin Island. Initially the structure housed either a boardinghouse or a bordello (no one is certain which, or perhaps it was both) serving the nearby mills. But in the 1880s, the St. Anthony Inn opened at the site. Renowned for its Gilded Age furnishings and the first electric chandeliers in Minnesota, the inn catered to visiting royalty, ex-presidents like Rutherford B. Hayes, and touring celebrities such as Mark Twain.

The inn closed finally during the Great Depression. Empty during the war years, the building was donated to the city in 1955. For forty-some years, the Minneapolis city administration stored excess furniture and office supplies within the neglected historic walls.

About a year after they were married, Nick and Lena spotted the dilapidated structure on one of their long bike rides down the riverbank through the St. Anthony area. They bought the building from the city after a series of successful cases put their tiny law firm in solid financial territory. Like many other affluent couples, they briefly flirted with the idea of opening a bed and breakfast at the site, restoring the name of the St. Anthony Inn. But the realities of their flourishing practice made that idea unworkable, for which Lena at least was truly grateful. She and Nick eventually renovated the top floor and lived there during the last year of their marriage.

After the divorce, Lena leased the first floor of the building to a restaurant. The second floor consisted of offices, mostly unused. The third floor was converted into condos. Lena lived alone in a suite on the remodeled fourth floor.

Harvey Larson worked for Lena as building manager, handyman, sometime private investigator, and occasional Nick wrangler. A burly ex-marine, he lived rent-free on the third floor, which gave Lena a sense of extra security; though the island was in the middle of the city, it felt dark and isolated at night. Harvey was also very good at tracking Nick down when necessary, which was often enough in the years following the divorce that he and Nick had become good friends.

As Lena and Nick approached, Harvey held open the door to the lobby, nodding a smile to Lena and tilting a questioning look at Nick as he passed by. Nick put a finger to his lips. Harvey nodded and gave Nick a subtle thumbs-up.

Under Lena's meticulous direction, the lobby had been restored to gilded elegance using early-twentieth-century photographs of the St. Anthony Inn. She had installed the elevator only after extensive (and expensive) negotiations with the St. Anthony Historic Preservation League. The glittering silver doors of the elevator were matched by ornate antique mirrors on the opposite wall. Nick and Lena surrogates waited for the elevator in infinite regression. Lena's doppelgängers smiled to excess.

"Doesn't this violate the divorce decree?" Nick asked.

"Yes," said Lena, still smiling.

"So basically you could have me shot at any time?"

"Yes," said Lena, still smiling.

*　　*　　*

For the first time since the divorce, Nick and Lena walked together over the uneven hardwood bands of the fourth-floor corridor. Lena entered the apartment, leaving the door open. Nick hesitated.

Lena looked back.

"You coming in?"

"I never thought you'd ask me that again."

"Don't touch anything."

"Now, that sounds like you."

Nick took a few steps into the large foyer and halted, reexamining the space.

"You've changed things."

"For the better."

Nick drifted into the living room.

"You've changed the lighting," he said.

"And."

"You bought a new rug."

"And."

One after another, Nick enumerated each piece of furniture. Then he laughed.

"You got rid of every piece of furniture we ever had sex on."

"Except one," Lena replied.

"Which one?"

"Well, I guess technically the washing machine isn't furniture."

Nick nodded.

"We'll always have spin cycle."

In the living room, Lena checked her messages. Preston's voice filtered through the room: "What are you thinking of, letting him back into your life? Do you know the definition of insanity? Call me. Maybe I can get you out of it."

Lena looked at Nick. "Wait right there," she said finally.

She left the living room and headed down the hallway. Nick sampled the chair that had replaced his recliner, setting Sancho on the back and sinking into the plush. Lena charged back into the living room with a stack of music CDs. Nick struggled to get to his feet.

"I've been meaning to give these to you," she said.

From across the room, she sailed a CD at Nick like a knife-edged Frisbee.

"Hey—"

She flipped another. Nick dodged.

"Wait—"

Another. Nick jumped.

"What—"

Nick held up his hands. Lena paused.

"Tell me," she said.

Lena launched one more, which soared over Nick's head and bounced off the mantel over the fireplace. He picked it up and examined it carefully.

"You broke Nat King Cole."

"Tell me why," she insisted as she zipped one more at him. He caught this one and held it up for her.

"And David Bowie is cracked."

She held up the next one for him. He saw the label and pointed.

"No! Not that one," he pleaded.

Lena brandished the CD like a martial-arts weapon.

"Tell me why," she demanded, "or John Philip Sousa is a casualty of war."

"Why what?"

"You knew the judge would order supervision. And you knew I would agree. Now what I want to know is why?"

"Lena, I had no idea the judge would do that."

Lena tested the wind factor and started winding up for the launch.

"Wait!" Nick shouted, then softly, avoiding her eyes: "This is hard."

Lena waited. Nick finally looked up.

"I don't think I can get through this alone."

Lena removed the CD from the plastic case and pressed the disk between her palms.

"I mean it!" she warned.

Nick smiled and shrugged.

"Okay, okay. You want to know why?"

Lena paused, then nodded.

"You still feel guilty about the divorce," Nick explained. "I'm giving you one last chance to make it up to me."

Lena was speechless for only a moment.

"That is absolutely ridiculous! I have nothing to feel guilty about."

Nick settled himself back in the new chair.

"I know that," he replied. "But *you* don't."

Lena stomped over to Nick, poised to either argue or attack, then dropped the CD into his lap. Nick pulled his long legs up into lotus position and spread his hands wide.

"If it's not guilt," he asked, "then why?"

Lena started to respond, then stopped.

She started again.

And stopped again.

Finally she said: "Work. Go. I have to. Here. Stay. Do not leave."

She grabbed her keys and purse and left quickly. Nick bounced mildly, testing the overstuffed chair. He held Sancho up.

"Who do you love?" he asked.

Dark eyes glimmered with recessed illumination.

*   *   *

Lena strode back and forth in front of her desk conversing with the air. The telephone headset swung perilously at each sudden period.

"But there must be. I know that but. This is a condition of. Yes. Please. Could you hold, please?"

After Nick left the firm, Lena was overwhelmed. But it was not the caseload that made her distraught; she welcomed the opportunity to focus on something other than her personal life. And it was not the duties of running a successful law firm; she had far more business acumen (and far more interest in the financial aspects) than Nick had ever had, and she had been running the firm, more or less, for some time.

It was not even being alone that had bothered her, as such. With Nick gone, Lena was overwhelmed by the silence. Nick was never quiet. Even on the few occasions when he wasn't talking, he was always buzzing about the office, humming, reciting poetry, singing, rustling papers, shuffling books, bustling around in an urgent search for the books and papers he had just rustled and shuffled.

After he left, the lack of noise in the office was nerve-racking. Any sound but the ringing of the telephone was welcome. Lena invited clients in without cause and took them to lunch more than necessary. She spent more time reorganizing than reading, because the shuffling noise was many times more satisfying than the occasional turn of a page.

Sharon, a refugee from the Midwest comedy-club circuit by way of Twin Cities Temps, had been her sardonic salvation. Several years before, Sharon had left unfinished her biography of Laurence Sterne and tried her luck as a stand-up comedian. Life on the gritty road of comedy and even grittier one-night stands finally wore her down, so she took a break, bought a condo in the Uptown area of Minneapolis, and applied for work through the temp agency.

Ward and Grant was her first and only position. After a week, Lena hired her outright as office manager, grateful for both her wit and her editorial skills. Sharon speculated that they had been friends for a thousand lifetimes. Privately Lena suspected something of the same sort.

Sitting outside Lena's office, Sharon was now thoroughly engaged in *Anna Karenina*. On the opposite wall, she noted the appearance of a shadow, vaguely human in form, with a disheveled halo. The shadow gestured dramatically.

Lena balanced on one leg while poking her head out the door of her office, *en point au décolletage*. The halo wobbled in concert with a circlet of hair sticking up through the metal band of her headset.

"Get my house on the phone, please," Lena requested.

"You must have one of those smart houses," Sharon noted.

"No. I mean, call my house."

"I'm pretty sure you're already here."

"No. Look. There's a man at my house."

"About time."

"Not that kind of man."

"Is there another kind?"

"It's Nick."

Sharon grabbed for the phone.

"Should I call an ambulance? Fire department? SWAT team?"

Lena closed her eyes.

"Just. Get him on the phone."

Sharon nodded. Lena pirouetted back to her desk and took the caller off hold.

"Hello? Look, anything will—what? An animal shelter is perfect. He loves animals. These are live animals, right? Could you hold on, please?"

Lena switched calls.

"Nick? Oh, hello, Dr. Richardson. You can? Wonderful. When? He'll be there. Thank you."

She switched back.

"Hello? When should he? He'll be there. Oh. One thing. There's a puppet. P-u-p-p-e-t. That's a good question. If you find out, let me know. Thanks."

She hung up and slumped into her chair.

"I'm the one who needs a psychiatric exam."

Sharon entered *glissade,* her headset securely ensconced.

"No answer. I'm getting your—"

Frantically, Lena gestured to Sharon.

"Hang up the phone. Hang up the phone. Don't get the—"

"Want to leave a message?"

*   *   *

The phone in Lena's living room was ringing. Nick looked over but didn't move. A deep voice emerged from the TV: "Today is E day.

"E is for Exciting.

"E is for Excellent.

"E is for Electricity."

A cartoon figure stuck a finger in a light socket and lit up. Nick chuckled.

The voice switched to the answering machine, but it was Nick's own voice. Nick Then said to Nick Now: "Hi, Nick and Lena can't come to the phone right now, so leave a message and we'll call you back in three point four minutes."

There was laughter, then a beep, then silence. Nick covered Sancho's ears.

*   *   *

Lena struggled into the apartment, managing the heavy door while carrying mail, keys, briefcase, and a grocery bag.

Nick cradled Sancho in the chair, legs dangling over legs dangling over the arm, enrapt in a Charlie Brown special—*A Midsummer Night's Peanuts*, with Snoopy in the role of Puck.

"Little help, please?" Lena asked.

"Sure."

The puppet came flying directly at Lena. She dropped mail, briefcase, and grocery bag, spilling all three over the floor of the foyer. She held on to the keys. And she caught Sancho.

"Thanks," Lena muttered.

Nick got up and walked over to Lena, examining the debris.

"You weren't much help," he complained to Sancho.

He kissed Lena on the cheek, gathered the groceries, and smiled.

"Nice message on the answering machine," he said.

Arms full, Nick headed for the kitchen.

"Just. Shut up," Lena called after him.

Nick, heading back out of the kitchen, shook his head.

"We never talk anymore."

He looked at Lena, silent for a moment.

"Whatever happened to us?" he asked.

Lena estimated the distance, judged the trajectory, charged forward for about ten feet, then launched herself into Nick, knocking him down and sitting on him.

"Oh yeah, now I remember," Nick said.

Lena shifted her center of gravity off Nick's solar plexus, against the solidity of the wall.

"You exhaust me," she sighed.

Nick moved next to her, and her head tilted down against his shoulder.

"Sorry," he whispered eventually. Lena didn't say anything, but settled in deeper. He waited a few moments before speaking again.

"Guest room, I assume," he said.

"You know what they say about assumptions."

"What?"

"Sometimes they are absolutely right."

Nick slowly straightened, stood, and stretched his back and neck, which cracked and creaked audibly. Then he reached down to help Lena up. He held her hand in both of his for a second, then traveled slowly down the hall toward the guest room.

The hallway was unlit. As he piloted his way along the wall, his fingertips skipped automatically over the pictures hanging below his eye level. In the dark, the content of the photos was not visible. At one time, the frames had held photos of trips they had taken together, mixing business with pleasure at speaking engagements all around the world. Nick had been highly sought after as a speaker on environmental legislation, and Lena had begun to develop a reputation of her own on legal issues related to international human rights.

At the door to the guest room, Nick's fingers drifted down to the antique door handle rescued from a dustbin in the basement. Before entering, he announced loudly to Lena's silhouette, framed softly in the incandescent foyer: "I just want you to know I'm locking my door tonight."

He disappeared into the room. The door clicked shut.

Lena also moved with assurance down the darkened hall. At the door, she whispered: "Nick?"

"Yes?"

"I just want you to know."

"Yes?"

"I'm locking your door too."

Lena chunked tight the padlock Harvey had installed on the door, then walked back into the light. Nick heard her whistling her way down the hall. An eyebrow raised to meet the challenge.

*   *   *

Lena woke to dark eyes staring down at her. Sancho leaned against the lamp on her nightstand, holding a crimson rose.

She sighed, then explained to Sancho: "It's not you."

She picked the puppet up and held him for a moment. Then she placed him on the bed, put on her pink silk robe, dumped the rose in the trash, and walked out of the bedroom.

Nick's door was still closed and padlocked. She dialed the combination, slipped the padlock out of the ring, enclosed it in her fist, and knocked. The guest room door toppled inward off its hinges like a stop-action colossus. Closing her mouth, she moved back up the hall.

The kitchen was nearly as large as the living room. The original stone fireplace, tall enough to stand in, contrasted with the recently acquired stainless-steel appliances at the other end. Whenever she lit a fire (which was not often), the reflection transformed the kitchen into a brushed scarlet inferno.

A wood-block island in the middle of the kitchen bridged the eras. Nick sat on a stool by the island, doing the crossword, stirring his coffee with a hinge pin. Lena shuffled in wordlessly, sat across from him, grabbed the paper, and examined his answers.

"These are all wrong."

"In what way?"

"In the way of not being right."

"They fit."

Lena looked closely. The words did fit in the spaces. And they did fit with each other. But they had nothing to do with the clues.

"They give you clues so that you can get the answers. They don't give them so you can at all costs avoid the right word."

"That's what they'd like you to believe," Nick said, taking the paper back.

"It's my crossword. Don't abuse it."

"Fine," he said and continued his work, entering the correct answers this time, though upside down and backward.

"Coffee?"

He poured her a cup from a pewter decanter she didn't know she owned. She took a sip.

"Look. This isn't going to work unless—"

She took another sip.

"This is good coffee," she continued.

Nick inhaled the arousing perfume of the brew he'd bought at Sebastian Joe's a half hour earlier.

"Thanks," he said.

Then Lena slammed down the coffee mug.

"Damn you, Nick," she complained. "You are *not* going to turn me into a commercial."

"I'm sensing that something is wrong."

He looked up from his crossword. Lena's long hair was free and tangled and her slightly bloodshot eyes crinkled as she squinted against the morning. Her robe slipped open, revealing rumpled blush pajamas, whose three unbuttoned buttons briefly took his breath.

"Look," said Lena, pulling her robe closed. "This is not going to work unless you stop this."

"Stop making coffee?"

"Yes. No. Yes. Stop trying to do whatever you're trying to do. Whatever that is. Not that I ever understand what it is. "

"I'm just trying to show my appreciation."

"Stop it!"

"What?"

"Being nice to me. It creeps me out."

Nick smiled.

"I could send roses. ..."

Lena stood, managing to stamp both feet at once.

"No roses! I mean it, Nick."

Lena began circumnavigating the island, round and round, as she spoke. Nick swiveled on his stool to track her progress.

"Look," said Lena north by northwest.

Then "Look," west by southwest.

Then "Look," east by southeast. "You'll be here until you complete your community service, which should be around four weeks. So the only way this is going to work is if we have as little contact as possible. So. So. So I'm going to get ready for work and then I will drive you to the animal shelter."

She stopped. Nick continued to spin on the stool until she grabbed his shoulders, and then composed herself.

"Now," she said. "I'm going back to the bedroom."

Nick started to rise. Lena interjected her hand palm up.

"Stay."

Nick stayed and sipped his coffee.

"Now, that's good coffee," he noted and smiled like the Mona Lisa.

*   *   *

Lena massaged the shampoo into her hair with one hand while holding her cell phone out of the shower with the other. She yelled beyond the hazy glass divide into the blooming fog of steam.

"Hi. I got your message but I can't talk about it now. Everything is arranged. He's seeing Dr. Richardson and volunteering at the animal shelter. What? Yes, the animal shelter. It's not that funny. Okay, it is that funny. Thanks for yesterday. It meant a lot. I'll call you later."

Bubbles slithered down Lena's body while an avalanche of suds dangled over her brow. She closed her eyes and slipped her face under the torrent of the shower. The water enfolded her, descending into a milky whirlpool at her feet.

Lena lifted onto her toes and reached toward the sink. Her torso inclined against the flimsy rigidity of the glass shower door as her hand sought desperately for somewhere dry, when a furry paw slipped the phone from her grasp.

"Get out of here, Nick," Lena warned. "I mean it. Or when you get to the animal shelter I'm having you neutered."

Lena turned off the shower and listened. No sound. She tiptoed over the chilly tile and checked the door. Closed. She looked back. As the steam parted, she saw Sancho on the sink next to her phone, bath cap on his head, washcloth strategically placed, from which emerged the crimson rose.

Lena smiled and sighed.

"It's still not you."

*   *   *

Lena's car passed through the broken chain-link gate and stopped at the top of the circular driveway. A single green metal door was the only apparent entrance to the massive two-story cinder-block fortress that constituted the Hennepin Animal Shelter. An asphalt courtyard marked with yellow stripes lay between the surrounding barbed-wire fence and the dirty walls.

"I take it the word 'shelter' is a euphemism," Nick muttered.

As he opened the car door, Lena put a hand on his arm.

"I think you should leave Sancho with me."

"You're right," Nick agreed. "This is no place for him."

He handed the puppet to Lena and got out of the car. The Porsche sped away before he could change his mind.

At the door, Nick hesitated but finally stepped inside. A short passageway opened into a wide rectangular reception area. On the walls, deteriorating corkboards displayed faded legal announcements, regulations regarding every conceivable aspect of shelter operation.

A woman sat behind a desk in the lobby, so short that her bright saffron blouse was almost entirely concealed by the clutter on the desk. The nameplate read:

Alice Wilson, Ph.D.

Director, Hennepin Animal Shelter

Nick approached slowly.

"My name is Nick Ward," he said.

She didn't look up.

"There's a chalk line in front of the desk," she said. "If you can tell me what it means, we can use you. If not, good luck somewhere else."

Nick looked down. Beneath his feet, a straight line was drawn in yellow chalk.

"It means a very thin person was killed here recently."

Alice didn't respond.

"It means you're the queen bee and I'm the worker bee."

Alice still didn't respond.

"It means this is where the desk goes."

Alice wrenched her eyes up from the papers covering the desk. She examined Nick silently for a long time. Then she looked back down and said: "Go on in."

Nick's eyes narrowed.

"I was right?"

Alice didn't look up.

"You were right the first time."

She pointed down the hall. Nick backed slowly away from the desk and continued down the passageway.

"Scary," he whispered, shaking his head.

"I heard that," echoed behind him.

He hurried down the corridor, passing several empty offices and finally reaching a double-bolted door. He pulled it open and froze in place.

The room was cavernous, a warehouse-sized abyss, dim in spite of long racks of dusty fluorescent lights suspended above. Spidery thin girders braced the high ceiling. Beneath the iron web, steel cages extended into the distance, row after row a football field long. Dozens of them. Maybe hundreds. From where Nick stood, no animals were visible. But howls and yelps echoed through the cinder and steel wasteland.

On a table by the door, Nick discovered a wine crate. Inside, a litter of kittens slept amid the din, tiny chests of black and white fluttering in an intricate confusion of shifting paws and twisting tails.

Nick proceeded down the center aisle, wandering slowly between the steel enclosures, observing right then left. There were a few unoccupied cages, but even those gave evidence of recent habitation. A blanket. A dish. A chewed-up toy. But most of the cages were occupied. Each inhabitant (all canine) was identified with a white three-by-five card taped to the door of the cell.

3224 Bloodhound mix male.

3226 Spaniel male neutered.

3227 Alsatian female.

3228 Beagle male puppy.

3231 Sheepdog/husky mix male.

3232 Shepherd mix female spayed.

3233 Schnauzer mix female.

3234 Labrador retriever mix male neutered.

3211 Wolfhound male.

3211 lifted his shaggy head. Great eyes flashed in the vibrating light as he began to stand, slowly unwinding from front to back until his enormous muzzle was even with Nick's chest. The dog unwound further, lifting his paws against the steel cage front until Nick looked directly into the huge eyes, black in the slash of sunlight that poured through the high window. The dirty beam of light fell to Nick's feet, spotlighting the dusty slab on which he stood, highlighting the great beast's profile.

Nick took out a pen, scratched out "3211," and wrote: "Wolfram."

"Now I know why I was sent here," Nick said.

The dog's pink ears pricked up.

"Then you're doing better than I am," a great penumbrous voice responded.

Nick spun around. The tall man before him wore a dark-green uniform with "Ralph" emblazoned on the left breast. His hair was cropped, and he wore thick leather work gloves that might once have been green also. Nick held out his hand and said: "Nick."

Ralph put a leash in Nick's extended hand and said: "Ralph."

Nick looked curiously at the leash.

"Am I supposed to wear this?"

Ralph didn't smile but finally said: "They told me you were funny."

"Who is that really scary woman out front?"

"That's Alice. She's my wife."

Nick started to laugh. But Ralph wasn't joking.

"I liked her immediately," Nick said.

Ralph and Alice had met at a party twenty-seven years earlier. Alice was studying management science and statistics at the University of Alabama. Ralph was in a master's program in wildlife conservation at Auburn. After enduring month of jokes about their *Honeymooners* namesakes, they decided they might as well get married. When the opportunity to work together beckoned, they moved their family (two girls then seven and nine) to Minnesota, where they accepted their current positions at the shelter. Alice ran the front (administration, budget, public relations) and Ralph handled the back (animal care, management, property maintenance). The home-life division was more intricate.

Ralph put a huge arm around Nick's shoulder. Nick's knees sagged slightly under the weight.

"Your job is very simple. Walk the animals. One at a time. On a leash at all times. Got it?"

Nick nodded again.

"Think so."

Ralph took off his right glove. A jagged scar like a bolt of lightning crossed his palm diagonally. He flexed his fingers slowly.

"You fish?" Ralph asked.

Nick nodded.

"Lobster mostly. Catch and release."

Ralph extended his open hand.

"Welcome to the shelter," he continued. "This could be your destiny."

Nick took his hand.

"It wouldn't surprise me."

*　　*　　*

Observing carefully as Lena paced in front of her office windows, Sharon rocked back and forth in the doorway to get the timing right, then stepped in to intercept.

"Busy?"

Like a pinball hitting a bumper, Lena immediately reversed direction without uttering a word. Sharon stepped back.

"There's a call."

Lena's path altered to curve around the desk, but still she said nothing.

"It's Cross from Luria Corporation. He's offering one million but he has to know within the hour," Sharon said.

Lena did not pick up the phone, but her pacing became amorphous, though her seemingly haphazard pattern managed to cross beneath every acoustic tile in the ceiling. Sharon stepped back to the door. Before pulling it discreetly closed, she asked: "Do you know the definition of insanity?"

*　　*　　*

Preston held the punching bag for Lena as best he could. She punched. He ooofed.

"Want to talk about it?" he asked.

"What's there to say I haven't already said a thousand—" Three quick side kicks. Ooof. Ooof. Ooof. "Times."

"Ever wonder where the term sidekick came from?" Preston asked.

Kick punch-punch combination. Ooof. Ooof-Ooof.

"Why can't I hate him?" Lena huffed.

"Apparently the phrase 'Kemo Sabe' wasn't from an actual Indian language."

"It would be so much easier."

"The word was invented by a writer on the *Lone Ranger* television show."

"I hate everyone else."

Punch. Ooof.

"No, you don't."

"No. I don't. Of course I don't. I'm about to be a duly recognized humanitarian."

"You're a what?"

Lena paused, leaning on the bag.

"Nick used to be on the board of directors of I swear every animal welfare and environmental organization in the state. After the divorce, when he dropped out of circulation, I stood in for him temporarily. At least I thought it was temporary. I kept thinking he'd come back eventually. And now they are giving me this award for meritorious humanitarian service to the community."

Preston stepped back.

"I have a surprise," he said.

"What?"

"I found someone to take him."

Lena kicked, missing the bag but not Preston, who collapsed backward. She sailed through and over him, landing on hands and knees facing his feet, with her thighs on either side of his head.

"I'm not exactly sure how to react to this," Preston commented. Lena didn't move.

"Who?"

Preston didn't move either.

"A group home. A good one."

A crowd of gym shorts loomed above them. Lena carefully extricated herself.

"Really?"

Preston tilted his head off the floor to nod.

"Tell him tonight," he croaked.

From the floor, Lena gave the bag one more punch.

"Don't I always?"

*　　*　　*

Lena's apartment took up only about two-thirds of the upper floor of her building. The rest was a rooftop balcony, forty-nine feet wide and twenty-three feet deep. Bags of soil, empty planters, and unopened envelopes of seed lay scattered against the wall.

The eastern side of the balcony allowed an early-morning sunrise vigil over the Mississippi River. On the opposite side, the sunset highlighted the silhouette of the cityscape of downtown Minneapolis, shining towers reflecting the evening transmutation like sparkling palaces in the clouds.

Absorbed in that later spectacle, Nick sat on the balcony. On the table next to him, a half-filled wineglass cast back the intensity of the blood-stained horizon. The cloud palaces were burning.

Lena emerged from the balcony doors.

"I thought you weren't supposed to drink when you're taking medication."

Nick raised his glass and adjudicated the luminous show, gauging the process against the cast of the liquid. The clouds flowed to cobalt.

"I'm not."

Lena paused.

"Not what?"

Nick was silent.

"How'd it go at the animal shelter?" Lena continued.

Nick lowered the glass and took a sip.

"They have animals there."

"That would have been my guess."

He looked up at her.

"In cages."

Lena sat next to him and put her hand on his arm. Her fingertips pressed his bicep.

"Nick. You know that the charges against you can be reinstated. If you do anything out of line, you could end up in prison. Or involuntarily committed to a psych ward. This isn't a game."

She removed her hand.

"I'll be good," he nodded. "Want a drink?"

Lena shrugged.

"Sure."

He handed her his glass.

"Did you know that sunset is sunrise backward?" he asked.

They both stared out at the softening light.

"And memory is imagination in reverse," he said.

Lena took a sip, then peered into the glass.

"What is this?"

"Hawaiian Punch."

*   *   *

The phone rang. Lena spun in bed, hesitated, then groped for the receiver.

"What? Oh, hi. No. I couldn't. It's just. He's very fragile now. I know. I know. I'll tell him this morning. I promise. I'll call you later."

Lena threw on her silk robe and went looking for the flannel one to put over it.

In the hallway, she hesitated in front of Nick's door. She reached for the wrought-iron handle, then released it and knocked gently. No answer. She made a hasty check of the hinges, then swung the door open and slipped inside. No one.

On the pillow, she found a note in Nick's scrawl: *There's fresh coffee in the kitchen. See you tonight.*

Lena sat on the side of the bed and pulled back the covers. Sancho was underneath, furry noggin askew on the pillow. Lena slipped under the sheets and snuggled close. She exhaled, then drew the covers up over her head.

*   *   *

Ralph carried the wine crate through the maze of cages, trying not to look at the other animals, and went out through the back door.

The five kittens, probably about six weeks old, had been brought into the shelter thirty days earlier. None had been adopted. Now, according to the rules, none would be. Originally the time limit had been five days. Ralph and Alice had lobbied to expand that to thirty, and management had reluctantly agreed, under the condition that adoptions increase concomitantly.

Behind the shelter, Ralph unlocked the gate, placed the box carefully in the chamber, and sealed it. At the side of the chamber, he twisted a brass lever. Gas hissed inside.

Ralph and Alice had also asked to switch to some of the newer synthetic gases, or possibly to lethal injection. Studies had determined that these methods were faster and produced less stress on the dying animal. Although carbon monoxide gas was generally thought to be effective, there were anecdotal reports of extreme suffering before the animal lapsed into unconsciousness. And more than one handler had died from CO gas poisoning. But the other methods of euthanasia were more expensive or required additional handlers, so the change had not been authorized.

The kittens inhaled the deadly gas. In a few moments, they receded into unconsciousness. Minutes later, their hearts failed. Soon after, all brain function ceased. The fragile remains cooled and constricted.

After fifteen minutes, Ralph unsealed the chamber. According to the recommended procedure, five minutes was all that was necessary. But young animals with tiny lungs sometimes took longer to die.

Ralph removed the crate. The dead kittens were curled up together as if sleeping. He carried the litter to the biological waste disposal container and gently positioned the kittens inside.

Back in the shelter, he removed the gloves, washed his hands, and drifted past the cages to the front lobby. He sat by Alice and held her hand. Neither spoke.

*   *   *

Nick dragged himself into Lena's apartment, exhausted by the efforts of the day. Lena was lying on the sofa, surrounded by a barricade of paper.

"How'd it go?" she asked.

Nick collapsed into a chair.

"It kept going and going. I must have walked a hundred animals today, round and round an asphalt courtyard. I'm still dizzy."

Lena tossed Sancho over to Nick.

"He's been waiting all day," she said.

"I'm exhausted."

"Come on."

"No. No. No. Okay."

Lena picked up the remote control for the stereo.

"Ready?"

Nick stood up and nodded. Lena clicked the remote. *The Liberty Bell March*. Loud.

Nick and Sancho began to march, barely going through the motions. Lena looked at him scornfully.

"Oh, come on."

She joined them, sliding her hands along an imaginary trombone. Nick fingered one-handed an invisible E-flat cornet as Sancho led the way with an Unreal piccolo between his paws.

Around the room.

Over the sofa.

Around the chair.

Into the kitchen.

Around the island.

Between the stools.

Down the hallway.

Into Lena's bedroom.

When the music ended, they collapsed together on the bed, Sancho between them. Nick was breathing hard. Lena laughed between gasps.

"Sometimes," she said in a breathy whisper.

"What?"

She paused.

"Sometimes I miss your world."

They relaxed together, arms touching, breathing in sync. Lena inhaled deeply. She didn't look at him.

"What do *you* miss?" she asked.

Nick didn't answer for a time.

"I miss being annoyed," he replied.

Lena spun around to him.

"Me too!"

Nick continued.

"I miss being awakened at five A.M. by the sound of either a coffee grinder or a dentist's drill, I'm not sure which."

"I miss seeing your footprints in the new-fallen snow and knowing that you are leaving wet tracks all over the oriental carpet."

"I miss the fog of hairspray in the bathroom."

"My hairspray is infused with rare floral essences from the rain forests of Borneo, harvested by an eco-friendly reforestation project run by the indigenous tribes in the Taman Nasional Danau Sentarum in Indonesia. My hairspray is a natural religious experience."

"Can I get an 'amen'?"

She slugged him on the arm.

"Violence begins when imagination fails." He rubbed his bicep, smiling. "It's the eternal paradox. Love is annoyment."

"Annoyment?" Lena considered. "Is that a word?"

"Questioning my word choice. I miss that too," Nick said, swiping Sancho away from her and setting him on the nightstand. "That's very annoymentish."

"You're the expert."

"Be it known," Nick declared, "and published in two newspapers of general circulation that we, hereinafter referred to as the Defenders of the Innocent, seek no enmity with your kind."

He leaned back and closed his eyes.

"You know what I miss. I miss all of that annoying kissing."

"That was extremely annoying," she agreed.

Nick opened his eyes, looked at her.

"Maybe we should annoy each other."

He leaned closer.

"Right now."

Closer.

"On the lips."

Lena shook her head.

"Absolutely not. Probably not. What was the question?"

Nick kissed her.

"Are you annoyed?" he asked.

"Yes, I am extremely annoymentated."

He tried to kiss her again, but Lena pulled away.

"I think that's all the annoymentacity I can handle. You should get some sleep."

Nick smiled.

"Funny thing is, this is a bed."

Lena smiled back.

"Funny thing is, it's not your bed."

Nick nodded.

"I see your point. Yeah, we're pretty tired. We should get some sleep."

Lena touched his shoulder.

"Isn't it better when the music is real?" she asked.

"The sound comes and goes. The music is always real."

The Wandering Bark

Oscar accelerated in elongated steps down the steep bank, heading in the direction of the lagoon, a narrow finger of water that stretched into the community at the northern end of Lake of the Isles. At the bottom of the decline, he slowed to a stroll and headed across the sward to the inner path, one of two asphalt rings encircling the lakeshore.

Swept up the slender channel on a southern breeze, Nick's voice guided Oscar along the path.

"In the early 1800s," the voice recited, "the chief lumberjack of the northern woods was the legendary giant and frontiersman Paul Bunyan. But one day in the summer of 1836, Paul lifted his head and looked far out over the Minnesota territory and the great forest that he loved. Everywhere he saw the desolation that he and his fellow lumbermen had wreaked. And he realized that the ruin he had caused could never be undone. Devastated by this vision, Paul grew despondent and great tears began to fall from his gigantic eyes."

Ambling past the blue flag iris that emerged still glistening from the green water, Oscar was escorted along the lagoon edge by a squadron of Canada geese, who bowed in concert as they passed the kingfisher perched on a bulrush. Nick's voice still floated toward Oscar like the narration in a nature film.

"For weeks that summer, Paul traveled all over the Minnesota territory, from logging camp to logging camp, from grove to ancient grove, begging forgiveness from the trees he had wronged. But the voices of the trees had been stilled forever by the axes and saws and spikes of the lumbermen. As he walked in silence, ten thousand tears fell across the land, and each tear formed a lake."

When Oscar reached the point where the lagoon flowed into the larger lake and the path turned off to the west, he stopped. Only a slender branch of water, a few yards at most, separated him from the northernmost of the two islands in the lake. One hundred yards across, a morsel of floating life, the island was covered by a chaos of spruce and pine, elm and aspen. A swath of tall grasses swayed along the narrow shore, alternately hiding and revealing the sign from the Minnesota Department of Natural Resources, a warning to would-be picnickers that the island had been set aside as a wildlife preserve.

"Finally, Paul could stand the guilt no longer," the voice continued. "He hurled his gigantic ax south, forming the bed of the Minnesota River. Then he took three giant steps north, creating three lakes: Lake Harriet, Lake Bde Maka Ska (Dakota for White Earth Lake), and Lake of the Isles.

"At Lake of the Isles, two huge objects fell from Paul's watch chain, forming a pair of small islands in the lake. One was his golden watch, which was larger than the great clock of London. The other was a silver, heart-shaped locket that held a picture of Paul's one true love: Beulah Heatherthorn, the gentle redheaded beauty he had left behind in Erie, Pennsylvania.

"Paul knelt at the top of Lake of the Isles to recover his precious possessions, but the tears so filled his eyes that he could not find them. Finally he took one step west, forming Cedar Lake, and was never seen in Minnesota again. In the summer, if you listen at the northern end of Lake of the Isles, you can still hear the silver locket beat with the sound of

Beulah's broken heart and the golden watch tick with the sound of Paul's lost years."

Oscar turned west and followed the path around an embankment. There he found Nick sitting on a park bench set back under the trees. A huge dog was draped over him, trapping Nick on the bench. Sancho balanced between the dog's enormous shoulders. Oblivious to the joggers and bikers and other park denizens circling around him, Nick rocked back and forth and told his stories to the lake.

"I was in the area," Oscar called out. "Thought I'd see how you were doing. Your wife told me you might be here."

Nick started, turned around as far as his canine companions would allow.

"Ex-wife," he corrected mildly.

"I followed your voice," Oscar explained.

"The water does that, I think. Or the wind. I was rehearsing. I might go back to teaching someday."

Oscar looked around.

"Nice spot."

"Welcome to my domain," Nick responded, sweeping his hand broadly across the horizon. The movement stirred the dog, who lifted his head, glanced at Oscar, sniffed once or twice, then returned to drowsy contemplation.

Oscar circled around to the side of the bench.

"So. How are you feeling?" he asked.

"Not wisely but too well," Nick responded.

"What does that mean?"

"It means ask a different question."

Oscar nodded, then turned his earnest attention toward Sancho.

"Nice puppet," he said.

"He prefers Unreal American," Nick replied.

"Oh. Sorry," Oscar said to Sancho. To Nick: "I was surprised they let you keep him at the hospital."

"I made a substantial contribution to the Lunatics' Ball."

"Where did you get him?"

Nick leaned back, extending his long legs and clasping his hands behind his head.

"Once upon a time, I wanted a dog. Lena didn't want a dog. I insisted that we get a dog. So she went out and got Sancho. And that's a brief history of our marriage."

Oscar nodded.

"Is it a boy puppet or a girl puppet?" he inquired.

"He's a him. You want to hold him? He doesn't bite."

"Really? Thanks."

"Often," Nick said.

Oscar gently accepted Sancho.

"He's so soft."

"Inside too. It's okay. He won't mind. He knows you."

Oscar held Sancho's head down and searched for the inner pouch.

"No, not like that," Nick corrected. "Stand up straight. Hold him up over your head. Then slip your whole hand in in one smooth motion, like a knight's gauntlet."

"I see," Oscar replied.

"I call it the Ritual of Joining," Nick explained. "It helps us clear our minds and focus on the mission."

"Kind of like the Green Lantern recharging his ring."

Oscar slipped his hand into the soft inner pouch. His fingers easily found the jaws and paws. Sancho twisted his head back and forth like an owl, intently observing the other park enthusiasts.

"He handles well," said Oscar.

"You should see him on the straightaways."

Oscar nodded, pointed to the huge dog on Nick's lap.

"What's his name?"

"Wolfram."

"Good name. He looks Spanish."

"He's Irish actually."

"That's what I meant. Irish."

"He's an Irish wolfhound. Largest dogs in the world."

Oscar nodded at Sancho.

"How do they get along?"

"Quite well, actually. Sheepdogs and wolfhounds have a lot in common professionally. Speaking of which, why aren't you at the institute?"

Oscar examined the bench, trying to find someplace to sit.

"That's part time, mostly nights, weekends, transport jobs. During the day, I work children's parties."

Nick brightened.

"Are you a clown?"

"I do animal balloons. Here's my card."

Oscar took a business card out of his wallet and handed it to Nick, who read:

The Amazing Oscar

Party Balloons

Balloon Animals

Party Animal

www.AmazingOscar.com

"I love balloon animals!"

Oscar took a couple of balloons out of his pocket, blew them up into long, thin cylinders, then twisted them into a hat with antlers. He crowned Nick with it.

"How do I look?" Nick asked.

Oscar offered his professional judgment: "In all my years as a party animal, no adult human has ever looked that good in a moose hat."

"Thanks," said Nick.

"Hey, I have a gig this afternoon. Why don't you come? You could handle the helium. I have this tank. It's easy. And kids love puppets."

"What would we do with him?" Nick said, patting Wolfram's bulky frame.

"We could pretend he's a pony."

Nick shifted under the huge dog until he could take a deep breath. He pointed out toward the lake.

"If you wanted to get to that island," he asked, "how would you do it?"

"Probably I wouldn't. There's a sign."

"I know. I put it there," Nick said. "But if you were going to. How would you?"

"You could swim. Maybe jump. With a running start. Or pole-vault. You could pole-vault."

Nick paused.

"I think I'd walk," he finally decided.

"You know, when I have a tough decision to make, I always ask myself: What would Spiderman do? Or Mister Fantastic. Spiderman was actually kind of neurotic. Which is understandable, I think. The pressures of being a superhero."

"Tell me about it," Nick said.

"Mister Fantastic was married to the Invisible Girl, whose brother was the Human Torch. Makes all the difference. Family. Superman's family was dead. Batman's, dead. Spiderman's, dead. There's a pattern there."

There was a long pause. The grave rhythmic stirring of Wolfram's chest was the only movement.

"When I have a tough decision to make," Nick said, "I always ask myself: What would I do in that situation? It makes it easier somehow."

"Good tip. Aren't you supposed to be walking him?" Oscar asked.

Nick looked at Wolfram.

"He's kind of a Zen dog. He likes to sit and think."

"Did you know that Zen is not a religion?" Oscar asked. "It's a practice, brought to the island of Japan in the twelfth century by a master named Dogon."

Nick looked over.

"*Mystic Existential Ninjas,* Issue 103," Oscar explained.

"You read a lot of graphic novels?"

Oscar snorted. Wolfram's ears jolted skyward.

"That's just a phrase some marketing geek made up so they could charge ten dollars instead of a buck. They're comic books. They were comic books when I was five and they're comic books now."

"I never understood why they were called that," Nick said. "I never thought they were funny."

Oscar's forehead forged a tiny wrinkle between his eyebrows.

"Some people believe they're called comic books because the books in the 1930s were collections of newspaper comic strips. *Terry and the Pirates* and *Dick Tracy* and *Flash Gordon* and *Jungle Jim.* Cervantes wrote the first comic book, you know."

"I'm familiar with it," Nick said.

"The French philosopher Henri Bergson said that comedy is the shared human modality of reacting to the unexpected."

Wolfram stirred.

"He also said comedy requires an unemotional observer. But I don't see how those two go together."

Nick nodded.

"Aristotle said that comedy is the celebration of the erotic impulse. Freud thought so too. He said jokes are psychoerotic manifestations of unconscious desires. And Georg Wilhelm Friedrich Hegel, well, he just wasn't funny."

Nick shrugged agreement.

"I think. I think." Oscar looked around, then whispered: "My theory is that comic books are about vision. All superheroes have x-ray vision or some kind of supersenses. That's why comics have all those bright colors."

Nick nodded.

"Thanks for clearing that up."

"There's no telling what you can learn from comics."

Nick picked up Sancho.

"He has supervision."

"Well, he should. He's a puppet."

"No. I mean, he has *super*vision."

"Really?"

"He's a sheepdog," Nick explained.

"So?"

"So he can see who is innocent."

"That's good," Oscar said. "Most sidekicks have lesser powers. I can't think of any sidekicks who have complementary abilities."

"He's not my sidekick. He's my partner."

"Oh. Well. That explains it."

Nick grew pensive for a moment, stroking the soft patch behind Wolfram's ear.

"What does an existential ninja do?" he asked finally.

"Nothing," Oscar replied. "It's what he *could* do."

"Ahhhh."

Oscar squeezed in, joining Nick and Wolfram on the bench. They sat without talking and watched the activities along the lakeshore.

Children played.

Dogs chased.

Geese swam.

Squirrels browsed in a never-ending quest.

Oscar passed his hand over Wolfram's shaggy coat.

"Smart dog."

*   *   *

The birthday party was being held in the backyard of a large house in north Minneapolis. Wearing the balloon antlers as his official badge, Nick arrived early with Oscar, passing under the party streamers hung in kaleidoscopic arches along the hedges. As promised, Nick helped blow up the balloons, helium specials that spun "Happy Birthday Jeremy" in the warm southern breeze.

Diminutive guests and attendant adults arrived in erratic procession. As the party commenced, Nick, Sancho, and Wolfram faded into the background to watch.

Oscar truly was Amazing. To the delight of the onlookers old and young, animal balloon sculptures soon filled the yard. There was a red-and-blue monkey holding something like a banana, a long yellow-and-green snake coiled and rising into the air, and even a purple-and-orange giraffe that stood almost six feet high. Nick insisted from the back that Oscar put glasses on it. The children turned and discovered him there, with Sancho.

The five-year-olds looked expectantly at the man with the puppet. Nick raised Sancho into the air and slid his hand inside.

The puppet lifted his head slowly and rubbed his eyes. Then he spotted the children and danced for joy. Nick harrumphed. Sancho turned and gazed at Nick for a long time. Then he dipped his shaggy head between his paws and shook it back and forth. The children hooted with laughter.

"Tell us a story!" they commanded.

Nick shook his head.

"Once upon a time," Oscar prompted.

Nick glanced around at the multicolored zoo Oscar had created, drew a big breath, and stepped forward.

"In the heart of a lake in the heart of a city in the heart of a land in the heart of the world there is an island in the shape of a heart.

"The island is home to many amazing animals: a purple-and-orange giraffe who recites poetry, a red-and-blue monkey who plays the saxophone, and even a yellow-and-green snake who juggles. But none is more amazing than the Magical Dog Who Never Sleeps. The Magical Dog forever stands on guard on the shore of the island.

"One fine sunny morning, a Knight in Blue Armor comes riding along through the forest and sees the island. And he thinks: 'Any island in the shape of a heart with a nearsighted purple-and-orange giraffe, a red-and-blue monkey who plays the saxophone, a yellow-and-green snake who can juggle, and a Magical Dog Who Never Sleeps must be a wonderful place indeed.'

"So the Blue Knight calls out, 'Oh, wise and wondrous Magical Dog, how may I get onto your island?'

"The Magical Dog replies, because all Magical Dogs can talk, 'Memory in reverse is Imagination.'

"'Hmmm,' says the Blue Knight. 'Should I swim to the island? Should I jump? Should I pole-vault?'

"But the Magical Dog only says again: 'Memory in reverse is Imagination.'

"'Ahhh,' thinks the Blue Knight. Then he kneels down by the water's edge and, seeing his reflection in the calm, shiny surface, dips his right hand through the image, lifts the water up in his palm, then casts the glittering droplets up into the air. Suddenly a rainbow stretches from the shore of the lake all the way onto the island. Then the Blue Knight stands and walks over the rainbow bridge onto the enchanted island.

"And the Blue Knight abides on the island in the shape of a heart while the purple-and-orange giraffe recites poetry, while the red-and-blue monkey plays marching songs, while the yellow-and-green snake juggles two pomegranates, a teacup, and the knight's very sharp sword. Finally the Blue Knight thinks that it must be time to leave, so he says: 'Oh wise and wondrous Magical Dog, this is a very fine island, but how does one get off?'

"'Beats me,' the Magical Dog replies. 'Why do you think I'm still here?'

"'No. Seriously,' says the Blue Knight.

"So the Magical Dog laughs and says: 'Imagination in reverse is Memory.'

"And so the Blue Knight kneels down once more at the water's edge and dips his left hand into his image and again casts the glistening droplets into the air. Once more a rainbow appears, and the Blue Knight crosses back over the many-colored bridge onto the lakeshore.

"But when the Blue Knight turns to say good-bye, he sees himself still standing on the island. So he asks the Magical Dog: 'Oh, wise and wondrous Magical Dog, why do I see myself still standing on the island next to you?'

"And the Magical Dog replies: 'On this island, there is no time. No day. No night. No past. No future. There isn't even any Now. There is only Always. If you are ever here, you are always here.'

"And the Blue Knight replies: 'Then I won't say good-bye,' and he turns and walks away.

"The End."

Nick and Sancho turned and walked away underneath the streamers.

"Who wants to ride the pony?" Oscar asked quickly.

*   *   *

Lena stood inside the door for a few moments as Nick and Sancho patrolled the perimeter of the balcony to a tune no one else could hear. Finally she stepped out.

"There's something I have to tell you," she said.

Nick turned to her.

"There's something I have to tell *you*," he responded.

Lena sat quickly and covered her eyes with her hands.

"I knew it. We're not really divorced, are we?" she said.

"Of course we're divorced," Nick replied, sitting next to her.

She uncovered her eyes.

"Sorry. My mind always jumps to the worst possibility."

"Thanks a lot. I was—"

"You slept with someone while we were married."

"No. I didn't sleep with anyone while we were married. That was part of the problem. What is the matter with you?"

"I'm just. I don't know. There's something I have to tell you."

"I know what we need," Nick announced, leaping to his feet.

"No."

"We need—"

"No!"

Nick lifted his right arm with a flourish.

"A balcony scene!"

"Oh no."

He knelt at Lena's feet, took her hand, kissed it.

"Let me not to the marriage of true minds admit impediments," he exclaimed.

Lena pulled her hand back.

"No Shakespeare."

Nick rushed to the balcony railing, draping himself against it.

"Love is not love which alters when it alteration finds."

He spun over the balcony railing, clinging to the iron trestle by his fingers and toes.

"Or bends with the remover to remove."

Flakes of paint rotored their way down thirty-some feet to the rocky ground below as the antique bolts began to wrench loose from the floor.

"Nick!" Lena pleaded.

Nick raised up on his toes, as though preparing to leap.

"O no!"

"Oh no!"

He vaulted onto the thin line of the railing. His voice dropped in volume.

"It is an ever-fixèd mark that looks on tempests and is never shaken."

Lena turned away. Nick inched slowly down the slender rail into her peripheral view. He spoke to the river: "It is the star to every wand'ring bark."

A step.

"Whose worth's unknown."

A step.

"Although his height be taken."

On the last word, Nick lost his footing. Lena screamed at his flailing shadow. But Nick caught himself, twisted in onto the balcony floor, rolled over to her and up, kneeling again.

"Ow. Love's not Time's fool, ow, though rosy lips and cheeks within his bending sickle's compass come."

Nick waited. He waited for a long time. A minute. Two. Lena did not look at him, but finally muttered: "Love alters not with his brief hours and weeks, but bears it out ev'n to the edge of doom."

Nick lowered his head into her lap.

"If this be error and upon me proved, I never writ, nor no man ever loved."

Lena pulled back, slid out, swept away, then halted in the doorway.

"Every time the phone rings, my first thought is that someone has found you somewhere, dead. My first thought. Every time."

Nick looked up at her. She stood just inside the doorway. The interior light flickered, revealing and concealing her silhouette.

"Is that a good thought or a bad thought?" he asked.

"Yes," she answered and vanished inside.

Nick picked up Sancho and stood at the railing.

"Any given sunset."

*   *   *

The phone woke Lena, who stared, then grabbed for it.

"Where is he? Oh. Hi. I was dreaming, I guess. No, I couldn't tell him. I just. Yes. Lunch. I can meet you."

*   *   *

Nick was preparing to walk his charges for the day when Ralph entered the cage room wearing wet gear, a poncho and boots. He threw a set to Nick.

"Put those on."

"Why?"

"Field trip."

Nick and Ralph left the shelter and climbed into a white van.

"Where are we going?" Nick asked.

"Not far. A pair of geese has decided to take up residence in someone's swimming pool."

"Not the mayor's, I hope."

"You know the mayor?"

"We're acquainted."

As the van pulled out, Nick shimmied into the slick outerwear.

"Who else keeps a swimming pool in Minnesota?" he asked.

Ralph shrugged.

"An optimist."

Fifteen minutes later, the van pulled up to a large house in southwest Minneapolis not far from Lake of the Isles. Ralph trudged around to the back of the van and opened the panel doors.

"So how are we supposed to catch these geese?" Nick asked.

"You'll see."

After searching a while, Ralph pulled out two long poles with nets and a flat vinyl case.

"What do we do with them after we catch them?" Nick asked.

"They're big birds."

"That's why I'm asking."

"So generally I like to roast them at medium heat for five or six hours."

Nick put his hand on Ralph's shoulder. Ralph turned.

"You eat them?"

"We relocate them."

Nick took the poles.

"I won't kill anything."

Ralph nodded solemnly.

"For your sake, I hope the geese feel the same way."

Ralph passed through a gate in the hedge at the side of the house. Nick followed him into an enormous yard, almost a park. The pool was located near the house, up from the English garden. About ten yards long, the blue cement pool was encircled by a raised white concrete walk surrounded by a weathered brick patio. In the deep end of the pool, farthest from the gate, two Canada geese cruised gracefully, unperturbed by the approaching men and equipment.

"They mate for life, you know," Nick said.

Ralph took one of the nets.

"So do humans. They just don't admit it as often."

Ralph strolled calmly but quickly over to the smaller of the two birds. He extended the pole and netted the goose without a struggle. Then he carefully drew the uncomplaining bird to the edge of the pool.

"That was easy," Nick said in admiration.

Ralph reached down, pulled the goose out of the net, and handed her to Nick.

"Be careful. She'll bite your ear off."

"I know the type," Nick replied.

The goose held still for a moment. Then a shudder ran through it up into Nick's arms, causing him to loosen his grip. Wings freed, the sturdy pinions assailed Nick vigorously, showering him, almost blinding him in feathers. Teetering on the cement ledge of the pool, Nick held the bird as far away from his body as possible, pulled on point several times by the frantic aviator.

"Careful," Ralph warned. "Those wings can break your nose."

"You tell me that now?"

The struggling goose squawked in alarm, at which point the mate, terrified and honking also, rose out of the water into the sky, circled the pool for momentum, and dived at Nick, who lost his grip on the captured goose and ducked too far. For one photo-finish second, he posed in peril, then toppled in stiff slow motion into the water. He breached the surface like a harpooned whale, stole a quick breath, then belly flopped once more into the pool.

Ralph extended the pole to Nick's grasping fingers and dragged him to the side.

"They mate for life, you know," Ralph commented.

As the pair of geese settled calmly once again into the deep end, Nick tried to shake himself dry. Ralph opened the black vinyl case and pulled out a small pistol with a long, thin barrel. He took practiced aim at one of the geese and fired the air-driven missile.

Without a thought Nick launched himself across the pool, arms extended, trying to get in front of the projectile. Once more he plunged in, then struggled up in knee-deep water.

Drenched and woozy, he tried to focus on the tiny dart protruding from his palm. He saluted Ralph, lofting his hand like a kid parading a newfound penny.

Ralph nodded, impassive.

"They told me you were funny."

Nick barked a laugh as he slipped back into the cool fluid blue.

*　　*　　*

Preston approached Lena's table at the restaurant, maintaining as much momentum as possible while winding through the narrow passages between mostly empty tables. When he reached her, he didn't sit.

"Why haven't you told him yet?"

"Sit down."

He glared at her.

"Please," she said.

"I pulled a lot of strings to set up this group home for him on such short notice."

"Will you please sit down? People are staring."

Preston glanced at the patrons scattered sparsely through the restaurant and decided to sit. He leaned across the table.

"He'll be better off. And you'll be better off."

Lena folded her hands on the table in front of her. Preston waited.

"I don't know how to explain it," she said finally.

"You never changed the message on your answering machine," Preston accused.

"I don't like the sound of my voice."

"Do you feel guilty?"

"You know, Nick would have a field day with that line."

"Just because you divorced him."

"'Sound of my voice.'"

"And took over his legal practice."

"He would have riffed for an hour."

"And he had a complete mental breakdown?"

"Yes!" Lena cried. "It's my fault. It's my fault. It's my fault," pounding the table, causing waves in the water glasses and eliciting stares.

Preston held up his hands to calm her.

"That's not true."

Lena shook her head.

"He's mentally ill, Preston. He's disabled, for God's sake."

"He's a nut."

"I left him."

"That's why they call them nuts."

"It's as if—"

"Because they crack."

Lena shot up out of her chair.

"My husband was in a wheelchair and I pushed him down the stairs!"

A gasp made its way around the room, then with Midwestern discretion the customers hid their heads in their menus. Preston took Lena's hand.

"Will you sit down?"

He lured her back into her chair.

"You did the right thing," Preston said. "The divorce was necessary. Your being together wasn't helping either one of you. The marriage was over."

"Right."

"He was acting crazy. Spending money crazy. Accepting crazy cases. You and the firm would both have gone bankrupt."

"Right. Right," Lena agreed.

"He isn't the man you married anymore. It's tragic but you have to think of him as gone and not coming back. People with this disease don't get better, and if they did, they still wouldn't be who they were before."

Lena ran her hands through her hair.

"But what if he can't make it?" she asked. "I don't think he can make it."

Preston took both of her hands this time.

"The captain does not have to go down with the ship, Lena. The captain is a beautiful, compassionate, valuable person that I, that I care about. Her job is to do her best and then save herself. Did you do your best?"

"I hope so."

"Then keep repeating: 'I have a right to my own happiness.'"

"I have a right to my own vodka. I need a drink."

Preston signaled their waiter, Stanley.

"Something is happening between us."

"Us?" Preston asked.

Lena shook her head.

"Nick and me," she said.

Preston jumped out of his seat.

"Not that, Preston," Lena reassured him. "I don't think."

Preston sat again.

"You don't think?" he hissed.

Stanley placed the drinks on the table.

"These are compliments of the manager. He asked if you would please stay in your seats. You're scaring the tourists."

Preston looked around.

"What tourists?"

Stanley shrugged.

"Okay, you're scaring me. Just keep it down. Please?"

*   *   *

Nick woke up soaking wet in a dark, damp, quivering metal cave. Two geese snoozed next to him, wings pinioned. Ralph was driving the van. Nick scooted up toward the front.

"Where are we?"

Ralph twisted partway around in the driver's seat.

"On our way to geese paradise."

"Which I hope is not someplace named paté."

Ralph turned back to the front.

"Trust me."

Nick shrugged.

"Well, you've inspired me so far. Why shouldn't I trust you?"

"You know, I thought you would have recognized a tranquilizer gun."

"Silly me. How did you get the geese in the truck?"

"I dumped you in and they just followed right after."

"Really?"

"Yep. Oh. I put some towels in the back. You know. Just in case."

*   *   *

After a lunch spent mostly in silence, Lena gazed into one of several empty glasses. Staring through the thick lens of the glass bottom, she watched Preston's face shrivel and warp and sink into the distant haze.

"I need to understand what is going on," Preston said quietly.

Sunlight shone and scattered through Lena's empty glass, refracting an oblong pattern on the white tablecloth: two flattened rainbows joined at each end.

"I have done everything I know how to do," she said.

She aimed the rainbows at Preston, at his pale shirt, then up his pale tie to his pale face.

"When he gets in trouble," she said slowly, groping for the words, "I'm the first one there. Other than the ambulance. Or the fire department."

"Or the SWAT team," Preston added.

Lena beamed the rainbows like a tiny spotlight across the finger where her wedding ring used to be.

"Nothing I do is—"

She paused.

"Enough," Preston added. "He uses your feelings to keep you from letting go."

Lena shook her head.

"You don't know him," she said.

"Do you?"

Preston moved his chair next to hers.

"Let me take care of you. And him," he said.

"How?"

"I'll find a way."

Lena put down the glass. The rainbows disappeared. She put her hand over Preston's.

"I'm so sorry for putting you through this," she said.

"There's nothing I wouldn't do for you."

*   *   *

The Minneapolis skyline was no longer visible through the rear window of the van. Nick lay quietly in the back, watching the geese, who had awakened and were watching him back.

"Trust me," he whispered.

The van soon pulled off the highway onto a dirt road. Branches lashed the windshield until the lunging vehicle halted, then backed up briefly.

Ralph turned around.

"We're here."

Nick slid toward the back and opened the doors. A wide meadow of flowers and tall grasses ran about a hundred yards down to the shore of a lake maybe half a mile across. Except for the small clearing, evergreens formed an impenetrable bulwark above the sturdy fortress of trunks. No trace of humanity was visible.

Ralph appeared at the back of the van and helped Nick out. Nick stood unsteadily on the ground, his leg muscles shaky and cramped, as a company of geese soared over the van and plunged onto the watery surface with a rainbow spray.

"I told you," Ralph said. "Geese paradise."

Nick reached into the truck and handed the geese one by one to Ralph, who held them at arm's length as he placed them gently on the ground. Nick knelt down beside them to deliver last-minute instructions.

"This is your new home. You'll be safe here. None of those irritating humans around to pester you," he said, glancing at Ralph.

Ralph knelt and freed the first bird. The powerful avian extended his wings and ran a few wobbly steps, then glided up and out over the lake. Nick hurried to free the second, having learned never to impede a mating goose. The pair sailed side by side in a graceful arc over the trees, then circled the two men before landing in the lake with a glittering shower.

Nick whispered: "'Beautiful bird; thou voyagest to thine home, where thy sweet mate will twine her downy neck with thine, and welcome thy return with eyes bright in the lustre of their own fond joy.'"

"What was that?" Ralph asked.

Nick shrugged.

"Shelley."

Ralph nodded.

"Amen."

*   *   *

Lena doodled mindlessly across a stack of important papers until Sharon casually pulled them away from her.

"Cross from Luria Corporation called again," Sharon said. "He's offering two million."

"I'm not here."

"I said you were."

"It's a mirage."

"It's Minnesota."

"It's snow blindness."

"It's summer."

"It's Minnesota."

"It's two million."

"I'll get back to him."

Sharon perched on the steel arm of the sofa.

"How was lunch?"

"I'm not hungry."

Lena pulled the papers back, picked up a pen, and began filling in the holes in the o's and p's and d's, damming the alphabet, as Nick called it, so the meaning can't escape. She had often complained about this habit of his, especially when she discovered the marks in papers about to be filed in court. Only recently had she discovered how satisfying it could be.

"Why don't you go home to your ex-husband?" Sharon asked.

Lena checked her watch.

"Can't. He's out saving the world."

Sharon leaned against the bookcase.

"I wish I had an ex-husband to not go home to."

"You want mine?"

Sharon struck her best Doris Day pose.

"You don't know what you're not missing."

Lena put down the pen and drifted over to the windows. To the west, city towers gave way to houses and apartments that gave way to lakes and parks then to farms and deserts and forests and mountains. The incline of the West. Civilization in reverse.

Sharon moved in at the desk and helpfully continued to fill in the holes in the letters. Lena spoke to the window.

"Nick used to send me roses. I don't know where he got them. He would never say. Deep crimson, they were called, but the color of the petals changed depending on the light. Under fluorescent light they looked black, outside in the sun blood red. At dusk they looked like a burgundy wine. I'd put them in a crystal vase on my desk and the whole room would seem like it was on fire.

"One day Nick bought me a dozen. Then he remembered I was out of town. So he chartered a jet to deliver them. I was in Geneva at the time. The Swiss customs agent apparently had a hard time believing someone would charter a jet just to deliver a dozen roses. So for eighty-nine thousand dollars, I got a pile of crushed petals and twelve sticks with thorns. When I got home, I filed for divorce. And that's a brief history of our marriage."

Sharon picked up the document and turned it to see whether it made more sense upside down.

"He meant well," Sharon noted.

"So did Karl Marx."

"Was he the one with the cigar?" she asked, doing an imitation with the pen. Lena walked back to the desk.

"I never heard of anyone getting divorced over roses before," Sharon continued.

"That was when, not why."

"So why?"

"Don't you have some work to not do?"

"I already didn't do it."

*   *   *

Lena slid open the glass door to the condo balcony, expecting to find Nick. The declining sun cast stark elongated shadows over the weathered planks. None she recognized.

*   *   *

The van pulled up to the shelter. Nick and Ralph began to unload the gear.

"You did good today," Ralph noted.

"That's what I live to hear."

"Why don't you come home with me for dinner?"

"This is so sudden."

"Alice will have everything ready."

"Okay," Nick agreed. "Let me make a call."

*   *   *

Lena reclined on the balcony, sipping a glass of wine. A small candle held out alone against the night. Her phone rang. She waited, then answered it.

"I wondered where you were. I'm here watching your sunset. Or I was. No, it's okay. Whenever. It's not house arrest. Just be quiet coming in. Yeah. Bye."

She hung up, blew out the candle, and went inside, closing the glass door behind her.

*   *   *

Ralph and Nick rolled to a stop in front of a house on Minnehaha Parkway. The four-story Victorian seemed to be built into a hill. Ralph led the way up the stairs to a moss-green veranda lined with buttercup-yellow gingerbread. He swung the door open and walked into a kiss from the waiting Alice, who then granted Nick a peck on the cheek. Nick stood frozen by the unexpected pleasantry. A second later, all three were inundated by dogs.

"We've adopted a few over the years," Ralph explained.

*　　*　　*

Lena lay on the sofa in a powder-pink cotton nightshirt, papers scattered around her, working. Her knees were drawn up beneath the nightshirt, hiding nearly all of her thick red socks. She alternated handfuls of Cheerios out of the box with sips of milk from a champagne flute. Her hair was captured in two long braids. Sancho perched on top of the sofa, supervising the activities.

Lena clicked on her small tape recorder and began to dictate: "Sharon, here are the notes for my speech at the London Convention.

"Title Identity and the Rights of Children new paragraph In the 1990 UN Convention on the Rights of the Child comma Article 8 defines the right of a child to preserve his or her identity without unlawful interference period But what constitutes that identity question mark The convention cites three elementary criteria of identity colon nationality comma name comma and family relations period But what else question mark What makes a child this child question mark Even our child question mark new paragraph To understand this comma we must examine how the law identifies a person period Under the law comma identity does not mean identical period A person is never the same as he or she was the day before comma either physically or psychologically period Cells grow and die by the millions each day period We gain weight or lose weight by the minute it seems period We add and lose memories in the same way period Our neurological pathways are continually altered by the sensible input we receive comma and by the internal feedback system that we refer to as ourselves comma our consciousness period new paragraph."

She stopped the tape and listened. Then she put down the tape recorder and reached for the remote control on the coffee table. The CD player clicked on: *The Liberty Bell March.* She tuned the volume very low and turned her attention to her papers. Her toes, emerging from beneath the nightshirt, marched to the music.

*　　*　　*

Ralph, Alice, and Nick pushed back from the table simultaneously. The dinner plates were empty.

"Thank you for a delicious meal," Nick offered.

"I noticed that you formed your mashed potatoes into a pyramid," Ralph mentioned.

"It helps the butter melt evenly," Nick explained.

"You didn't try the chicken," Alice remarked.

"I don't eat meat."

"How long have you been a vegetarian?"

"About five hours."

Alice's eyes grew wide.

"Actually," Nick continued, "I'm a geometrarian."

"What is that?" Ralph asked.

"I only consume foods in elementary shapes. Like circles or rectangles or pyramids."

Alice relaxed back into her chair.

Nick went on: "Someone once tried to convince me that broccoli florets grow in Fibonacci sequences. But for me, pure mathematics ended with Euclid."

Ralph leaned forward.

"Plus I don't like broccoli," Nick finished.

He smiled.

Then Alice smiled.

And finally Ralph smiled, then rumbled out a chuckle, then thundered a laugh that shook the condiments.

Nick looked through the doorway into the living room and spotted a piano. He turned to Alice.

"You play?"

Alice nodded at Ralph, who said with some embarrassment: "I play at it."

"He's good," Alice countered. "He plays every Tuesday night with some friends down at a little jazz club."

"Jazz?" Nick said. "Would you?" he added, nodding toward the piano.

"Go ahead," Alice told Ralph. "I'll get the dishes."

"Thanks, hon," Ralph replied. Then to Nick: "Good thing you're here. Dishes are usually my job."

"You two are so different," Nick said after Alice went into the kitchen. "And you're together all day and all night. How do you make it work?"

Ralph put his finger to his lips.

"Duct tape and Krazy Glue. I'll say no more," he replied.

Ralph and Nick crossed to the family room. Ralph sat at the piano and touched his fingers lightly to the keys.

"A good marriage," he continued, "is not a democracy. It is a series of contiguous tyrannies by mutual consent."

Ralph's hands curled into something slow and syncopated.

"Ahhhh," Nick responded.

"Marriage," Ralph announced, "is a partnership sustained by a common vision."

"How do you know?" asked Nick.

"She told me so," Ralph replied.

Ralph turned toward the kitchen.

"It's not always like this," Ralph added with warmth. "But it's like this enough."

Alice wandered in. Her hands, always busy with something, were now wringing a dishcloth.

"You like music?" she asked Nick.

"I love it," Nick responded.

"Who's your favorite?"

Nick stood at reverent attention.

"John Philip Sousa."

Ralph and Alice nodded but kept quiet. Ralph lifted *Stardust* to march time.

*　　*　　*

Lena woke to see Nick sitting on her bed.

"Sorry," he said. "I didn't mean to wake you."

She put her head back down.

"What time is it?"

Nick checked the clock beside her bed.

"It's tomorrow."

"Tomorrow," Lena slurred, trying to remember something. "Tomorrow. Tomorrow. You have an appointment with ..."

"Dr. Richardson, I know."

"He has to file a report with the ..."

"Court, I know. Go back to sleep."

He pulled the comforter up.

"What are you going to do?" she asked the pillow.

"I missed my sunset. I thought I'd watch you for a while."

"No. You. Okay. Good-night."

Nick settled back on the bed and pulled Sancho to him.

*   *   *

Lena felt pressure on her leg and woke suddenly. Nick was curled up asleep at the foot of the bed, his arm draped awkwardly over her thigh. Lena got up carefully so as not to wake him.

When the alarm went off, Nick jumped and rolled onto the floor. When he looked up, he saw Sancho with the alarm clock in his lap.

"Traitor."

Tempests

Nick leaned back in the chair. Sancho, riding on his lap, nearly tumbled off, but Nick caught him.

Dr. Richardson got out a notepad and sat down across from Nick.

"You don't have any books here," Nick noted.

"I can't read," the doctor replied. "So, how are you feeling?"

"Not wisely but too well."

The doctor closed his notepad.

"You know, maybe I didn't explain this properly, but therapy normally includes talking about yourself."

Nick considered.

"I'm not normal."

Dr. Richardson considered gravely.

"Me either."

Nick slid his hand up into Sancho's interior. Dr. Richardson turned his attention to the puppet.

Sancho moved leisurely at first, as if waking from sleep. He yawned. He scratched. His dark eyes scanned the room.

Dr. Richardson observed with careful curiosity: *The naturalness is uncanny, his control is effortless, as if his hand has somehow grown a consciousness of its own, a separate awareness, a distinct intention. He pays no attention to the puppet's actions at all, except when they are directed at him. An extraordinary performance: detailed, consistent, convincing. And slightly unnerving.*

The puppet who had become Sancho turned toward Dr. Richardson. The cherry tongue appeared as the jaws widened in a smile. The doctor found himself smiling back.

"Tell me about the puppet," Richardson said.

"Once upon a time, I wanted a dog. Lena didn't want a dog. I insisted that we get a dog. So she went out and got Sancho. And that's a brief history of our marriage."

Richardson nodded and smiled.

"Good name for a sidekick."

"He's not—I didn't name him. Lena did."

"Why did she pick that name?"

"It's a mystery."

The doctor returned the smile.

"You two spend a lot of time together?"

"We're divorced."

"I meant you and Sancho."

"We're just good friends."

The doctor laughed.

"You like him."

Nick and Sancho turned to each other.

"He's the best person I know."

"You talk as if he's real."

"Real is trickier than people realize."

The doctor laughed again, tasted his pen, then changed the subject.

"Staying on the meds?" he asked.

"Usually. Sometimes. Not really," Nick admitted finally under the doctor's gaze.

"I see."

"Do you ever watch movies on PBS?" Nick asked.

"Occasionally," said Richardson. "*Mystery*. The wildlife programs."

"You know how for a movie they put those black borders on the top and bottom?"

Nick held his palms outward, one over his forehead and one below his chin.

"That's what my brain feels like when I take the pills," he added.

Richardson made another note.

"Try and think of it as editing for *Prime Time*. We just take out the bad parts."

"You mean the exciting parts."

"I mean the dangerous parts."

"I'll try to remember that," Nick assured him.

Richardson paused, drumming the pad with the pen.

It's the job. To cure. So. Throw medication and therapy at the problems like politicians throw money. Maybe, somehow, the right buttons will get pushed. We have theories: dysfunctional families, dysfunctional neurotransmitters, sanity as chemistry. But our theories don't begin to approach the complexity of brain function. Not to mention mind function. And the soul? We pray it's not there. What pill can ever cure a soul?

During the doctor's silence, Nick's usually animated expression swallowed itself, three dimensions folding into one solemn surface. His eyes reflected sky as he focused out the window.

"What's going to happen to me?" he asked finally.

"Well, let's see," the doctor replied, going back over his notes. "You have a serious mental disorder. You're divorced. You have no job. You don't take your medication. My guess is you'll be dead in five years."

Nick shifted in the chair.

"Haven't you ever heard of a rhetorical question?"

"Sorry," the doctor replied.

Nick glared at the doctor.

"I'm not crazy," he whispered.

"We don't say that word here. We think it a lot but we don't say it."

"I'm not crazy," Nick repeated firmly.

The doctor leaned forward, gazing intently at Nick.

"No?" he challenged. "Then what are you?"

At the question, Sancho swiveled, cocked his ears, and gazed at Nick with equivalent intensity. Nick shrugged.

"I am. Imaginative."

The doctor nodded and scribbled in the notepad.

"So it would seem."

"So what do I do?" Nick asked.

"Was that rhetorical?"

"No."

"Well, one choice would be to take your medication, stay in therapy, and get your imagination under control."

Nick thought a moment.

"What's the second choice?"

Richardson closed his notepad.

"Make it a good five years."

* * *

Lena arranged the elephants on her desk in Traveling Circus order, alternating large and small. All of them had names, but only Lena knew what they were.

Names. Identity. Names. What is a name? What's in a name? A rose by. No. NO roses. Forget roses. Nick. What's in a Nick. A Nick is a nick is a nick. The knack of Nick. We don't really know. We don't really know who we are as much as we remember ourselves. Our stream of consciousness flows into an ocean of memory and by this memory, this correlated continuous database of personality and happenstance, we awake each day to reconstruct ourselves in the real world. Whether this reconstruction is the same is an issue, like the teleporter in a Star Trek *episode: when Captain Kirk is beamed up to the deck of the* Enterprise, *is he the same person he was on the surface of the planet? I wonder if our dreamselves have memories just as our conscious minds do? And if the lives of the dreamselves (and who knows how many there are) affect our bodies the way we do? If so, I hope my dreamself goes to the gym more often than I do.*

Lena didn't notice when Sharon entered the office.

"Cross is on the phone again," Sharon announced. "He's offering three million plus future royalties. He says to please call him back at your convenience."

Lena didn't respond.

Sharon walked to Lena's desk, pulled on the headset, and, in her best Lena imitation, announced into the phone: "Cross? Lena Grant. Three million plus royalties, and I want the fucking check on my fucking desk by the end of the fucking day. Thanks for fucking calling."

Then she hung up on him.

"Want some fucking coffee?" Sharon inquired.

*   *   *

As Nick strolled into the shelter, he noticed that Alice was not at her appointed place. Instead, Preston Winter sat behind her desk reviewing some papers.

"Doing your own investigating," Nick said. "I'm flattered."

"I've taken a personal interest in your case," Preston noted.

"How am I doing?"

"Surprisingly well, unfortunately."

Nick crossed his arms.

"Do you enjoy what you do, Preston?"

"The pay is low, but the benefits are good and I get to have people killed."

"I'm happy for you," Nick said. "Where is everybody?"

"Back with the veterinarian. Some dog is sick."

Nick rushed toward the cage room.

"See you later, Preston."

"You certainly will," Preston agreed as he stuffed papers into his briefcase.

Back in the cage room, Nick found Ralph standing outside Wolfram's enclosure, looking worried. Nick hurried up beside him.

Wolfram was lying on the floor of his cage, his breathing labored and shallow. A veterinarian knelt by him. Alice stood by his side.

"We found him like this early this morning," she said.

"Will he be okay?" Nick asked the vet.

"Don't know," the vet responded. "He's been in a cage for a month. That's hard for an old dog, especially one his size."

"He's been here a month?" Nick asked.

"Come day after tomorrow," Alice told him after a quick glance at Ralph.

"So. So what do we do?"

Alice shook her head but the vet responded: "We wait. Call me if anything changes."

The vet packed up and left.

"He's a great dog," Nick said to Ralph. "I'm surprised he's been here so long."

"He's old and he eats like a horse. People don't want a dog like that," said Alice.

Wolfram lifted his great head off the floor to see Nick, then tried to get up but couldn't. He lay back down, struggling to breathe.

"Okay if I stay with him?" Nick asked.

"Sure," said Ralph and Alice simultaneously.

*   *   *

Ralph looked back in. Nick was sitting on the floor with Wolfram, his hand across the dog's neck.

"Any change?" Ralph asked.

Nick shook his head.

*   *   *

Alice's figure filled the door of Wolfram's cage. Nick and Ralph had moved a little table and a couple of folding chairs into the cage. They were sitting next to Wolfram, playing chess.

Alice shook her head.

*   *   *

The overhead lights went on. Alice reappeared at the door to the cage. Nick and Ralph were still playing chess.

"Thought you could use some illumination," Alice offered.

"It's a popular opinion," Nick replied.

*   *   *

Nick and Alice were at the chessboard. Ralph dozed on the blanket next to Wolfram. Both were taking smooth, shallow breaths until Ralph stirred.

"What time is it?" he asked, blinking away the bleariness.

"Almost midnight," Alice replied.

"Why don't you two go home?" Nick offered. "I'll call you if anything changes."

Alice considered and nodded.

"Anything, you call us."

Ralph and Alice left. Nick brought in a small lamp from one of the unused front offices, then switched off the overhead fixtures. The tiny lamp formed a circle of light on the floor. Nick relaxed on the old blanket next to the huge hound, pulled out his cell phone, and dialed Lena.

"Hi. I was pretending you were worried so I could call and tell you not to be worried. One of the dogs is sick. I'm going to stay. I don't know, could be all night. Sleep well. Bye."

Nick looked at Wolfram, who had awakened and shifted his head across Nick's knees.

"Do you play chess?"

*   *   *

Lena opened the steel door to the cage room. She was wearing an old sweatshirt and tights, a St. Louis Cardinals baseball cap, a ponytail, and white sneakers. She passed under a rainbow of streamers and balloons and wandered down the first row of cages adorned with Day-Glo posters. In the dim light, she strained to read the message on each.

Watson: A male bloodhound mix, Watson loves long walks on the beach in search of anything.

Alonzo: This spaniel male was neutered while training for an Olympic fencing medal. He loves children, riding in the car, and the films of Frank Capra.

Fanny: A wily Alsatian female best known for her impersonations of French cabaret singers of the 1950s.

Pal: Beagle puppy. He's a puppy. Everybody loves puppies.

Rufus: This male sheepdog/husky mix is a champion chaser who can find a tennis ball in any kind of weather. Rufus is housebroken and prefers Plato in the original Greek.

Grendel: This female shepherd mix needs no leash and loves other pets. She recently saved Timmy from a burning barn.

Annabelle: Female schnauzer mix. A loving mother of twenty-seven, since retired, Annabelle has a wild side and can frolic through a meadow with the best of them.

Huck: Labrador retriever-mix male. Sweet-natured and very playful, Huck is a wonderful swimmer, loves to play in water, and recently received critical acclaim for his existential novel Woof!

Wolfram: This well-fed male wolfhound possesses knowledge beyond human understanding.

She found Nick in the last and largest cage, sitting on Wolfram's blanket with one hand across the huge dog's neck.

"You look like a sixteen-year-old escaping to spend the evening with her boyfriend," Nick commented.

"I was bored all alone," Lena replied. "So I thought I'd come down and be bored with you."

Nick lifted his arm. Lena slid under it, resting her head on his chest.

"By the way, you don't play chess," she said.

He nodded.

"That explains so much."

*   *   *

Nick opened his eyes and promptly shut them again. The morning sun shone starkly bright even through the dingy windows above his head. He tried to stretch his cramped legs but found himself trapped. A sleeping Lena suffused his lap in a fall of strawberry blond. Wolfram dozed with his snout across Nick's knees.

Ralph walked in.

"A ménage à trois," he said, eyebrows raised. Nick looked down at his sleeping charges.

"In a menagerie no less," Nick replied.

Lena opened her eyes, stood up, and stretched.

"I'm Lena," she said, offering Ralph her hand.

"Ralph."

Lena nudged Nick with her foot.

"I have to get to the office."

"Thanks for being bored with me," Nick said. Lena nudged him again.

"It was a first," she said and ambled down the aisle, drawing every male to attention, regardless of species. At the double door, she turned and waved. Ralph looked at Nick, who hadn't stirred.

"You let her go?"

"It was a mutual decision. No, it was more like mutually assured destruction."

Ralph stooped to check Wolfram, ran his hand over the still form. Wolfram hadn't yet lifted his head.

"No change?"

"Not much."

"Well, it's probably just as well. Tomorrow is E day."

"E day. What's that? We send him somewhere?"

"In a way."

Nick slid his legs from under the dog and rolled onto his knees to face the big man.

"What?"

"E is for Euthanasia."

"You're going to kill him?"

"Policy. If they haven't been adopted in a month, then ..."

Nick looked back at Wolfram.

"You can't be serious."

"A month is a lot. In many shelters, they get only a few days. Let me show you something."

Ralph stood and hauled Nick to his feet, then led him to the rear of the shelter and out the back door. Ralph opened the gate, walked inside, and put his hand on the gas canister.

"This is carbon monoxide. It produces unconsciousness in seconds. They just go to sleep."

"How do you stand this?" Nick asked. "You love these animals. I know you do."

"It's for their own good," Ralph argued. "Is it better for them to run around loose, starving to death, hurting someone or hurting themselves?"

"Some people say the same thing about me," Nick said. "I can't believe this goes on here. This is Minneapolis. The capital of Nice. There must be some other way."

"You don't understand the issues," Ralph tried to explain, his own voice rising. "Neutering and adoption programs don't come close to solving the problem. Millions of animals every year come into shelters all over the country. Where would we put them? What would we do with them? People want brand-name pets. They don't want generics."

Nick shuddered.

"I can't let this happen," he said decisively.

"We've been here for fifteen years," Ralph said. "You think we haven't tried to change this? Change it if you can. Too bad you're not still a lawyer. I bet you knew the governor personally."

Nick walked back inside and slid onto the floor, his back against a cage. Ralph sat beside him. For a while, nothing was said.

"I've had years to learn to deal with this," Ralph said. "You're a good man, Nick. Don't come around tomorrow."

Ralph stood, waited a moment, and walked away. Nick watched him recede, then stood rapidly and quick-marched out front. Alice was sitting at the desk. He raced past her without speaking.

"Hey?" she asked.

Nick ignored her, banged open the front door, and walked out.

*   *   *

Lena was on the sofa, holding Sancho on her lap.

The legal fiction of identity reaches past our ever-changing stream of physicality and personality to seek that which is, if not the same, at least continuous. We identify a person physically by external appearance. In criminal procedure, we have the eyewitness and the ubiquitous lineup. We hold each other responsible for the actions that are performed by a body. But we have found that for real identity we need to look deeper, or differently. We look to handwriting or fingerprints or DNA. But even this is not conclusive, because the law also recognizes in rare instances a multitude of identities within a single body: the multiple personality, the insane individual who is not in possession of his or her faculties. Not in possession. If we are not, who is?

*   *   *

It was late when Nick dragged himself into the apartment. He wandered aimlessly for a few seconds, then slumped into his chair. Lena waited for him to speak. He didn't.

"Bad day?" she asked.

He didn't answer.

"Want to talk?" she prompted.

Nick turned his face to her without really looking at her. After a second, he stood and walked back into his bedroom. Lena heard the door click softly shut.

"We never talk anymore," she murmured.

She cleared up her work and followed him back to his bedroom. She put her ear to the door, listening for a moment, then opened it. Nick lay on the bed, holding Sancho, staring at the ceiling.

"Alice called," Lena said. "She told me."

Nick didn't turn to her, but kept staring up.

"Do you know how many animals are euthanized in animal shelters each year? Do you have any idea?"

Lena sat next to Nick on the bed.

"No," she said.

He didn't look at her.

"Neither did I. And tomorrow, it's Wolfram."

Lena braced his shoulders and pulled him around to face her.

"There's nothing you can do," she said, then softened. "I'm sorry."

Expression drained from Nick's face. He pulled away from her and walked to the window.

"I can't do nothing."

"I'm speaking as your attorney," Lena said.

"Are you?"

She didn't respond.

"We could adopt him, Nick said."

"I can't have this discussion."

"I'm just saying."

"There is no *we*, Nick."

Nick stiffened and tucked himself safely away.

"We'll figure out something," he said.

Lena shook her head, started to speak, stopped, then turned and left the room.

Nick pulled a card out of his wallet, then picked up the phone and dialed.

"Oscar? It's Nick. I need your help. The Minions of Euthanasia must be thwarted by the Agents of Anthropomorphosis."

* * *

Lena lay on her bed. She heard a door slam, got up and opened hers. Nick's door was wide open. His room was empty. She closed her bedroom door and sank down against it.

* * *

In the morning, she opened Nick's door a crack, then pushed it wide. He was on his bed, dressed, or still dressed.

"Morning," Lena said.

"Morning."

She stepped into the room.

"When did you get in?"

"Late. Sorry."

"Aren't you going to the shelter today?"

"It's E day. They said stay home."

Lena put her hand on his shoulder. He didn't pull away.

"Call me if you need anything."

He didn't respond.

"I'm sorry, Nick. I really am."

Nick shrugged.

"It's life. Or not."

* * *

Alice sat at her desk. Ralph sat nearby.

"You may as well get it over with," Alice said.

Ralph walked reluctantly back through the shelter, stopping at Wolfram's cage. The old dog looked up. His tail wagged briefly.

"Soon it won't hurt anymore."

Ralph knelt down and slid his green leather gloves under Wolfram's frame. His muscles surged and he curled the dog against his chest, lifted one knee then the other, and stood. He shuffled slowly to the back door of the shelter and out, struggling under the weight of the massive canine. At the exit, Ralph froze in place. The gate leading to the chamber stood open.

Attached to the chamber itself, a balloon floated. The logo read:

Killing Is Easy

Then the other side flipped around in the breeze, and Ralph read:

Comedy Is Hard

Ralph shook his head as he lowered Wolfram gently to the ground. The huge snout lifted into the air and sniffed, sensing something not right.

Ralph untied the balloon and watched as it drifted up in a slow spiral, out of the enclosure, over the fence and trees, disappearing finally in the morning sun. Then he squatted down to test the chamber, twisting the handle on the gas canister.

A blast spurted in his face. He inhaled involuntarily. Gasping, he looked at the canister.

The rubber hose had been cut.

He backed away, coughing, and shouted for help.

"Alice!"

Ralph's voice didn't carry. It sounded odd. Higher in pitch. Registers higher. Wolfram lifted his head and howled.

Ralph looked again at the gas canister. The label said HELIUM.

"What the hell?" he squeaked. "Alice!"

Ralph looked up to where the balloon had flown and laughed out loud. To Wolfram, he announced in a chipmunk voice: "Well, old boy, I guess you get a reprieve."

*   *   *

Lena stormed through her front door, slamming it behind her.

"Nick!"

She threw off her jacket and purse and charged into the living room.

"Nick!"

She headed down the hallway to his bedroom. She didn't knock this time but threw the door back on its hinges, punching an S-shaped dent in the wall with the antique door handle.

Nick and Sancho were on the bed watching CNN.

"I had to!" he explained.

"Helium? You substituted helium?"

"I'm playing for time."

"Where did you get helium?"

"Minneapolis is a party town. You can get the stuff on any street corner: balloons, streamers, cone hats, whatever you need."

Lena sat on the bed.

"Alice had no choice," she told him. "She had to report to her boss, who called the judge. The charges have been reinstated and the judge has ordered you back to the institute. You have to turn yourself in tomorrow. You're going to be involuntarily committed or go to prison. There's nothing I can do."

Nick smiled.

"You never support any of my projects," he said.

Lena spun away in fury.

"I hope you can laugh when that door slams shut on the next ten years of your life."

"Good thing I've only got five years to live."

Lena shook her head.

"You know, it just occurred to me. You always say that I left you. But the truth is, you left me first. Every time told a joke instead of talking to me, you put one foot out the door."

Nick paused, then: "I must have had a lot of feet."

Lena nodded, shrugged, rose slowly, and moved to the door.

"Who do you love?" Nick asked softly when her back was turned.

The question caught her.

"You mean 'whom.'"

"I know the difference."

She turned.

He was looking directly at her, not accusing, not penetrating, merely posing, as if he were her professor again, as though the answer were academically intriguing but nothing more.

"I don't understand," Lena said after a moment.

"No, I don't think you do," Nick agreed. "But then maybe I don't either."

"Are you asking about Preston?"

"No."

"Then?"

Nick sat up, put Sancho to the side.

"Who do you love?"

She leaned her head against the door, eyes concealed in a curtain of blond hair.

"I don't know who you are anymore."

"We are who we imagine. So are you."

Her hand curved tightly around the door handle.

"I don't know what you're trying to tell me."

Her wrist twisted. The door clicked open.

"Wait," Nick said.

She turned back once more to find Sancho hurtling through the air to her. She caught him and held on.

"You shouldn't be alone tonight," Nick said.

"You're right. I shouldn't."

She left the room, not slamming the door but closing it tightly.

Nick began to pack his few things, stuffing them hard into a suitcase. Before he finished, he slumped on the bed.

The door creaked. He looked up.

"You shouldn't be alone tonight either," she said.

*　　*　　*

Lena and Nick lay in bed.

"That was unbelievably annoying," Nick said.

Lena tipped his face toward her. Her eyes mirrored darkly in his blue. She shifted up high on the bed so she could look down at his face.

"They say the definition of insanity is doing the same thing over and over again and expecting a different result."

"I don't expect anything."

He pulled her down.

*　　*　　*

Lena sat on the washing machine, naked and sweaty, leaning against Nick.

"That's what I like," she whispered in his ear.

"What?"

"Extra starch."

She began to giggle.

Nick pulled back and gaped at her.

"Our last minutes together and you're telling jokes?" he asked. He wiped away a pretended tear. "I'm so proud."

Too exhausted to laugh himself, he still managed carry her back to the bedroom.

*　　*　　*

When we read a book, our minds, our minds assemble the words and spaces and punctuation into a text, and our imagination assembles bits of text into a character. In life our minds assemble the elements of experience (words, looks, touches, actions) into memories, and from those memories our imagination constructs a persona. Even those we love exist only in our imagination. Only. Only...

*   *   *

Lena and Nick lay in her bed, eyes closed. She rolled over to him, her head pressing his chest.

"I just want you to know."

"Yes?"

"I just do."

"Okay."

She eyed the shuttered windows for a sense of sunrise.

The Bending Sickle

Nick kept forgetting about the handcuffs, dragging one hand with the other as he chatted amiably with the police officers. He knew them; they were friends who often stopped to swap stories as he circled Lake of the Isles. He was their neighborhood watch, as the squirrels and geese were his.

The police car circled through the parking lot, heading for the emergency entrance to the Golden Valley Psychiatric Institute. The officers opened the rear door, carefully helped Nick out, and escorted him inside.

Oscar was waiting, dressed again in his lab coat, a ravaged *Spiderman versus The Rhino* hanging out of the left pocket. He removed Nick's restraints quickly, all too aware that escape was impossible. Oscar recognized the ancient forms. Protasis. Epitasis. Catastasis. Catastrophe. The Old Ones knew. Sophocles. Horace. Stan Lee. Jack Kirby. *The Mighty Thor 154* to *157*, the greatest comic epic of the modern era. The Mangog, last survivor of a holocaust and imbued with the power of a billion billion extinguished souls, seeks to bring about Ragnarock, the end of days. *Now Ends the Universe.* The God of Thunder fights, is defeated, rises again, and foils the enemy with the aid of his faithful companions.

The forms ruled.

Comic books.

No telling.

Oscar led Nick through the labyrinth of bland back corridors, into the elevator to the ninth floor, through the locked doors, and back to his room.

Nick lay down on the tiny bed.

"Sorry, Nick," Oscar said and shut the door with a muffled thud.

*　　*　　*

Nick started from sleep as Lena dropped her briefcase on the tiny white table. She tossed the puppet to him.

"We need to prepare your testimony for the competency hearing tomorrow," she said, not waiting this time for Nick to speak first. He raised his right hand.

"I solemnly swear to tell the truth, the whole truth, or nothing but the truth."

Lena grabbed a gavel out of her briefcase and banged the table, just missing Nick's left hand.

"That's '*and* nothing but the truth,'" she amended.

"Can't I just pick one?"

Lena removed a legal pad and pen from her briefcase, slipped off her shoes, and leaned precariously backward on the two rear legs of the chair, resting her feet on the bed.

"What were you doing at Lund's grocery store on June 11?" Lena asked.

Nick picked up the puppet and began to pantomime the events.

"We were on a routine training mission. Suddenly things got hot. We spotted the perp assaulting the victims, so we identified ourselves and attempted to intervene."

"Training for what?"

"Defending the innocent."

"And why do you do that?"

Nick lifted Sancho like a stone tablet.

"And God said: 'Behold the Defender of the Innocent. Unless you shall be as one of these, you shall not enter the kingdom of heaven.'"

"Did he say this to you in person?"

"Of course not."

"Good."

"It was on C-SPAN."

Lena nodded to Sancho.

"Why him?"

"He's a sheepdog."

"So?"

"He can see who is innocent."

Lena put down her notebook and pen.

"You can see whether someone is innocent?"

"I can't. He can."

Lena leaned forward to look at Nick. Sancho leaned forward to kiss Lena on the forehead with his fuzzy pink tongue.

"How. Does he. What?" she asked.

Sancho stood at attention and saluted with his paw.

"Love," Nick replied.

"You can see that?"

"I can't. He can."

She drew his conclusion.

"So if I loved you, I would be considered innocent?"

"By reason of insanity."

"I'll take your word on that."

"Thank you, Ms. Grant," Nick said and turned to Sancho. "No more questions."

Lena closed her notebook.

"Nick. If this goes beyond tomorrow, beyond the competency hearing, we need to find you a new lawyer. It's not smart for me to represent you."

"Can't decide whether you want me to win?"

"No," she said. "I can decide."

Nick waited. Then Sancho's paw pointed to Lena.

"We want you," Nick announced.

Sancho nodded vigorously.

*   *   *

"May I come in?"

The voice belonged to Preston Winter.

The bedsprings groaned as Nick sat up.

"Be my guest," Nick said. "Or am I yours? I forget."

Preston sat in the chair and leaned in over the wobbly wooden table.

"I've decided to put you out of your misery."

"But you just got here," Nick responded pleasantly.

Preston continued, unwilling to interrupt his rehearsed speech.

"I can't see Lena hurt this way any longer. I'm going to end her suffering. And yours."

Nick folded his arms. "Our tax dollars at work."

Preston paused. "You object to euthanasia?"

Nick nodded. "Too many syllables."

The lids of Preston's eyes lowered slightly. He would not lose control, despite the intense turmoil. The stakes were high. An ex parte communication could cost him his job. He knew Nick knew that. What he was about to propose could cost him everything, or win it.

"It's from the Greek, you know. It means 'a good death.'"

"Why are you here?" Nick asked.

"You're a smart guy, Nick. I thought, maybe, you would do the right thing."

Preston moved next to Nick.

"Look at this place. Imagine a lifetime in here, a lifetime of drugs and restraints and therapy and more drugs until finally there's no you anymore. You're gone. And as bad as this place is, prison is worse. Much worse. You know that. You've seen it."

He edged closer.

"Imagine what it will be like for Lena with you here or in prison. You lose. I lose. She loses."

Nick put his arm around Preston's shoulder and escorted him the few paces to the door.

"I wouldn't watch any more *Godfather* reruns if I were you, Preston."

Preston smiled.

"Your family will be taken care of."

He stopped smiling.

"Take care of yourself, Nick."

*   *   *

Preston and Lena spoke quietly outside the courtroom doors.

"They're adding charges. Destroying government property. Interfering with a government operation. Reckless endangerment."

Lena's mind raced.

"Those are felony counts."

Preston nodded. "They think he's some kind of animal rights terrorist," he added.

"They want jail time?"

"No deals. He's committed or he goes to jail."

"Can't you do anything?"

Preston shook his head.

"If the judge rules that he's competent, he's going to prison," he told her.

Lena began pacing in front of the doors.

"You're telling me that to keep him out of prison, I have to commit him to a mental institution."

"Yes. The judge must decide that he is unable to stand trial. If that happens, commitment is a certainty."

"It won't work. Whatever I try, he'll see through it."

Preston's expression was brittle.

"Not if he still loves you."

Lena collapsed on a bench.

"How can I do that to him?"

Preston edged down next to her.

"Maybe you shouldn't," Preston answered firmly.

Lena shot him a trapped look.

"How can I not?"

*   *   *

Oscar escorted Nick into the same small courtroom that had been used for the arraignment. Like pieces on a chessboard, they moved into the previous diagonal juxtaposition.

Sharon sauntered through the courtroom doors, pulling a litigation case behind her. She set it on the table where Nick was sitting and then took a seat in the gallery not far from Oscar. She eyed Oscar and the handcuffs with curiosity. Oscar pulled out *Daredevil 106*, which he had folded twice and stuffed into his back pocket. Sharon moved closer.

"Vintage Marvel," she noted.

"You like comic books?" Oscar asked.

"I love them. I'm a big Mr. Fantastic fan," she replied.

Oscar reached into his pocket, pulled out a business card, and handed it to her.

"How amazing are you?" she asked.

A dog barked.

Nick spun around.

Wolfram was sitting by the door, shoulder high to a very nervous bailiff. Attached to his collar, a helium balloon fluttered in the air conditioning. The logo read: BREAK A LEG.

Nick waved to Wolfram, then to Ralph, who was sitting in the aisle seat, barely able to restrain the colossal dog, and then to Alice, seated next to Ralph. Ralph petted Wolfram and gave Nick a thumbs-up. Alice shook a finger at Nick and edged the corners of her mouth into an anxious smile.

Preston and Lena strode into the courtroom together, pacing briskly down the center aisle, bursting in unison through the gate, then splitting at right angles like a marching band from a very small school that couldn't afford any instruments.

Lena edged in next to Nick at the defendant's table. Preston sat at the prosecutor's table. Both looked grim.

Nick turned to Lena.

She shook her head.

He looked away.

Lena took out some papers, then set her watch on the table. The bailiff stood.

"All rise."

Nick recognized Judge Anne Ritchfield from the arraignment.

"Sit sit sit," she ordered, shuffling through her papers, then surveying the hearing room before motioning for the bailiff.

"There's a dog in the courtroom," the judge whispered.

"Yes, Your Honor," replied the bailiff.

"This one looks real."

"Yes, Your Honor."

"Don't tell me: he's a material witness."

The bailiff nodded. The judge sighed.

"Call the case."

The bailiff turned to the court.

"State versus Nicholas Ward."

"Well, I see we're all here once again," said the judge. "Wait. Where's the puppet?"

"Oh!" said Lena, reaching into her litigation case and extracting Sancho. Nick reached for him immediately.

"I want to remind everyone," the judge declared, "that this is a competency hearing, not a trial. Which means I make up the rules as I go along. You can object if you like but don't expect me to care. Any objections?"

"Your Honor," Lena began, standing. She got halfway out of the chair.

"No?" the judge interrupted. "Good. Call the first witness."

Preston began to stand, then looked at Lena, who was frozen in a halfway standing position that to Oscar resembled the Egyptian hieroglyph for indecision. For a moment, Lena and Preston were a silent calliope, sitting and standing, until finally Lena slid into her seat and Preston attained full height.

"The state calls Dr. Henry Richardson," he announced.

Dr. Richardson entered the courtroom briskly and took the witness stand. The bailiff approached him.

"Do you solemnly swear to tell the truth, the whole truth, and nothing but the truth?"

Dr. Richardson did. Preston, hoping to proceed quickly, remained at the prosecutor's table and discharged his questions with pace and precision.

"Doctor, you are a psychiatrist?"

"Yes. In practice for twenty-one years."

"And you are treating the defendant?"

"Yes."

"Have you formed a medical opinion about the defendant's mental condition?

Dr. Richardson looked at Nick.

"Mr. Ward suffers from a psychiatric condition known as delusional disorder."

"Can you describe that for the court?"

Dr. Richardson straightened his tie, after which his hands dropped down to the railing in front of the witness box. His fingers played with an imaginary cigar.

"Certainly. Patients with this disorder have beliefs that they maintain regardless of compelling evidence to the contrary."

"Thank you, Doctor. In your opinion, is the defendant competent to understand the charges against him?"

Dr. Richardson paused.

"Mr. Ward is highly intelligent, often lucid, and his legal knowledge seems, so far as a layman can judge, intact."

Preston stood and emerged slowly from behind the table to highlight his most important question.

"Again, in your professional opinion, is the defendant able to participate in his own defense?"

The doctor paused again, longer this time. His face was troubled.

"That is a much more difficult question. His condition is not predictable and can change rapidly."

The judge broke in.

"Doctor, is Mr. Ward's condition controllable by medication?"

This time the doctor answered quickly.

"Medication can be helpful. There are whole new classes of antipsychotic drugs that might be efficacious. But in Mr. Ward's case, extended hospitalization may be required to find a medical regimen that will consistently alleviate the symptoms."

The judge nodded. Preston stepped up.

"I have no more questions, Your Honor."

The judge looked at Lena.

"Your witness, Ms. Grant."

Lena stood and smoothed out the front of her suit. Her hands were trembling slightly.

"Hello, Doctor," Lena said pleasantly. "I have a simple question. What's wrong with him?"

The doctor said in his wisest voice: "As I said, my diagnosis at this time is delusional disorder."

"Is that what is wrong with him?"

Dr. Richardson looked at Nick, hoping for either a clue or a dispensation. He found neither one in Nick's eyes, which reflected only amused curiosity.

For twenty-one years, Dr. Richardson had dealt with the most difficult of institutionalized cases. Too many of his patients were like Greek tragedies: good people with a fatal genetic flaw that would ultimately destroy not only their own lives but the lives of those around them. He did what he could. Sometimes it worked. Sometimes it worked for a while. Often it didn't work at all.

"That's what we're telling the insurance company."

"So basically he's crazy."

"We don't—"

"Is that why he drives me crazy?"

"It's not—"

"Is there some crazy bug? How is it transmitted? Sexual contact? A sneeze? Gravitation?"

"Counselor," the judge cautioned.

"The German philosopher Immanuel Kant—"

"Why doesn't he love me enough to be normal?"

"Counselor."

It was a question Richardson had heard many times, in many forms. His only answer was another question.

"If he were normal, would you love him?"

Lena glanced at Nick, knowing the answer but unwilling to give voice to it. She stepped away and walked a shaky path back to the defendant's table.

"One last question, Doctor. Could stress be a factor in setting off the delusions? For example, the stress of a trial?"

"Very likely. Stress is often a critical factor," the doctor responded.

"That's all," said Lena as she sat.

"Thank you, Doctor," the judge said. "You may step down." Dr. Richardson took a seat in the gallery close to Nick.

Lena glanced at Preston and nodded, then looked to the judge.

"Your Honor, may we approach?" she asked.

The judge waved them forward. As Preston and Lena reached the bench, Nick leaned down, removed something from Lena's litigation case, and passed it surreptitiously to Oscar.

"Your Honor," Lena said. "I feel that both the state and my client would be best served if he were in a place where he could receive proper treatment for his illness."

The judge stopped her.

"Ms. Grant, I only have one decision to make here today: whether your client is competent to stand trial."

"Your Honor, he talks to a puppet."

"Ms. Grant, do you have stuffed animals?

"Well, yes."

"Do you ever talk to them?"

"Well. Yes."

"I talk to my car," said the judge. "My son talks to the dog. My husband yells at the football players on television. Sometimes he even waits for them to answer. Yet, except for my son, that does not seem to preclude any of us from acting competently."

"No, Your Honor," Lena agreed reluctantly.

"I need proof. Step back."

Lena and Preston stepped back in tandem. Lena turned to him.

"I have to do this?" she asked without hope.

"He'll be better off."

"There's no other way?" Lena asked again, searching Preston's eyes for bureaucratic salvation. Preston shook his head.

"Well," Lena sighed, "what woman wouldn't jump at the chance to drive her ex-husband crazy?"

The judge waived the bailiff over.

"What happened to the dog?" she asked.

The bailiff scanned the room. Wolfram was missing.

"Maybe it went for a walk," he replied.

"Well, if it's not here when it's called to testify, you're in trouble."

"Yes, Your Honor," the bailiff responded.

"Ms. Grant, let's get going," the judge called out. "We only get two weeks of summer here. I'd like to enjoy them."

Lena nodded. "Your Honor," she asked, "may I have a minute to confer with my co-counsel—I mean my client?"

"Any objection?" the judge asked Preston.

"No, Your Honor."

"Make it fast," the judge ordered.

Lena walked over to Nick and leaned across the table.

"It wasn't a dog," she said.

"What?"

"That story you tell: you wanted a dog, I didn't, you insisted, I bought Sancho. It's a good story. But it's not true."

Nick shook his head.

"I don't understand—"

"You didn't want a dog."

"I don't—"

"You wanted a child."

"I—"

"I didn't buy Sancho. You did. You bought a new stuffed animal every day. And every day I tried to imagine what life would be like for our child."

Lena touched Nick's cheek. She could almost hear the drums in his mind begin to roll and the piccolo to trill.

"You're an amazing man, Nick. You're brilliant and funny and surprising in so many ways. You do so many things so well. But I'm just not sure that love is one of those things."

She took her hand away but would not look down.

"And I couldn't do that," she said. "I couldn't have our child go through life feeling the way I felt."

She took a breath.

"So I told you I wanted a child too. Just not with you."

Lena felt, with the professional certainty of one who performs such acts for a living, that she had broken him again, just as she was certain now that she had broken him before with the same statement. And she marked the moment in her mind with the color that she reserved for those acts for which she could not forgive herself.

Nick picked up Sancho. One side of his mouth curled up as he bent to whisper to her: "We are. Imaginary."

He cradled Sancho as he walked away, then carefully balanced the puppet on the dark polished railing as he sat in the witness stand.

"Ms. Grant," the judge said. "Are you ready to proceed?"

Lena turned hastily to the judge.

"I call Nicholas Ward to the stand."

The bailiff approached Nick.

"Please stand and raise your right hand."

Nick stood. The puppet tumbled off the polished railing down to the floor. As the bailiff leaned over to pick him up, Nick calmly slid the weapon out of the bailiff's holster. The bailiff felt the motion, grabbed, but too late. Nick raised the hand with the gun, barrel pointing at the ceiling.

"I solemnly swear to tell the truth, the whole truth, and nothing but the truth. All of the above."

The bailiff stood still, unwilling to move.

"Thanks. I'll take him," Nick said as he retrieved Sancho. "You can stand down," he directed calmly, motioning the stunned bailiff back with the weapon. The bailiff glanced at the judge, then complied. All other motion in the courtroom had ceased.

Lena fought her shock and confusion, gathered herself.

"Nick, are you crazy?"

He smiled.

"Why do people keep asking me that?"

Underneath Nick's familiar tone she recognized something new and struggled to classify it.

"Put down the gun," she ordered.

As Nick shoved the cold mouth of the gun barrel hard against his temple, he turned to Preston, who stared, unbelieving, mouth half open.

"What we need here is a good death," Nick announced calmly. He surveyed the room and observed the diversity of expression.

Ralph: wondering if it was all a joke.

Alice: worried that she had known it all along.

Preston: shocked and guilty.

Dr. Richardson: unsurprised and riveted.

Oscar: protective of Sharon.

Sharon: protective of Lena.

The judge: powerless and angry.

And finally Lena: terrified but undefeated.

Nick continued: "I mean, it's our proposal. Our method. Our Solution."

Nick went on, his voice quiet, reasonable, chilling: "Inconvenience deserves a death sentence."

Nick turned toward the judge without removing the barrel from his temple.

"But let's not shut it away this time. Let's not hide it in an animal shelter or slaughterhouse or nursing home or prison cell or concentration camp. Let's get it out in the open where we can see once and for all exactly what we are responsible for."

He ran his hand along the slick mahogany surface of the judge's bench.

"Where better for this sacrifice than here?"

Nick waited for an answer. Finally Preston spoke.

"Put it down, Nick," he said. "That's not what she wants. It's not what anyone wants."

Lena glanced around for help, to the judge, to the doctor, to Oscar, to Preston. No one moved.

She looked at Nick. The picture she saw was preposterous and her mind rebelled. Nick hated guns, had never held a gun in his life. She closed her eyes and tried to bring the world into focus again.

All she could think was how sad Sancho would be.

With that image, she sensed the entropy of the universe reverse itself as the fragments of Nick fused in her consciousness and the shattered mirror was whole again.

She took a step toward Nick, holding his eyes with hers, willing him into conjoint awareness. Preston lunged out to pull her back but halted at Nick's warning glance.

"There's something I have to tell you," Lena said quietly.

She continued a step, her voice little more than a whisper: "'Whenever any species is listed as a threatened species pursuant to subsection (c) of this section, the Secretary shall issue such regulations as is deemed necessary and advisable to provide for the conservation of such species. The Secretary may by regulation prohibit with respect to any threatened species any act prohibited under section 1538(a)(1) of Title 16 Chapter 35 of the US Code in the case of fish or wildlife.'"

A step.

"'The term "fish or wildlife" means any member of the animal kingdom, including without limitation any mammal, fish, bird (including any migratory, nonmigratory, or endangered bird for which protection is also afforded by treaty or other international agreement), amphibian, reptile, mollusk, crustacean, arthropod or other invertebrate, and includes any part, product, egg, or offspring thereof.'"

A step.

Inches away.

She put her hand on his arm, imagining her three fingertips like pebbles tossed in a lake, radiating concentric waves of love and serenity through his arm, torso, heart, mind.

Nick cocked his head, tipping the gun barrel up into the air.

"Are you pregnant?"

Lena tipped her head to match his.

"Are you crazy?"

The gun slipped to the floor as he answered: "No more questions."

Nick sank without another word into the witness chair, giving Sancho, who was now in Lena's arms, a brief nod. The bailiff quickly retrieved the gun and handcuffed Nick. The judge peered at Preston.

"Cross-examination, Mr. Winter?"

Preston shook his head.

"Bailiff. Take Mr. Ward to his seat."

The bailiff escorted Nick to the defendant's table. Oscar moved up and sat next to him.

"We rest, Your Honor," Lena said.

"If counsels will waive closing remarks?" the judge asked.

Lena and Preston nodded. Judge Ritchfield continued: "Mr. Ward, medical testimony and other evidence indicate that you have an uncontrolled mental illness that prevents you from fully participating in your defense. The court finds that you are not competent to stand trial on these charges."

Oscar clapped. Nick seemed not to register the remarks. Lena looked down. Preston looked unhappy.

The judge went on: "The court also finds that this condition renders you a danger to yourself and to others. Consequently, I am ordering you confined to an appropriate psychiatric institution until such time as medical evidence shows your illness to be under control. Good luck, Mr. Ward. Court is adjourned."

The judge stood and quickly left the hearing room. Lena took Nick's hand.

"Oscar will bring you out front. I'll meet you there."

Preston's eyes followed Lena to the door, then he gazed at Nick with a puzzled expression. He spun around behind the prosecutor's table, staring at the wall. Oscar escorted Nick out of the courtroom, flanked by a couple of bailiffs.

"Is it all set?" Nick asked in a whisper.

"All set," Oscar replied.

*   *   *

Outside the courthouse, Nick and Oscar waited by the rear door of the institute van. Lena soon emerged from the building with Sancho, followed closely by Sharon.

Nick whispered to Oscar: "I need to speak to Lena alone."

Oscar spoke to the bailiffs, who agreed, but continued to watch Nick closely. Nick gestured Lena into the shadow of the court building.

"I have that stupid awards banquet tonight," she said hurriedly, "But I'll be over first thing tomorrow."

He took her hands as best he could with his wrists restrained.

"You think this is your fault, don't you?"

Lena shouted "Yes" inside but responded: "No."

"Well, it is," Nick said.

Lena was speechless.

"You saved me," he continued.

Lena shook her head.

"You know you're going back to the institute, don't you?" she asked.

Nick laughed. A car pulled up behind Lena. Before she could turn to see who it was, Nick drew her close.

"I have a favor to ask you," he whispered.

"What?"

"I want you to take care of Sancho."

"Why?"

"He's a puppet."

"So?"

"Well, he can't take care of himself."

Lena looked down, then nodded.

"Sure," she said, laughing, unsurprised finally that with everything that had happened this was what he worried about.

"Do you know what this means?" he asked.

"Is it absolutely necessary?"

"You are now officially a Defender of the Innocent."

Nick kissed her on both cheeks like a legionnaire, then lingered on her mouth.

"Thanks," he said.

"There's that word again."

Lena and Nick rejoined Oscar, who was conversing intently with Sharon at the back of the van. Oscar reached for Lena's hand, deposited something cold in her palm.

"I assume this means I don't get the Porsche," Oscar said.

Lena gave him a puzzled glance, then examined his gift.

"These are my car keys. How did you—"

"Time to go," Nick said, climbing into the back of the hospital van.

Sharon moved close to Lena, never taking her eyes off Oscar.

"Do you know the definition of insanity?" Sharon asked.

"Yes," said Lena. "It starts with an L."

Sharon nodded.

"By the way," she said, looking over Lena's shoulder, "nice dog."

Lena twisted around. Her Porsche was parked behind her, top down. In the passenger seat, towering over the windshield, sat Wolfram, observing all with blessed serenity.

"Oh, no."

She turned back to Nick.

"Oh, no!"

Oscar slammed the rear door of the van. Nick waved through the window.

"You. I am not. There is no way."

The van pulled slowly away.

"Come back here!" Lena cried.

Finally she approached the colossal hound.

"Do you remember me?" she asked sweetly.

"Are you hungry?

"Are you really a dog?"

*   *   *

Sipping a snifter of Hawaiian Punch, Lena sat in lotus position in her office chair (her outfit for the evening hanging behind her). Her desk had absorbed the sunset radiating through the windows, a Turner skyscape enshrined in crystal. The reflection transfigured the walls, entrancing her. Blue to yellow. Sunrise backward. Orange to red. A rainbow smeared out over time. Blue to violet. The happy refraction of the reality circling in the dark.

She tried to identify the moment when the color changed. But she couldn't.

There was no moment of change.

Only change revealed.

* * *

The banquet room was full, seats occupied mostly, but not entirely, by women. On the wall behind the dais, the banner proclaimed:

Minnesota Business Women

Humanitarian Award

Preston Winter hurried into the room and found Lena seated on the dais next to the podium. He caught her eye, waved her over.

"Something has happened." Lena said flatly. Not a question.

"He's missing," Preston replied. "And so is the van from the institute. And so is the driver."

Lena moved unsteadily. She didn't make it all the way to the chair, but collapsed onto the steps of the dais. Preston knelt beside her.

"He wouldn't hurt anyone," she said.

"After what we saw in court today, can you be sure?"

"I'll come with you," she said. "I know where to look."

Preston took her hand.

"No. I called Harvey. He's helping us look. You go home in case Nick calls. If he contacts you, call me immediately."

A gray-haired woman in a long gown moved to the podium. Lena saw her, gestured to Preston to wait, and returned to her seat.

"Thank you all for coming tonight," the speaker announced jovially, "and for helping us honor the winner of this year's Minnesota Humanitarian Award. As you know, the award is given each year to the nominee who does the most to make the rest of us feel guilty."

A smattering of laughter rippled through the crowd. Preston sat by the side of the dais.

"Tonight's honoree certainly qualifies with her constant dedication to charitable causes throughout the city, the state, the nation, and the world. Please join me in welcoming tonight's Humanitarian Award recipient: Elena Grant."

Lena stood up at the applause and walked to the podium. She shook hands with the emcee, then gazed out at the seated crowd.

"What does it mean to be a humanitarian?" she asked. "Vegetarian means someone who eats vegetables. Proletarian means someone who also eats vegetables, just not as many. Although I am an attorney, and have from time to time been referred to as a man-eater, I hope that's not why I am being honored today as a humanitarian."

The audience laughed. Preston applauded.

Lena continued: "We grow up thinking that heroes carry guns and badges, or briefcases and gavels, or stethoscopes and scalpels. And they do. But sometimes they carry pencils. Sometimes they carry books. Sometimes ..."

Preston stopped smiling. Lena's voice grew sharper, more brittle.

"They aren't always the easiest people to be around. They are driven by priorities the rest of us may not understand, priorities they aren't always very good at explaining.

"But in their love and gentleness, their honor and selflessness, their oddity, their veracity, their vulnerability, their empathy, they shape the world. They enrich the world. And they make the world proud."

Preston's jaw was taut. His eyes reflected her pain. Tears began to sneak down Lena's face. She ignored them.

"I am proud to accept this award in their honor. We don't always know their names. But we will always remember their gifts. Thank you."

Lena returned to her seat. Preston moved to her immediately. The emcee walked back to the podium.

"I. Uh. Thank you, Ms. Grant. Very. Heartfelt."

Lena hurried out the door of the banquet room, pursued by Preston.

"Well," the emcee covered, "I think it's obvious we made the right choice here tonight."

*   *   *

Lena opened her eyes to a rotated world, then realized she was lying on the floor of her apartment. Wolfram guarded one side, Sancho the other. The phone lay nearby. It was ringing.

The trio stared at the phone for many long minutes as it rang. Finally Lena crawled over, lifted the receiver, listened, then closed her eyes.

"Where did they find him?"

She nodded.

"I'll be right there."

She didn't write it down.

No Man

Wolfram walks a crooked path, through the park and down the bank, along the lagoon. Lena follows, one hand on his leash, the other cradling a gray-and-white bundle to her breast.

Past the ambulance.

Past the fire department.

Past the SWAT team.

Past Preston, arms crossed.

Past the park bench, past Sharon, to Oscar, who reads aloud from a Day-Glo three-by-five card: "I had no choice. I tried to stop him but I couldn't. There was nothing I could do."

"Congratulations," Preston says. "Those are the exact words you need to say to avoid being charged as an accessory. Almost as if an attorney had prepared your statement."

Sharon slips one hand in Oscar's and covers his mouth lovingly with the other.

"As the American philosopher Ralph Waldo Emerson once said, 'Good as is discourse, silence is better, and shames it. The length of the discourse indicates the distance of thought betwixt the speaker and the hearer. If they were at a perfect understanding in any part, no words would be necessary thereon. If at one in all parts, no words would be suffered.'"

"I don't—"

"It means shut up."

"Ahhh," Oscar murmurs, nodding into Sharon's palm.

Lena slides gracefully between Oscar and Preston. Wolfram claims his usual place, eclipsing the bench.

"Whose dog is that?" Preston asks, pointing at Wolfram, then thinking better of it and pulling his hand back to safety.

"Whosesoever he wants to be," Lena replies.

"And what are you doing with that puppet?" Preston continues. Lena ignores him this time.

"Where is he?" she asks.

Preston gestures toward the water.

Lena spins.

In the heart of a lake in the heart of a city in the heart of a land in the heart of the world there is an island in the shape of a heart.

Nick is there. But not alone. Cats of all ages and shapes and colors luxuriate in the morning sun. In Nick's arms, a bundle resolves into kittens.

A German shepherd mix bursts through the brush.

Then a Labrador.

Then a beagle.

Watson.

Alonzo.

Fanny.

Pal.

Rufus.

Grendel.

Annabelle.

Huck.

Then more and more of all shapes and sizes, orbiting Nick in concentric blurs.

"How many?" she asks.

"Every animal in the shelter," Preston replies, then twists around back to Oscar.

"How did he get those animals on the island?"

"Well ..."

"Don't tell me he walked on water."

"Sort of, he did," Oscar explains. "The channel is only a few yards wide right there and not very deep. So we, he, unloaded the animals and drove the institute van into the lake. It sank, but the top was only an inch below the surface. Then Nick started marching around and around pretending he was playing a musical instrument and the animals began following him and pretty soon they were all marching around and around, the cats and dogs, even the puppies and kittens, and then Nick marched down to the shore and right across the top of the van onto the island and they just followed right after him."

"Was he playing a pipe?" Preston asks.

Oscar ponders.

Lena turns back to the island.

"It was an E-flat cornet," she says.

Nick connects, smiles, stirs. Scrambling kittens around his feet, he leans on the sign.

A policeman and a fireman report to Preston, who orders crossly: "Get those animals off that island."

The world swirls. The colors rush together, remix, then whirl back into place, repainting the day. A thrill surges through her till she can barely breathe. But she laughs anyway.

"You can't do that," she manages to say.

"Why not?" Preston demands.

She collects herself.

"That island is a state wildlife preserve. It takes an executive order from the governor to remove any animals."

"How do you know that?"

"Nick is an expert in wildlife regulation."

Preston turns to the policeman.

"Well, then, get *him* off there at least."

Lena shades her eyes.

Nick points to the sign, then to himself.

"You can't do that either," she announces.

"Why not?" Preston demands again.

"The legislation doesn't distinguish between human animals and other animals. He gets just as much protection as they do."

"How do you know that?"

"We drafted the legislation for one of his wildlife groups. Nick thought it was funny."

Preston storms in a circle, all red in the face and shouting.

"Well, he has to come off there sometime and when he does he's going down for kidnapping or dognapping or catnapping or something."

She tries not to smile, fails.

"You can't do that."

Preston stomps like Rumpelstiltskin.

"Stop saying that!"

Then he sighs.

"Why not?"

Lena manages to look serious.

"Because the judge has already found him incompetent to stand trial. When he comes off the island, he goes back to the institute. But I don't think he's coming off anytime soon."

"Why not?"

"Because someone called the media."

Satellite trucks herd through the narrow lane that encircles the lake. Gaggles of cameras overflow the lakeshore while packs of reporters jostle each other, shouting questions to Nick.

"Looks like every local media outlet in town. Not to mention CNN."

One by one, for the cameras, Nick frames each dog and cat and puppy and kitten. And tells their names. Their stories. Their hopes and dreams.

The cameras capture each one: home free.

Preston makes a funny face.

"What does he want?"

Lena turns to Nick. He places his fist to his forehead, extends his middle finger, and wiggles it subtly, not quite the secret sign of the International Brotherhood of Crustaceans.

Lena turns back to Preston.

"He wants the governor to issue a moratorium on nonmedical animal euthanasia throughout the state and provide additional funding for shelters and adoption programs."

"That's political blackmail. The governor won't agree."

Lena sets her feet wide apart, hands on hips. The salmon merino sweater tied around her neck drapes down her back, rippling in the breeze.

"He'll agree because it's a fucking election year and otherwise he gets to condemn puppies and kittens to death on fucking national television."

Preston revolves, arms whirling, a windmill in a cyclone, shouting, furious, into the air: "Get me the fucking governor. Get me the fucking governor!"

Then he stops. Slowly he turns.

"Tell me," he says.

"What?"

"Tell me that he didn't plan all this from the very beginning."

Lena closes her eyes.

"He doesn't make plans. He has visions."

Preston sighs, nods, releases.

"We never imagine we're not the hero," he says.

Lena kisses Preston gently on the cheek. He waves her down to the lakeshore. She drops Wolfram's leash, threads through reporters and cameras and Ralph and Alice and geese and squirrels and trees and grasses, down to the water's edge.

"You're an animal," she calls.

Nick laughs. The backdrop blurs. Amethyst empties the day of shadow. The topaz sun evaporates the mist, unveiling chalcedony trees and emerald grass. Butterflies hover in sapphire suspension.

Wolfram ambles past in stately solo procession, gliding without hesitation across the water's surface. Nick greets him solemnly with a bow.

Lena peers down through the glimmery beryl reflection, through the mirrored sardonyx purl, through the lake of sunrise fire. The path is there.

And then in the midst, diffracted, refracted, reflected, Nick floats, bobbing softly upside down in the clouds, eyes glowing jasper, transverse but whole.

"It occurs to me," his image expounds, "that if I'm not mentally competent, those divorce papers I signed may not be valid."

Lena opens her mouth to speak. No words. Nick steps out from the bank, lowering one knee to the blazing water.

"I imagine that I will annoy you for as long as we both shall live."

Lena's sheep-caught-in-the-headlights look dissolves. The ritual of joining begins.

No more questions.

True Minds

All together now.

We love who we imagine.

So love you.

The world through button eyes is a Revelation.

The Delusion Delusion

Henry Richardson, MD, Ph.D.
Minnesota Journal of Alternative Psychiatry
Volume 12

An English philosopher named Gilbert Ryle once proposed that all human behavior could be explained by referring to observable activity. In logical behaviorism, as he called it, there was no need to refer to anything inside a person. There was no 'Ghost in the Machine'.

No mind.

No spirit.

No soul.

We psychiatrists liked that idea. So we started to come up with lists, lists of behavior. To identify any disease, we just check off the behavioral components on the list.

√ Inflated self-esteem
√ Decreased need for sleep
√ Racing thoughts
√ Rapid conversation

These add up to mania.

Include cycles of:

√ Diminished pleasure

√ Hypersomnia

√ Fatigue

√ Suicidal ideation

Then you have bipolar disorder.

The purpose of this scheme was to preclude the need to look inside a human being. We don't really know what's happening inside, and we can't just start opening people's heads to find out.

(Not while they are alive anyway.)

Oh we can look at brain scans and see that something is happening. Lots of neurological fireworks. But we don't really know what it represents at any level of detail. To say nothing of what it means.

My patient has at once time or another exhibited all of the symptoms of bipolar disorder. Nevertheless, my diagnosis is delusional disorder. Let me explain why.

First, he is nonresponsive to any of the standard medications for depression or bipolar disorder, or any combination of medications that I have tried in during the time that I treated him, both as an inpatient and an outpatient.

Second, he appears to have unabated intentionality and complete volitional control. His behavior, however bizarre it may at first appear, makes sense to him within his particular worldview. And if you spend much time around him, it may begin to make sense to you in a way that is often disconcerting.

Third, though he has been sometimes debilitated by his illness for extended periods, often he is more than able to cope with the world around him. He is in fact able to compel it, to shape it, and make it conform to what he himself calls his visions.

His delusion derives primarily from what I have come to call Imaginative Dissonance, the constant pressure between what he imagines the world could be and what the world actually is. This is the disorder of Visionaries, and I suspect there is no cure.

Delusion is the democratic illness. A delusion is a false belief that the patient maintains despite substantial contrary evidence. How do we determine the belief is false? If the belief is contrary to the beliefs of the majority, it is considered false. We all know what we know, right? We know what is true and false. God? True. Aliens? False. Evidence? Who needs it, really?

So what is this patient's false belief?

I don't know.

The obvious choice is the sheepdog puppet named Sancho, his constant companion. He treats the puppet as real, but calls him Unreal or Imaginary. But I suspect for this patient Unreal isn't not real. Is that false?

The patient marches (literally) to the music in his head, a very different drummer, with an entire marching band besides. I hear music in my head. Is it unreal?

This patient is quite capable of making complicated distinctions, and living his life on the basis of those distinctions. The problem is that he won't tell us what beliefs he acts on. He simply acts. Perhaps his delusion is that he believes he is not delusional.

Because here's the thing:

Either he is delusional.

Or we are.

Let Me Count the Ways

"Obviously," replied Don Quixote, "you know little about adventures."

—Miguel de Cervantes

Feeling Out of Sight

Lena,

Dante wrote of L'amor che move il sole e l'altre stele. *I know that my love cannot bridge the space between us or recover the years we have lost. But I also know that time and space have no claim on the love that I feel, always and everywhere, for you.*

Nick

PS—Sancho misses you.

How Do I Love Thee?

Lena Grant stepped off the elevator on the skyway level of the Wells Fargo Center in downtown Minneapolis, slipped quietly down the deserted corridor until she reached the atrium, paused as she took two deep breaths leaning against the Italian marble wall near the museum with the working telegraph, slid into the historically accurate fully restored red and gold stage coach, hunched down low on the rear bench, and sang, very softly, the Wells Fargo Wagon song from *The Music Man.*

The lobby was deserted, except for the lone security guard at the front. Lena was sure he was aware of what she did. But he was discreet enough not to notice her singing and she was discreet enough not to mention how little affect his thermos of coffee was having.

Qui tacet consentire videtur was the common law maxim: silence gives consent, as Nick would surely have reminded her, after which he would have quoted the entire summation by Thomas More at his trial for treason in 1535, then perhaps a chapter or two of *Utopia*. Lena was a superb attorney, but she did not have her husband's legendary legal memory.

De facto husband, not necessarily *de jure*, she reminded herself. Nick had signed the divorce decree. But was he competent to do so? Nick had suggested that he was not. But in making that argument, wasn't he contradicting the argument?

How can he argue that he wasn't competent if he was competent enough to argue competency?

Lena sat upright, rocking the coach. Exactly, she thought. This was exactly what being married to Nick was like, even when you weren't. Nothing was what it was, and everything was something else entirely that you had never imagined or anticipated.

She couldn't live like this, she decided. And she was going to go home and tell Nick to his face. After no more than three more choruses.

*   *   *

When Lena and Nick decided (had they decided?—she couldn't remember an actual decision) to move back in together, Lena moved out of the building she owned on Hennepin Island and bought a small home near Lake of the Isles in southwest Minneapolis. She accepted without understanding Nick's deep connection to the area, especially the lake and the islands.

And she loved the area herself, would often take her bike out on the paths connecting the Lakes. She and Nick would race, seeing how many circuits she could make riding while Nick and Wolfram walked. It wasn't really a race; she knew Nick held back for the sake of Wolfram, whose frame had many of the issues that dogs his age (whatever it was) experienced. But Wolfram would not be left behind when Nick went to the lake, and Nick did not have the heart to insist.

On the days when Lena was busy (which was most days) and Nick was not volunteering at the Hennepin Animal Shelter, Nick and entourage still wandered the paths by the lakes. Lena did not know what they did, or why, or with whom. But as long as it didn't end up with an ambulance or the fire department or the SWAT team en route, she was content. Nick was not the sort of man who could enjoy being inactive.

Sitting on the stoop in front of her home, Lena lifted the mail slot to listen. It was something she had started doing when things were stressful, which lately had been most days. Fortunately, the front door was hidden from the street by a tall hedge, so the neighbors would not likely spot her. And the colony of sparrows (hundreds from the sound but more likely ten or twelve breeding pairs) that lived in the hedge did not seem to object. The chatter from the throng sometimes made it difficult to hear through the slot, especially towards evening. But they had lived there longer than she had and seemed to tolerate her well enough, so she felt she should return the favor.

As she listened, she hoped for a clue to Nick's state of mind. Sometimes the clue was musical: *The Liberty Bell March* meant a joyful Nick. *Brandenburg Concertos* meant he was working on something. For a long while she had not heard them, but they had recently reappeared in the repertoire. *Songs of the Auvergne* signaled an introspective Nick (Te Kanawa version), or a romantic one (Von Stade).

If the clue was not musical, sometimes it was still aural. Nick would be speaking, on the phone, or to Sancho or Wolfram, or to other audiences unknown and probably unknowable to anyone but him. Or he might be reading poetry out loud to his imaginary (sorry Imaginary) assembly. Yeats or Shakespeare were his favorites, Cummings or Browning (E. B. not Robert) hers.

When this happened, she would settle in on the stoop and listen. Nick was an enthralling reader: his comprehension, diction, evocation; the flow of the sounds; the voice itself–subtle and wry, soft yet forceful– reminded her of being in his class in Law School.

And then sometimes he was silent, which left her completely unprepared.

Lena did not know any normal people in in normal relationships, but she suspected that most of them did not have to sit outside their houses after work. Or maybe they did. Maybe they should. Maybe her relationship wasn't so odd after all. Maybe it was the model for modern major marriages.

Lena stifled most of a laugh, hoping Nick did not hear. Lena didn't know if Nick knew that she listened. With Nick, you could never discount the possibility of theater, even if you were not the audience. Even if the audience was Imaginary.

The sun was down, and it was starting to get chilly for a Minnesota September night, which meant cold most other places. Minneapolis tended to be a few degrees warmer than most of Minnesota. Lena didn't know if it was the confluence of the Mississippi and Minnesota rivers that altered the climate, or the Urban Heat Island Effect (which she originally thought was one of Nick's tall tales but turned out was an actual meteorological phenomenon), or something different.

Something different would not have surprised her. There was a charm to the city that she understood but could not describe. Maybe it was because charmed creatures like Nick existed there, or maybe charmed creatures like Nick existed there because of Minneapolis.

There had been some magic even in her surprising choice of Minneapolis as a destination after graduate school. She just couldn't decide if it was white magic or black magic. Most likely it was neither black nor white but rainbow magic, like everything else in her life, beautiful and fragmented and ephemeral.

Destination. How much destiny is in destination? Would she have been happier in a black and white life? She wondered from time to time. Was it her love that made Nick extraordinary or the extraordinary in Nick that made her love? Doctor Richardson had asked her that once.

Preston. Preston would have given her a normal life, offered her one, in the marital interstice that ended what seemed decades before, but was really only a year and a half. Less than that. Preston would have loved her. She didn't love him but she could have eventually. Maybe. He was a good man. And they would have had one of those just so houses on the lake shore, given just so dinner parties, had just enough of just so children. She could have chosen that path after the divorce. Or could she? How much destiny was in destination?

The ancient Greeks had worshipped three goddesses linked to the idea of destiny: Ananke, goddess of Necessity whose mate was Khronos, Time; the Moirai or Fates, the three sisters who spun out the threads of life; and Tyche, the goddess of Fortune, who brought abundance. Necessity. Fate. Fortune.

She thought about the houses around her, the great houses, the smaller homes like hers just blocks away, the duplexes, triplexes, condos. Were they the site of happier lives, more fulfilling lives?

She knew better. Life was life no matter where you lived it. And she knew that despite the trials that she had experienced, she was both gifted and blessed by the life she had now. Whatever the necessities, whatever her fate, she counted herself fortunate.

Still. She was sitting outside her front door in the cold, listening in silence to silence.

She stood, got out her key, and entered.

*   *   *

Each evening when Lena entered the foyer of her home, she would open the door wide to remove her key, shut the door, then turn the inside lock, then the deadbolt. She would let her briefcase slide to the floor near the umbrella stand, drop her keys in the ceramic dish on the black lacquer table that she had inherited from her mother, then turn and toss, actually toss, her coat onto the wooden rack in the corner. About nine out of ten times the coat would land properly on the peg; occasionally it would plunge to the floor. Lena would stare at it for a moment, give a small laugh, then pick it up and try again.

From the foyer, Lena could see Nick sitting on the floor, using the piano bench as a desk. A yellow Number 2 pencil notched with bite marks wagged up and down in his mouth as he examined his work. Sancho supervised from above, propped up against the music stand with *Liebestraum No. 3* as his backdrop.

Lena let her briefcase slide to the floor, dropped her keys in the dish, then turned and tossed her coat onto the wooden rack, successfully. Then she turned to Nick.

"What are you doing?"

"Ahahahahahahaha," emerged from Nick.

"Please take the pencil out of your mouth."

Nick complied.

"I'm writing you a love letter."

Lena thought for a moment.

"No really. What are you doing?"

Nick put the pencil back in his mouth and said emphatically:

"AHAHAHAHAHAHAHA."

Lena paused. It was odd, which with Nick often meant it was true. Nick frequently composed little notes to her signed by Sancho and his troop of stuffed animal companions. And sometimes he would text her, making up secret codes on the fly based on wherever he happened to be, so they would read like:

The butterfly skips across the daisies of Greenland

which he would later explain meant he was stopping by the grocery store for pistachio ice cream. But never could she recall any physical notes or letters from Nick as Nick, whoever that might be at the moment.

"Can I see it?"

"It's a first draft."

"I don't mind."

"I'll show it to you later."

"Later when?"

"After the next time we aren't together."

Lena drew back her hand. This was something they both knew was a possibility, but they had never spoken of it. They had been married, then divorced. This was a trial...trial what?

Remarriage?

Repatriation?

Lena was not sure, nor was she sure it was going to work, nor was she sure what options she had whether it worked or not.

"What makes you think I will leave you again?"

Nick looked at her and something flashed in his eyes, a passage of emotions so swift and complex as to be unreadable.

"I know things."

Lena felt a shiver pass through her, starting at the back of her neck and passing down both sides and meeting in the middle of her stomach. He did know things, things only he knew. Sometimes these things did not exist. But sometimes they did.

"Can I see it please?"

Nick handed her the paper.

"You have to promise to act surprised the next time you see it."

The note was in Nick's large elegant script, which for some reason always had a hint of the Renaissance for Lena. She read the note three times, then handed it back to Nick.

"This note would not bring me back to you."

Nick looked at her sharply.

"What would?"

She recognized that tone as the one that would have brought whatever she mentioned to her doorstep in the morning. She thought of saying the mocha espresso gelato from the café across the lake, because she really did want some. But she knew Nick would not stop at buying a cone.

He would buy the store.

Or the building.

Or the Italian company that made the gelato.

Or Italy.

He was reading Dante again. There was no telling what could come from that. So she said:

"This note will not bring me back to you because I will never leave you."

"I know," he said. "I'm going to leave you."

She felt that shiver again, but steadied.

"Maybe. But you're not taking Sancho."

*   *   *

As Lena came down stairs, she found Nick sitting in the breakfast nook drinking coffee and reading the comics page of the Minneapolis Star-Tribune to Sancho, who was gazing out the window at the squirrels who lived next door.

In the beginning, Lena thought Sancho was a substitute for, or at least a reminder of, what was missing in both their lives: a child. But now for Nick he had evolved into a familiar of sorts, like the bird, the owl, Merlin's owl, in *The Once and Future King*, Nick's favorite book, which he read (out loud to her) at least once a year. Or a channel, connecting Nick to something, or something to Nick. Or even an alter ego, not that Nick needed any more of those, in her opinion.

Nick looked up at Lena's approach, as did Wolfram, who lay dozing at Nick's feet (and halfway into the kitchen).

"Sterling deposition today," she announced.

Nick nodded.

"I read the draft of your brief. You didn't site *US v. Holt*."

Lena picked up her coffee and sipped.

"I know," she said. "I thought *Lamprey v. State* was sufficient."

Nick closed his eyes, and she knew he was reviewing the Lamprey decision in his head. He nodded again.

"Probably right. You usually are."

"As you always said in class, briefs should be."

Nick smiled.

"I used to say that, didn't I? A little obvious for me."

"You were speaking to eighty students who hadn't slept in two years. You needed to be obvious."

Nick picked up Sancho, who continued to stare out at the squirrels, who were now starting to stare back.

"The rhyming couplets were also very helpful," Lena added, kissing him lightly on the head.

"What time is it?" he asked.

"Half past I want you out of the house," she responded.

Nick nodded.

"I think we need our clock fixed. That time comes around a lot."

Lena ran her hand through his hair, pulling lightly, then smoothing it back.

"I need to review this brief and I just focus better when you aren't here," she said.

Nick rose quickly and slid his arms around Lena's waist.

"Are you saying I'm a distraction?"

Lena disentangled herself.

"That is not the word I would use."

"What word would you use?"

"The word I need has not yet been invented."

Nick held his hands up in mock surrender.

"I see. Well, I think we are due for Lake Patrol anyway. What do you think, Wolfram? Shall we sally forth with Sancho?"

Lena glanced at Wolfram, unable to control the impulse to expect him to respond.

Wolfram lifted his enormous head and looked at Sancho. Wolfram's mysterious orbs and Sancho's button eyes glittered in the morning sunlight, giving Lena the impression that they were communing telepathically.

"Good," she said. "Enjoy."

Nick picked up Wolfram's leash and nodded. Wolfram raised his regal head and allowed Nick to fasten the snap on his collar, then began the tenuous process of rising. Wolfram insisted on the leash, would not walk without it, and Lena sometimes wondered if it was for Nick's benefit, to keep him tethered to something.

"Don't rescue anyone," she added.

"Or anything."

"Or need to be rescued yourself."

"And remember you have a 1:00 appointment with Doctor Richardson."

"I remember," Nick called as the cavalcade exited.

*   *   *

Nick and Oscar sat together on a bench outside Dr. Richardson's office at the Golden Valley Psychiatric Institute. Wolfram lounged at Nick's feet as Oscar held Sancho while reading one of the mildly mangled comic books he collected obsessively.

The office door opened and a voice called out: "I'm ready. Are you?"

"You know," said Nick. "Every once in a while I hear this disembodied voice that thinks it knows everything."

"I heard that," said the Voice.

"It's beginning to worry me," Nick added.

"Me too," said the Voice.

*   *   *

Doctor Henry Richardson, Chairman of the Department of Psychiatry and Medical Director at Golden Valley Psychiatric Institute, and Nick's therapist, sat conducting Scriabin's *Fourth Symphony* with his unlit cigar while quietly observing Nick.

During his therapy sessions, Nick didn't like to talk about himself. So they generally filled the first part of the session listening to music, the second part talking about music, and the third part with Nick evading questions. It seemed to work for both of them.

"You always wear the same suit," Doctor Richardson noted.

"No. I always wear a different suit," Nick replied. "It just looks the same."

The sessions were no longer court-mandated, and neither participant pretended that therapeutic improvement was being made, but Richardson still hoped it might, if it turned out that therapeutic improvement was indicated. His training told him it was, his intuition whispered something else. He enjoyed the puzzle and hoped for the best.

Nick never missed a session. Richardson suspected that he simply enjoyed the company of someone who had seen enough in life to wonder instead of judge. Plus, it gave Lena someone to talk to about Nick who might be on Nick's side occasionally, which he likely regarded as a bonus.

Scriabin's piece was 22 minutes, a bit longer than usual, so when it ended Richardson skipped the second part and plunged right into questions.

"So, how do you feel?"

Nick wiggled his fingers.

Doctor Richardson blinked.

"Sorry," Nick said. "That was my mother's one joke."

"Let's change the subject to you. You seem more anxious than usual. Do you feel anxious?"

"Only when I listen to that piece."

"You didn't like it?"

"No. I did. I do. It's Extra Spiritual."

"Do you feel spiritual?"

"It's a little early for me. But if you're offering."

"I need to restock. Next time maybe."

Richardson stood.

"If you don't talk to me, I'm putting the music on again."

Nick turned away.

"I don't negotiate with terrorists."

Richardson scratched his beard. He had grown it the previous year, wondering if it would create an air of gravitas. But the sparkle in his eye apparently undercut that impression. And the resemblance to Santa Claus had for better or worse not gone unnoticed by his patients.

"Are you still working at the animal shelter?"

"Yes. Several days a week. Taking care. Walking. Feeding. Cleaning."

"But."

"I like it. It's good work. And Ralph and Alice are inspiring. But it's hard to. It's not."

"It's not?"

"Enough."

Richardson made a few quick cryptic marks in his notebook.

"What would be enough?" Richardson asked.

Nick was silent for a long moment.

"I don't know."

"I think you do."

Nick shrugged.

"I think I need to go back to work."

Richardson leaned back in his chair and put his hands behind his head.

"Practicing law? Is that even possible?"

Again Nick shrugged.

"My license was never suspended or revoked. There was no allegation of misconduct. I just stopped practicing. Attorneys have issues, just like people."

Richardson gave a little nod.

"Lawyers now are about half my private practice. The Legal professions suffer from mental illness at a much higher rate than the norm. But I was thinking about all the publicity. Could you maintain a practice again?"

Nick shrugged again.

"I would probably get some very interesting cases."

"No doubt. Would you go back to your old firm? With Lena?"

Nick paused.

"That could be tricky."

"Have you mentioned this to her?"

"Not yet. What do you think?"

Doctor Richardson closed the notebook.

"I think you should talk to Lena."

Nick nodded, and his hands moved as if he were looking for Sancho.

"Do you think it is a good idea?" Nick asked.

Now Richardson paused, then opened his desk drawer, took a lighter, lit the cigar, leaned back in his chair, thoroughly enjoyed two long puffs, then extinguished it. He leaned across the desk and spoke slowly.

"I think, for you, that work is a good idea," he said. "But you would need to carefully control any associated stress. I'm not sure that practicing law is right choice."

Nick waved the smoke away.

"I see. Thanks for the advice."

Richardson got up, and opened the window.

"Don't want to lose you Nick," he said.

"As a patient?"

"As you."

*　　*　　*

Lena was trying to decide how to deal with the elephant in the room. Elephants actually. Lena found them in her travels across the world and brought them home with her. The stuffed animals that roamed her office had come from Nick, and they represented his imagination. The elephants were Lena's choice, and they were made of sterner materials like porcelain, brass, and jade. Her favorite was a miniature Carnelian elephant from India.

Lena generally kept them on a special shelf behind her desk. Now she had set them carefully onto the clear glass surface of her desk and pondered their configuration.

She had used the Traveling Circus arrangement before (alternating large and small). But she needed something more concentrated this time. She finally decided on a tight circle in the far right corner nearest the door, with the trunks facing out. Defending the herd.

Sharon came in from the outer office and watched the meticulous process silently. After several minutes of careful trial and retrial, Lena held only the carnelian miniature in her hand.

"What's the name for a baby elephant?" Lena asked without looking up.

"I thought they already had names," Sharon responded.

"They do. I mean, what do you call a baby elephant? A baby dog is a puppy. A baby goose is a gosling. A baby lion is a cub. What do you call a baby elephant?"

Sharon frowned.

"I know there's a joke there somewhere. Give me a minute."

Sharon's sense of humor, too oblique for the Comedy Club circuit (line line punchline beat beat beat vague chuckle), usually found an appreciative audience in Lena. But today Lena was not paying attention.

"I know I know this," Lena said. "But I can't remember."

Sharon looked suspiciously at Lena.

"Are you pregnant?"

Lena's eyes widened but her concentration on the baby elephant balanced in her palm did not waiver.

"No. I. No. Please. No."

Sharon waited. Finally, Lena met her intense gaze.

"I think maybe Nick is like Jesus," Lena announced.

Sharon paused, trying to work out the logical transition.

"Because you aren't pregnant?" she asked.

"No. I. No. Please. No."

Sharon shook her head.

"Nick is not like Jesus. That walking on water bit was a trick."

Lena smiled, sighed, smiled again, frowned, and sighed again, remembering the moment Nick had walked out onto the water at Lake of the Isles.

"It was a good trick," Lena agreed. "He had me there for a second."

"Me too," Sharon admitted.

"No. I mean. What I mean is. The thing is. Nick loves everyone. Just. I'm thinking. Maybe. Like Jesus. No one in particular."

Sharon nodded, satisfied with the explanation if not willing to concede the resemblance.

"A baby elephant is a calf," she said.

Lena smiled, relieved, and placed the carnelian calf safely in the middle of the herd.

"Right," she said. "I knew that. I just kept thinking it had to be something more..."

"What?"

"Complicated."

*   *   *

Lena missed her balcony. Her old apartment on Hennepin Island had spectacular views of sunrise over the Mississippi, and she had loved sitting out there in the morning drinking coffee and preparing mentally for the day's activities. The peace outside generated the peace inside, so she could regenerate the peace outside, which was as she saw it her job, her place in the world.

The sun had not yet risen, and neither had Nick. Nick was nocturnal. She was not. She rose before he did. She went to bed before he did. This blissful disconnect in their schedules had always been a source of serenity for her. Many things were abundant in Nick's presence. Serenity was not one of them.

Lena opened the paper to the crossword, folded it four times, and put Nick's favorite pen on top. She did not look at the crossword herself.

She thought to ask Nick about his session with Doctor Richardson, then thought to make a note about it. In the past she had relied on mental reminders. But in the Nickian universe, physical or electronic notes were required.

She was reaching for her iPad when she heard a noise upstairs. Nick was up. That meant she could finally grind the coffee beans. She knew Nick would not have objected to the noise, but it would have risked her time of tranquility.

At some point, she was going to have to confront this growing issue she had of not feeling comfortable in her own home, or anywhere with Nick. She loved him. But being around him for long periods was getting more and more difficult. It was one of the reasons she had asked for the divorce in the first place. She required a minimum amount of normalcy in her life. And however much Nick understood and respected it, he simply could not provide it.

She heard footsteps on the stairway, but it was four softly padded ones, and knew that Wolfram was making his gentle descent. The problems in his hips sometimes caused his back legs to slip out from under him if he went too fast, so it took him some minutes to navigate the stairway. But he would not sleep downstairs.

The coffee was dripping into the carafe by the time Wolfram padded into the breakfast nook. She was perusing some papers when his huge head lowered into her lap. She scratched him between the ears, at which point he lowered himself gradually at her feet. He was tall enough that he could do this without moving his head. Lena inhaled the aroma of the coffee, yearning. She knew that she would be trapped until Nick arrived.

* * *

Lena heard Nick walking down the stairs and wondered that he sounded like Wolfram. Slow, soft, reluctant steps. He turned the corner into the kitchen and she saw why. He had not dressed—no blue pinstripe suit, his standard uniform. Instead, he was still wearing the t-shirt and boxers he had worn to bed. The only usual accessory was Sancho folded in his arms.

She smiled to think that the puppet was the normal part of the morning. This was definitely her life. The smile disappeared quickly as she began to examine the possible options.

Nick was not feeling well.

Nick was going to try and get her to come back to bed.

Nick was collapsing emotionally and taking the known world with him.

Wolfram lifted his head to greet Nick, and cocked his head at Sancho when Nick set him on the table. Lena, released, started to get up, but Nick anticipated her, poured two cups of coffee, and slid into the nook, pushing the crossword out of the way, and whispering:

"We have to talk."

Uncounted disastrous possibilities flashed simultaneously through Lena's mind. Then she laughed. This was what it was like to be in her husband's head, her flawed ill beloved genius husband. No, Nick would imagine everything working out, everything succeeding, the marriage, the whales, and the world would be saved. And somehow, except for the marriage, it would.

Then her eyes widened: she had used the H word. He was her husband. Till death do they part. And probably not even then. Nick would find her in the Afterlife. And what was worse: she wanted him to. She could not choose anymore; they were both beyond choice. But if she could, she would choose him, the true unending horror of the eternal happy ending.

"You're in a good mood," he said.

"Why shouldn't I be?" she said, reaching for Sancho and pulling him into her arms. "I am surrounded by the ones I love. Completely surrounded."

Nick's left hand drifted toward the crossword, stopped, then curled in.

"I had a good session with Hank Richardson yesterday," Nick said.

"Good. Good. It's good that it was good."

"It's good that you think so."

"I made a note to ask about it. Or did I? I meant to. I'll make a note to start making notes."

Lena set Sancho down on the table and reached for the crossword herself. She stared at it for a minute, as if it were in a foreign language, one she was not fluent in.

"Hank and I were talking about you," Nick said.

"Me?"

"You."

Nick claimed the pen for himself, clicked it, and started drumming it on the table, making little blue dots on the table cloth. Lena stared at the dots. Morse code? Braille? Hieroglyphics? Maybe some ideographic language like Aztec or Akkadian. She was startled from her analysis by the sound of his voice.

"I told him," Nick said, "that I thought it would be helpful if."

"If?"

"If I came back to work."

Lena dropped the crossword.

"At the firm?"

"Yes."

"Our firm?"

"Yes."

"Ward and Grant?"

"That's the one."

Lena took the pen from Nick, clicked it shut.

"That's where I work," she said.

"That's the point!" Nick responded. "We could spend every minute of the day together. Think of it."

"I'm thinking of it."

Nick waited a moment.

"What are you thinking?" he asked.

Lena nodded and said "Noooooooooooo."

"You're nodding and saying no. That's a little hard to interpret."

Lena nodded again and said "Nooooooooooo."

"Maybe we should discuss this later."

Lena nodded again and said "Nooooooooooo."

Lena stood.

"No. No no. No!"

"Well, that's intelligible at least."

Lena noticed that she was holding the pen like a knife, and set it down. Nick reached out and moved it away from her, but did not pick it up himself.

"Nick," Lena began. "Nick. You can't. Come back to work. You can't. It's. Too. Stressful. Too stressful for. You. You have found a little bit of normality, a little tiny precious bit. And you know. I mean, you know. That stress can make you, you know, make you, you know, you. You can't handle the rigors of practicing law any more. You can't. I can't. Watch you put yourself through that. Ever again. Nevermore."

"I understand there is a risk but."

Don't say it, Lena thought. Don't say it. Don't send our life back down the rabbit hole.

"I'm bored."

Lena screamed.

Nick paused.

"So it seems," he said "that this is a longer discussion than I anticipated. We'll talk later."

"Sure."

"You have a good day."

"Sure."

Lena grabbed her briefcase and keys and sped out the door.

Nick sat back down, picked up the crossword, and began to rapidly fill in his answers.

* * *

When Lena entered, Doctor Richardson was standing on the couch in his office conducting Barber's *Adagio for Strings*. She paid no attention to him, walked to the chair in front of his desk and semi-collapsed into it, dropping her keys and briefcase in front of her, and her head into her hands. She waited quietly until the piece was complete and Richardson returned to the desk.

"I think I missed my calling," he said, clicking off the amplifier.

Lena's voice filtered through her fingers.

"If you did, then the rest of us are hopelessly lost. So, maybe you did."

"Are you feeling lost?"

"Can you be lost in the life you insist on?"

"I take it Nick talked to you about coming back to work."

Lena screamed.

"Sorry," she said. "I can't seem to control that reaction."

"Don't worry. That happens a lot in here. And sometimes it's me. It's healthy. Screaming is a common affective vocalization we inherited from our primate ancestors."

"Were they married to Nick too?"

"I take it you are not in favor of the plan."

"He doesn't make...you know."

Richardson nodded.

"What was it like when you first started working together?"

Lena was surprised by the question. It was an area of her memory she had walled off, because to approach led to too much grieving, and worse, too much hope.

"It was his idea. We were already married. I hadn't even passed the bar. But he wanted it so much."

"And you didn't?"

"I did. I probably did. I thought, maybe, offices next door to each other. He'd have his practice and I'd have mine. And we'd meet in the hallway after work and drive home together."

"And working in the same office, how was that at first?"

"It was. Perfect. We were the best legal team I have ever seen. We complemented each other in ways I never imagined. It was effortless and. Perfect."

Richardson crossed his arms, giving her a minute to dwell in that memory space, which he suspected was not one she visited often. Then he learned forward.

"But it changed."

"It did. Or maybe it didn't, until the end, when everything changed. Or maybe in the beginning I didn't notice things I should have. Signs. There were signs. I think there were signs all along. The animals. Sancho! And he would do things, introduce me to trees. Dance in the rain when there wasn't any. Point at the sky during the brightest daylight and say there's Mars, there's Venus, there's galaxy EGS8p7. He had this, this, vision is the right word, I guess. This unique, oblique, magnificent vision of everything and he seemed to see it all at once. He wasn't tied down to what was in front of him, but he didn't miss what was there either. He didn't miss anything. It was charming. And seductive. And thrilling. I should have seen though. Then. But when life is that good..."

"Sure."

"And then. So fast. It all collapsed so fast."

She stopped. Again, Richardson waited.

"And now? How is it now?

"Now?"

Lena searched for a way to explain.

"Imagine living in a firehouse. You spend all your time staring at the bell waiting for it to ring. You don't want it to ring. You know it means wanton destruction. But you know it's going to ring. And you can't stand the waiting. So you need it to ring."

"Vivid. Go on."

"When the bell goes off, I'm all action. I can handle anything. I wonder sometimes if that is how Nick feels. Invincible. Able to leap tall buildings and such."

"And after?" Richardson prompted.

"After. After. Each time the recovery period is longer and longer. And I have become so sensitive that the slightest change in Nick sends these precursor waves of trauma and anxiety and grief. It's like in quantum physics—the waves spread out before the event."

Lena paused.

"When I am at work, I can forget about the bell for a little while. Then I get home and I can stand it, and I can even enjoy our life together. But if I lose that sanctuary, which is certainly what will happen if he comes back to work, then everything will collapse again."

Doctor Richardson nodded.

"Did you tell him that?"

"Not yet."

"You should."

Lena shook her head.

"Is it ethical for us to talk like this?"

"You ask that every time you come here."

"I know. I feel like I'm going behind his back."

"Yes, it's ethical as long as I charge you. Or don't charge you. I can't remember which. Our billing department handles the ethical decisions."

Richardson got up from his desk and walked to a cabinet in the corner. He opened it, removed the vinyl disk from the turntable, and slipped it back into the album cover.

"You're a purist," Lena said.

"No. I can't really hear the difference between analog and digital. I just want to."

He returned to the desk and looked at the album cover.

"I sometimes imagine that our lives have musical scores that that most of us can't quite hear. But Nick can; his is the *Liberty Bell March* of course. I think mine might be the *Adagio for Strings*, with that unattainable sostenuto and the unresolved dominant chord at the end. What do you think yours would be?"

"White noise. Every possible note with no discernible pattern."

Richardson thought for a moment, then smiled.

"Maybe."

Lena was afraid to ask, but did anyway.

"What do you think it is?"

Richardson shrugged.

"I don't know. But I bet Nick does."

*　　*　　*

When the doorbell rang, Lena was on the floor in the den running through her yoga routine. She was wearing pink leggings and a T-shirt Nick had worn to bed for years, before she had appropriated it. There was writing on the front, and a picture of a boat, or maybe a bird. She could no longer make out the writing, which was part of its comfort. Nick would remember, but she liked not knowing.

Lena rose and stepped carefully around the papers spread on the floor. She had planned exactly where to position them so she could read while holding some of the poses. Her instructor had thought this defeated the purpose; but for Lena it was all one. Reading kept her from thinking about anything except what she was reading.

She opened the door and found Nick looking down at her. She was in her bare feet, so he stood close to a foot taller than she did. It was still a startling juxtaposition. She didn't think of him normally as so tall. But then she didn't think of him normally, she thought, and almost laughed.

She was tall herself, and had seldom had a partner make her feel short. The first time she had felt that way, they had been dating a few weeks, if you could call it that—neither one of them dated really, they simply found someone compatible and absorbed them into their routine where possible. He had a class to teach that morning, she was planning to study at home. He had leaned down to kiss her in bed, but at his touch she had rolled out and stood up. She was naked, he was fully dressed in his blue pinstripe suit and unicorn tie and he seemed enormous, as if he were bending to keep from touching the ceiling. She had stepped up on his shoes and kissed him. She felt the impulse to do the same now.

"Is it safe?" Nick asked.

"No. You interrupted my yoga so I'm very dispeaceful."

"Sorry."

Nick stepped inside and the height disparity seemed even greater.

"Why did you ring the doorbell?"

"I lost my keys. Maybe in the park somewhere."

"I'll call the locksmith tomorrow. I have him on retainer."

Lena shut the door and headed back down the hallway to the den.

"That's my t-shirt."

"Not anymore. Possession is whatever," Lena admonished with a wave of her hand.

"That's not actually true, you know. The law is nine tenths of the law."

"So you say."

Lena paused.

"What's the other tenth?"

Nick smiled.

"Never mind," Lena said quickly. "I don't want to know."

"What are you doing here?" Lena asked, settling back into Lotus position. "I was coming to get you."

Nick stopped at the doorway to the den, knowing better than to get in Lena's way in while she was mid-transition. Plus standing outside gave him a better view of the proceedings.

"Thought I'd save you the trouble."

Lena morphed into seated angle pose.

"It's no trouble. I like coming to get you. It means you aren't here."

"It also means I am going to be here."

Lena pulled her legs into bound angle pose.

"There's good and bad in everything."

Nick leaned against the doorframe.

"Aren't you glad I'm here?"

"Quiet. I'm concentrating on my hips."

"So am I."

Lena stood.

"You're not going to let me finish, are you?"

"I'm just trying to say I'm sorry."

Lena gathered her papers and brushed by him, marching down the hall.

"You're sorry. I'm sorry you're sorry. We're sorry together. This doesn't feel like love. I don't know what it is, but–"

"L'amor che move il sole e l'altre stele."

She stopped and turned back.

"No Dante. You want to talk, let's talk."

He smiled and pulled her close.

"I don't need to talk."

She pushed him away and continued down the hall.

"My love is strengthen'd, though more weak in seeming; I love not less, though less the show appear."

She didn't stop or turn.

"And no Shakespeare either."

"There's no balcony here anyway."

"Exactly."

"I'm feeling handcuffed."

"You should be used to that by now."

Nick caught up to her, close behind but not touching.

"Nick, what are you–"

He stepped closer and his hands encircled her waist. He pulled her close, leaned his head down, and whispered.

"How do I love thee?"

Lena turned and slid her arms around Nick, not encircling him, but sliding her hands up his back, supporting him, as he did to her. They held on for a moment, enveloped in one another. Then she raised her head from where it rested on his chest and looked up. He lifted her up, far far up, and she kissed him. It was neither fast nor slow, quick nor long. There was no dimension of time to at all.

Then he carried her upstairs.

After, as they shared the same pillow, staring up at the ceiling, she asked:

"What is love?"

"You're asking that now?"

"I mean. I know what love is for me. What is it for you?"

Nick started to speak but she cut him off.

"No Dante. No Shakespeare. No either of the Brownings. What is it for you?"

Nick's hand slid down her body to find her hand, and entwined his fingers in hers. She pulled his hand up to her lips and kissed it.

"Is it something you feel?" she asked.

She turned to look at him. He looked thoughtful, maybe taking her questions seriously for once.

"Do you love me Nick? Sometimes I think I'm just part of what is wrong with you."

"You are everything that is me."

"That sounds so wonderful and makes no sense at all."

She pulled his hand to her breast and held it there for a while.

"I don't want to lose you again."

"Are you sure?" Nick said, laughing.

"No," Lena said. "But if I do lose you, I want it to be my decision."

"You can't lose me. Even if I'm not here, I'm here."

Lena took a moment to ponder the possible permutations of the phrase.

"See, that's the thing I don't get. To me you're here or you're not. And I'm trying to keep you here by not having you here. See?"

"That makes perfect sense."

"We can't work together Nick."

"I understand."

"Do you?"

"It's what I do."

As Men Strive for Right

At the point nearest the island, Wolfram lies down in front of Nick's bench. His shaggy coat, grey at the edges, provides enough protection from the chilly ground, though it is no longer a match for winter snow.

Nick places Sancho on the bench, then sits, lifting his legs high over Wolfram's frame.

Two geese fly up from somewhere between the two islands that give Lake of the Isles its name, gliding gracefully up in a long elliptical spiral, circumnavigating the island twice, then diving earthward in a dizzying arc, splashing into the narrow channel that separates the shore from the lake. Beads of water leap up in the wake of their passage, invoking rainbows. The pair paddle slowly down the channel and wander into the tall grass that guards the tiny nearer island a stone's throw (or bus length) away.

After a decent interval, the local squirrels approach the bench, having negotiated an uneasy truce with Wolfram, who could not have chased them if he wanted to, and would not have wanted to if he could. Nick pulls peanuts out of his side pocket and rewards them for their courage.

One of the squirrels loses heart and, dashing back up a tree, hovers face down, tail twitching nervously. Nick follows, speaking softly. But as he approaches, the squirrel sidles round

215

to the opposite side. Nick rounds the tree, only to find that the squirrel has eluded him again, clutching close to the bark on the far side.

"A pragmatist I see," Nick states. "Much to admire in that." He drops a few peanuts at the foot of the tree and rejoins his team.

Nick walks down to the water's edge, examining the zizia aurea and rudbeckia hirta that flutter in the slight northern breeze, and the asclepias incarnata and verbena hastata that shudder farther up the bank.

Wolfram growls a warning.

Something splashes.

Drops again glitter in the afternoon light.

Something floats in the lake.

Long.

Thin.

Serpentine.

Another flies over their heads, spins out over the narrow channel between the shore and the island, landing in the grass and alarming the geese, who flee into the air.

A mad roar erupts.

Nick turns and sees that it is only a Giant. In front of the Giant, a Golden Retriever cringes on the ground, terrified by his wrath.

An arm heavy with muscle reaches for a branch, long and thick and crooked with a knob at the end, and rips it off the tree. The Giant limb whirls the giant limb like a demon windmill, as the Giant mouth spits curses at the Golden.

Nick stands and begins the Ritual of Joining. He lifts Sancho into the air and thrusts his right hand inside the silken gauntlet, slender fingers insinuating the jaws, flexing, ready.

They charge to the rescue. Wolfram joins the formation.

The club is raised to strike.

The Golden cowers.

The weapon descends.

Nick speeds forward, catching the giant wrist.

"You could put someone's eye out with that."

The Giant is furious, yet puzzled. He tries to free his wrist, and can't, and can't understand why he can't. Nick speaks again in a soothing and courteous manner.

"A wise man once said: 'an eye for an eye, and soon the whole world is blind'."

Fear blurs the Giant's eyes.

Conceit narrows them.

Deceit vacates them.

The massive shoulders slump, the arm begins to drop, and Nick lets go. Then the Giant whirls to strike again at the Golden. Wolfram barks a warning.

"Sancho!" Nick roars.

Sancho leaps toward the Giant and sinks his tooth into the bulging wrist.

The huge face swings back around, curdling in grim derisive laughter. But his voice croaks, his eyes widen, and his face grows rose red then snow white. He begins to sway. His legs crumple like beanstalks.

Nick catches him toppling and lays his wilting frame gently in grass. The Golden whimpers in gratitude for her deliverance and glances shyly at Wolfram.

The mission complete, Nick and Sancho disengage. From Sancho's silken interior, Nick pulls their secret weapon, a tranquilizer dart that Nick has borrowed from the animal shelter.

Nick pulls out his cell phone, dials 911, reports the fallen foe, then announces: "There are none so blind as those who are unconscious."

Old Griefs

Oscar got up from his desk on the ninth floor of the Golden Valley Psychiatric Institute, unlocked and opened the double steel doors, and listened.

Silence.

He enjoyed his job as night attendant on the ward. He liked to think of himself as more concierge than guard, doing what he could to make the patients' (hopefully short) stays as pleasant as possible. He had seen enough tragic cases come and go, or come and not go, that his open heart recognized the limits of healing, if never the limits of hope. So he did what he could.

He returned to his desk, and the mildly mauled edition of Marvel Team-Up 91. But neither Spider-Man nor Ghost Rider could hold his attention.

Oscar had always wanted a nickname. When he was seven, he tried to get his friends to call him Scar, but it didn't take. He was not a Scar, and deep down he knew it. For one thing, he didn't have a scar. He did have a red birthmark on his left thigh that was shaped vaguely like a whale. But he couldn't warm up to Moby.

Nick of course had the perfect nickname: Nick.

Short.

Strong.

Slightly wounded in a deeply masculine way.

Oscar was not jealous. He knew he was not a Nick. And, on balance, he knew he wouldn't want to be. He admired Nick, loved him (in a deeply masculine way), and preferred his company to almost anyone else. But he wouldn't want to be him.

Anyway, being Oscar was suddenly pretty wonderful. After all these months, it was still something of a shock that Sharon was in his life. Like, all the time. How did that happen? He wasn't quite sure.

Oscar had met Lena through Nick and Sharon through Lena. Sharon was Lena's, well, she said assistant, but he knew better. Oscar was a student of superhero relationships, had published his thesis on his blog at www.amazingoscar.com, which he also used to advertise his part-time gig making balloon animals for children's parties and to display his gallery of balloon animal artistry.

Superhero relationships evolved in three categories: associate, sidekick, and partner, with a fourth category of teammate reserved for semi-permanent multi-hero collectives such as the Avengers or the Justice League. Sharon was Lena's associate at least (though she lacked a law degree), but verged on partner.

Oscar respected Sharon immensely, for her uncompromising mind and sly humor, her intense eyes and elusive smile, and was deeply surprised to find that she was interested in him. Maybe more than interested, though Oscar hardly dared imagine it.

And so he needed a nickname even more. Because without it, he didn't see how he could possibly keep Sharon in his life. A nickname was like a secret identity. Powers he had theorized didn't create the secret identity. It was the identity that created the powers, the Who that created the How.

Deeply engaged in speculation, Oscar didn't see Lena step out of the elevator.

"Where is he?" she asked.

Oscar jumped up at the interruption, his Teenage Mutant Ninja Turtle necktie bouncing over his shoulder.

"His usual room. I try to keep it ready for him."

"I'm sure he appreciates that."

"The police brought him directly here. They seemed nice."

Lena nodded.

"Barry and Hal. They patrol the Lake of the Isles neighborhood and are well acquainted with Nick."

*   *   *

It might have been Nick's usual room, or any other on the ward, for all the Lena could see. Like all the others, there was a bed, a chair, a table, and lots of white. All that distinguished this room was the sheepdog puppet who appeared to be asleep on the pillow, and her possibly but possibly not ex-husband. Not that he was possibly not. Then again possibly he was possibly not. He was certainly impossible.

"Comfy?" Lena asked.

"Like a home away from home," Nick replied, saving Lena from further ontological parsing.

He patted the tiny single bed.

"Join me?"

"I don't think so."

Oscar peeked around the door and waved.

"Hi Nick. Hi Sancho," he added.

Lena turned to Oscar.

"I'll call you if he needs you."

"You betcha," Oscar responded, all too familiar with the imminent peril behind the calm in Lena's voice. He left the door ajar and escaped down the hall, reminding himself to check in later and help clean up any debris.

"So," Lena said, "what's new?"

"Let's recap," Nick responded, "Sancho saved a dog at the park. I got arrested. Hal and Barry took the dog to the shelter, took Wolfram home, then brought me here. Oscar called Sharon who told you. You are going to meet with our favorite Assistant State's Attorney Preston, who will tell you that witnesses at the scene corroborate the story that the dog was being abused, so no charges will be filed. But he will notify the Animal Shelter that they should start an investigation into missing tranquilizer darts. You were going to say 'what were you thinking' but by now you have thought better of it and will just say 'I'll be back'. Did I miss anything?"

Lena paused.

"Preston's actual title is Assistant Attorney General," she said, and turned go.

"Have you thought about what we discussed?"

Lena stopped.

"It's crossed my mind."

"And which direction was it going?"

Lena's eyes narrowed.

"It might keep me out of trouble like this."

"Ha!" Lena said.

Then a deep breath.

Then: "I'll be back."

"Porto sventura a chi bene mi vuole," Nick said.

"Fu in quel dolore che a me venne l'amor," Lena responded, then left.

Nick made sure Sancho was comfortable, then settled in for a nap.

*   *   *

Lena slipped into the courtroom to watch Preston, admiring as always his sharp mind and succinct delivery. Preston was a fine attorney, and had turned down a number of offers to move into the private sector. When his boss retired, he planned to run for Attorney General, but that was years away. For now, he was content where and as he was, doing what he was doing. Content with work anyway, she thought, already regretting involving him again in her troubles with Nick.

The judge quickly ruled for the State, denying the motion in limine. As the parties filed out, Preston joined Lena in the gallery.

"You heard?" Lena asked.

Preston folded his arms and nodded.

"Anything to do with Nick they bring directly to me now."

She sighed.

"Sorry."

"Come on. Let's take a walk."

They left the courtroom, paused briefly at the coffee vendor in the courthouse lobby, then walked outside. It was a mostly clear day, only a few clouds in the Minnesota true blue sky, and in the bright sunlight almost balmy. Lena unbuttoned her long wool coat. She was a northern girl, attuned from birth to appreciate any vestige of warmth.

They strolled slowly side by side for a bit. Preston finally broke the silence.

"He's in GVPI?"

Lena nodded.

"How is he?"

Lena shrugged.

"No charges are being filed," Preston said. "Witnesses corroborate that the dog was being abused. I notified the shelter so hopefully he won't be getting his hands on any more tranquilizer darts. But he may, probably will, lose his certification."

Lena looked up.

"He was certified?"

Preston sighed.

"You can't give me an opening like that and expect me not to use it. It's not fair. I could bust something."

Lena almost laughed.

"Sorry," she said, aiming for sincere but edging into amused.

Preston laughed himself, started to put his hand on her shoulder, then pulled it back.

"Nick was certified in animal control a few months ago. You didn't know?"

Lena shook her head.

"I don't ask what he does during the day," she said. "If he loses that certification, does that mean he can't work at the shelter anymore?"

Preston shook his head, then automatically ran his fingers through his hair to make sure he hadn't disturbed it, and by doing so, disturbed it. Lena watched a few strands fall into disarray. He had good hair, Lena thought. He had good everything. He even had a good heart. She should have loved him. But she didn't. She never had, even while they had dated, during the years when she and Nick were...estranged was the best she could come up with.

"I don't think so," Preston said. "He can still work at the shelter. They'll just keep him away from anything sharp. Which is probably for the best anyway."

Preston took Lena's hand.

"How is he really?" he asked.

"I don't know," Lena answered. "I never know."

She looked around. They were standing in front of the Hennepin Government Center plaza.

"He wants to practice law again."

Preston laughed.

"I think the Bar Association may have something to say about that."

"They never took his license. He just stopped practicing."

Preston folded his arms again, a common mannerism for him. He didn't cross them, he folded the right over the left, as if he were hugging himself. Sometimes the fingers of his right hand started drumming on his left elbow, usually top to bottom but occasionally bottom to top. Lena had not decoded the message in this behavior, nor was she sure she wanted to know.

"He's crazy," Preston said. "He runs around with a puppet. Who would probably be his paralegal."

"Stop please."

Preston shook his head.

"Sorry. I just can't imagine it."

"He can. But that's not the worst part."

The drumming started.

"With him, whatever you think is the worst part isn't."

Lena laid her hand on his arm. The drumming ceased.

"The worst part is," she said so quietly Preston could hardly hear, "he wants to come back to the firm. To Ward and Grant."

Preston dropped his arms, forgetting the cup in his hand, which left a coffee trail on the sidewalk. Lena pulled back her hand. He turned away, then suddenly turned back to her with enough force that she lurched backwards a bit. Preston touched her shoulder this time, to steady her.

"Sorry," he said. "I just. We've had this conversation so many times."

Preston remembered his coffee, righted the cup and took a sip.

"If he is heading downhill again, you need to get out once and for all. I'm worried about you."

"Preston."

Lena put her hand to his cheek.

"You are a sweet man and a good friend. But..."

Preston nodded.

"I know. I know. You can't help the way you feel and I can't help the way I feel. And who knows really what he feels. It's a fucking mess. Oh. I'm sorry."

Lena laughed.

"You're right. It's a fucking mess. And I'm the one who is sorry.

*   *   *

Passing through the lobby of the Wells Fargo Building, Lena fought the urge to hide in the stagecoach during daylight hours and brooded her way up to the forty-fifth floor. With Sharon's perceptive collusion, she tried to concentrate on work for a few hours, but had little success, drifting off inevitably to contemplate her own dilemma.

Finally Lena gave up trying to work. She randomly stuffed papers into her briefcase and put on her sunglasses and coat. As she left she said one word to Sharon: Handle. That was her code that she would be out indefinitely.

Thank God for Sharon, Lena thought as she got into her car. Lena knew that a large firm would pay her more, a lot more probably, than she could afford to. That was actually an argument for letting Nick return to work; his reputation would bring in clients. Well, not his reputation now, she reminded herself. But his legal acumen had been semi-legendary at one point. Maybe it still was. Very few of her colleagues would broach the subject.

No, she thought. She couldn't think of that now. Just, thank God for Sharon. Lena didn't know what she would do without her.

*   *   *

"So what's the problem?" Nick asked, as Sancho moved Knight to KB4.

The chess board was set on the small table in Nick's room. Oscar sat on the chair, while Nick was on the bed, leaning back against the wall, Sancho on his right hand, a copy of Moby Dick in the other. Oscar concentrated on his opponent: Sancho.

"I'm down a bishop," Oscar replied.

Oscar responded with pawn e4-e5.

Sancho moved pawn to e5.

Pawn takes pawn.

Bishop takes knight.

"You and Sharon okay?" Nick asked.

Oscar shifted his head from side to side. But from every perspective, his situation looked grim.

"Sharon is a whole other story," Oscar said.

"Not going well?"

"Going wonderful for me."

Other knight to QB5.

"And for her?"

"No idea."

"And you never will."

Pawn to e3.

Sancho looked at Nick.

"Checkmate," Nick announced.

"I thought you didn't know how to play chess."

Sancho looked back at Oscar.

"I don't," Nick said. "But he has been playing since he was a puppy."

Oscar tipped over his king.

"You want my advice on how to have a lasting relationship with a beautiful intelligent woman?" Nick asked.

"Yes."

"Are you insane?"

"No. I want your advice."

"That is my advice."

"But..."

"In love, sanity is a liability."

"But you're not insane."

"That's my problem."

"I see."

Sancho turned to look at Nick, and nodded. Nick continued:

"Did you ever wonder why the term insane means not sane? Shouldn't it mean in sanity? Even the word insane is insane. The word has only been in use for a few hundred years. The Latin derivation is what is confusing, the root, insanus, in meaning not, sanus meaning well or healthy. Sanitas, sanitatis, sanitati, sanitatem, sanitate, sanitas. Another connotation of course is sanitation: clean. To be insane is to be not clean. I think there is something in this sense, that to be insane is to be comfortable in disorder, negative capability, as Keats put it, being in uncertainties, mysteries, doubts, without any reaching after fact and reason. The Catalan word for sane is seny, which I suppose makes sense because Catalan developed out of Latin, but the opposite of seny is rauxa, which is hard to translate but means not so much insane as irresistible exuberance. I could almost admit to that. Spanish has more words for insane than any language other than English, probably due to *Don Quixote*. It's a long book and Cervantes couldn't just keep repeating himself. Though Norwegian has quite a few words for insane also. All those nights without darkness I guess. Or all that Ibsen. Though he lived in Italy. Italian has pazzia, which is just fun to say: pazzia. The German word for insane is verrückt, which means displaced. I like that. It's gentle. To be insane is to be displaced. But am not insane, because I am exactly where I should be."

"In a psychiatric institute."

"Ironic isn't it?"

"That's one word for it."

Sancho began resetting the chess pieces on the neatly patterned board. Oscar frowned.

"If you're not insane, why do you know so much about it?"

Nick shrugged.

"It seems to come up a lot in conversation."

"Makes sense."

"And roses," Nick added, observing the restoration carefully, since Sancho sometimes confused bishops and knights. "Lots of roses. For no reason. Which is easy, because you're insane."

*   *   *

Lena pulled up outside the Hennepin Animal Shelter in her Carmon Red Porsche convertible and stopped. She loved her car, a present from Nick after they won their first case together. It was eminently impractical, a rear wheel drive convertible sports car in a city snow-bound six months or more a year. And Lena had almost fainted when she opened the envelope and found that Nick had charged the entire cost of the car to American Express. Still, the color was perfect, and the feel, and on a summer day's escape it was a glorious companion. These days the escapes came more often.

Even from the parking lot, Lena could hear the plaintive barks and cries of the shelter residents, and as always her heart responded. She had so much respect for Ralph and Alice, dedicating their lives to helping lost, homeless, and injured animals. Now that non-medical euthanasia had been banned at the facility (thanks to Nick and his contacts in the media, and now the Governor's office), the workload had become overwhelming. But they never complained, were relieved in fact to be done with a task they both found abhorrent. The shelter population had boomed as they both scrambled to care for the needy residents. Adoptions were up, but never enough. Budgets were up, but never enough.

Alice's desk in the front hallway was empty, so Lena checked her office. From the typing sound, she deduced Alice was there, though the tiny woman was hidden behind the computer monitor.

"Hello, Alice," Lena said. "Busy?"

"Yes," Alice replied, annoyed. "Apparently I need to inventory some animal control supplies."

Then she looked at Lena and softened. Alice knew the burden that Lena carried. Nick was a wonder among the animals but a terror among the humans. In her work, he was an enormous asset, but Alice could not imagine living with him. She loved Nick as a friend, but she knew that Lena's connection was deeper, far more complex, far more perilous.

Not for the first time that day, Alice thanked God for her own situation, a husband who put up with her moods and eased her anxieties, with whom life was easier if not easy, richer if not rich. They had struggled together to raise two children and put them through school, together in work they loved and felt important, together in lives enduring in affection and care. Together. She suspected this was not a life Lena would ever know.

"I'm sorry," Lena said. "I shouldn't barge in like this."

"Come in, come in," Alice said. "I'm just working on a presentation. Would you like a cup of tea?"

Lena sat down.

"Tea would be good."

Alice got up, filled a small crystal teapot with hot water, dropped two teabags in it, watched as the dark molecules infused the clear water, always fascinated by the pattern, different each time.

"Where is he?" Alice asked.

"Golden Valley for now," Lena replied. "But he'll be home soon. No charges are being filed."

Hints of orange and cinnamon diffused through the small space. Alice picked up a cup, porcelain with gold inlaid roses, one of three that had belonged to Ralph's great-grandmother. For years they had remained unused. Finally, Alice could not stand the thought of something so beautiful locked away, and brought them to the office. She turned to Lena.

"Milk or sugar?"

"Neither, thanks."

"Straight up it is."

Alice poured tea in two cups, slowly, careful not to spill. Then she brought one to Lena, and stood in front of her desk inhaling the scent from the other.

"Well, that's something at least'" Alice said. "I was afraid they would send him back there permanently. Or worse."

"Me too."

Alice took a sip.

"The dog is here, the one he saved. She's fine. Or she will be. You can tell him that."

Lena held her cup with both hands, enjoying the warmth.

"Oh that's good. I'm sure they will be relieved."

Alice took another sip.

"They?"

Lena laughed.

"I was thinking of Nick and Sancho and Wolfram. He treats them like humans so often, I'm beginning to think of them that way myself."

Alice didn't quite laugh herself, but leaned in toward Lena.

"I know what you mean," she whispered. "I've been in this field a long time and I've had more conversations with animals in the last year than the previous twenty. And you know what? Don't tell anyone, but, they understand. Especially Wolfram. That dog knows things."

Lena smiled and nodded. It was a common opinion among those who spent any time with the special dog. She could almost credit Nick's stories about his Fey ancestry (the pink ears were the telltale sign).

"What is the presentation for?" Lena asked.

"A convention on animal shelter design. It's something Nick got me interested in and now I'm obsessed."

"He can have that affect," Lena agreed. "Let me hear it."

Alice stood quickly, her smiling head appearing just above the monitor.

"Well, if you insist."

She paused.

"It's a draft."

Lena nodded.

"I only have the beginning."

Lena waited.

Alice took another sip, cleared her throat.

"As we continue to improve our care for animals, we need to look beyond slogans and recognize that the better we do our jobs, the more difficult they will become. The more animals we rescue, the more animals we need to care for long-term. This recognition will lead us to a new era of shelter design and organization: shelters that do more than shelter. Shelters that save."

Lena applauded.

"That's good. Nick inspired that?"

Alice pulled her chair out from behind the desk to sit next to Lena, then remembered her tea and recovered that.

"He did. He has some very unusual ideas about space."

"It would be unusual if he had an idea that was usual."

Lena got up to pour herself another cup of tea, but looking down she realized she hadn't taken a sip yet. She sighed and returned to her seat.

"I'm doing that all the time now," she said. "My mind is always somewhere else."

"I think I know where," Alice responded.

Alice set her cup down on the desk and reached for something.

"You need a hobby," she said. "Ralph plays the piano. I do origami."

She held up the figure of a moose that had once been a County budget directive.

"Just something for the hands to do."

Lena lifted the cup, both hands around it again.

"My hands are full. Or tied. Choose your metaphor."

"I know, dear."

Lena stood.

"Is Ralph here? I wanted to talk to him about Wolfram. I think he's getting worse."

Alice motioned toward the warehouse.

"He's in the back. We don't see each other much during the day. You want me to call him?"

Lena shook her head.

"Not yet. I came to talk to you too, if you have a moment. And that's actually what I came to talk to you about."

Alice gave Lena a puzzled glance.

"About Ralph?"

"About you and Ralph."

"Ah. Ask."

Lena inhaled the scent of the tea, finally took a sip.

"This is good."

"Maybe that's your hobby. Tea ceremonies can be very healing."

"Maybe Vodka ceremonies."

"That would work."

Alice stood.

"Come on," she said. "We can talk and walk."

"Some days."

They left Alice's office and headed for the wide metal doors that served as the entrance to what they called the 'warehouse'. It might have been a warehouse in an earlier incarnation. Lena remembered the first time she stepped through those doors. The cold cavernous space with the eerie fluorescent lighting had reminded her of a mad scientist's lair. She had avoided coming back ever since. It was just too sad and disturbing.

When Alice opened the doors, Lena was surprised to find the lighting supplemented by new windows and skylights. The cages were clean and colorful, almost cute. In the middle was a playground where the dogs could roam at will.

"This is amazing," Lena whispered.

"Thanks," said Alice. "Our primary focus now is to create an environment that will encourage adoption. We also do adoption fairs and the like, but when people visit here, we want to them to be able to envision the pet as part of the family."

"Did Nick do this?"

Alice looked around with pride.

"The design is mine. We're LEED certified now, a Green shelter. We're still making improvements when we can afford it. Nick did a lot of the painting. Ralph doesn't like ladders; hard to find one that will hold him. And Nick still does the names and animal descriptions. No one does that like him."

Alice pointed to a card on the cage of a sandy-haired canine. Lena read:

> Chance: this chow mix is the perfect watchdog. He'll watch you do anything and can tell time using only the look on your face.

Lena smiled. Very Nick, she thought.

"We're making progress," Alice said. "Nick is a big help."

Lena turned to Alice.

"That's what I wanted to talk about," Lena said. "Nick wants to come back to work."

"Here? He still comes here twice a week. I thought you knew that."

"I do. And I'm grateful."

"So are we. Nick has a gift; the animals trust him immediately, even when they are in pain."

Lena sat on a bench painted deep blue with thin perfectly placed red pinstripes.

"They sense a kindred soul."

Alice sat next to her.

"Could be. Plus, he gives Ralph someone to talk to. They can both talk for hours, about anything. I'm more of a listener myself."

"You're doing okay."

Alice laughed.

"I guess I am."

Lena put her hand on Alice's.

"What I meant was, Nick wants to practice law again."

Alice paused, nodded.

"I can understand that," Alice said. "I don't know much about it but I imagine he has a gift there too."

"Oh he does. I'm a very good lawyer. In terms of practicing law. Overall, I'm probably better than he is. But in terms of knowing and understanding the law, any kind, anywhere, I don't know many who match him. And in a courtroom, he has a rare ability to find just the right perspective that makes everything clear. Or he had."

"And you think he might have lost it."

"No. Maybe. I don't know honestly. But I think he might have lost the ability to use those gifts in a legal practice. And I think the stress of that would be very unhealthy for him. I don't know that he could handle it and maintain the little equilibrium we have."

Alice stood.

"So, you want him to work here? He could work here fulltime. We would be happy to have him."

Lena stood too and they both began walking toward the back.

"I wish that were a solution. But despite how rewarding this work is from him, and how much he loves it and you both, it doesn't engage his mind the way I think he thinks he needs. He wants to be the Nick that was. He wants to be the legal superhero, swooping in and saving the world."

Alice smiled.

Lena shook her head.

"But that is only half the problem, and that's what I wanted your advice on. He doesn't just want to practice law, he wants to do it with me. He wants to be my partner again."

"And you don't?"

Lena leaned back against one of the enclosures and closed her eyes.

"If I could have the Nick I married back, I might dare to try. But even then, the differences between us drove us apart. That's how the divorce happened in the first place."

"So why are you here?" Alice asked finally.

Lena sighed.

"I don't know. You and Ralph make it look so easy. I thought, maybe you have advice, a secret you can tell me."

Alice laughed then.

"If I knew the secret to a good marriage, you think I'd be working here? I'd be on Oprah every other day. No, have my own talk show, with Oprah as my guest. And a book. Ten books."

She paused and smiled.

"No, I wouldn't. I'd be here."

Lena sighed.

"So. I'm stuck."

Alice nodded, patted Lena's cheek.

"You are. Nick is a good man who will love you for the rest of your life whether you want him to or not. And my only advice is, learn to enjoy it. All of it. It's always all or nothing with men like him. And would you really want it any other way?"

"A question I keep asking myself," Lena said.

Then she held out her hand.

"Thanks, Alice."

"For nothing, I know."

"No."

Alice walked past Lena's outstretched hand and hugged her, an odd feeling as the top of her head pressed into Lena's breastbone.

"Ralph is?"

"Where the animals are."

*　　*　　*

The golden retriever stood on a table as Ralph carefully brushed her luminous coat. It was a delicate task, as the hair was matted in some places and skin had been torn away in others. The animal had been abused for some time, Ralph suspected. It was beyond his understanding.

As Ralph worked, the golden emitted an occasional low growl. But the sound filtered into the usual chorus of yelps and yips and hisses that serenaded him each day. He had grown up on a small farm, and still retained somewhat a farmer's complex attitude toward animals. They were not human, not family. Yet they were yours; you needed them, you understood them, you cared for them. He wondered sometimes if this distinction was what had allowed him to stay in this field all these years, with all the suffering he had witnessed.

But he didn't wonder often.

There was work to do.

Few people guessed that it was Alice who had the tender heart, who struggled every day to improve the conditions for these poor animals, who worked every night and weekend on adoption programs, improved regulations, enhanced care. It was Alice who dreamed of finding some land and creating a real home for hundreds of animals. It was Alice that kept him in this field. Her passion for this, and his for her.

Lena stood back and watched as Ralph groomed the reddish-golden fur. Such delicate strokes from such huge hands. Taller even than Nick, and far more massive, he looked like he should be wrestling alligators, not wrangling canines.

Lena could see that the dog was not enjoying the attention, had probably been taught all her life that attention meant pain. How long, she thought, does it take to heal from that? Was it even possible?

Lena moved closer and stretched out her hand toward the dog.

"Careful," Ralph said. "She's not sure of people."

"Will you find a new home for her?"

"The police convinced the owner to sign a release, so she won't go back there. I think we'll probably send her someplace that specializes in abused pets. She'll stay there until she's ready for adoption. If ever."

"Let me know what the costs are," Lena said.

"Nick already volunteered."

"Of course he did."

Ralph gathered the golden in his arms. She nipped in his direction, in surprise mostly, then settled into him. He placed her in a nearby pen, with food and water near. The golden curled in a corner, watching warily.

"What will happen to the owner?" Lena asked.

"Nothing," Ralph said. "Trade-off for not filing charges. But someone will be by to check on him."

Lena knew the someone would be Ralph, who would be very convincing.

"It's not right," she said.

Ralph shook his head.

"No. Does that surprise you?"

"I guess not."

Ralph closed the door to the pen. The golden seemed to relax a bit.

"Right is your husband's domain," Ralph continued. "Mine is what is possible, though sometimes we even get to what's best."

"Right. Best. Possible." Lena rehearsed. "I don't think Nick knows the difference."

"I'm not sure for him there is any. Here. Let's go to my office."

Ralph led Lena out the back door of the warehouse. On a cement slab, lawn chairs had been set up, with a table in between and a cooler to one side. Ralph took a seat, and Lena wondered that the chair didn't collapse under Ralph's weight. Ralph noticed the worried look.

"They have broken once or twice," he said and shrugged. "I just buy another."

Lena sat in the other chair, then noticed the metal holes in the cement where a chain link fence had stood, and she remembered. This had once been the location of a device for euthanasia. Now it was gone, thanks to Nick. Right. Best. Possible. Nick for sure.

"Drink?" Ralph asked.

"No thanks. I just had tea."

"Of course."

Ralph squinted up at the sky. The autumn air was chill, and there was even the scent of snow. Ralph had seen snow only once growing up in Alabama. Here it was too common to be remarked on.

"Are you here about Nick?"

"Actually, I wanted to talk to you about Wolfram. He is slowing down even more, his breathing seems shallower. I wondered if there was anything more we should do."

Ralph sighed.

"I'm afraid not, at his age."

"How old is he?" Lena asked.

"It's hard to say. We don't have any record. He just wandered in here one day. If I had to guess, I would say he was maybe fifteen, maybe even twenty years old, which is old for any dog and ancient for his breed. Wolfhounds seldom survive more than a decade."

Lena let the ramifications sink in.

"So he's just old, or is there something else?"

Ralph smiled.

"Being old is enough. Ask my digestion. Wolfram has conditions associated with age. He has spondylosis, a degenerative condition of the spine common in large breeds. He doesn't seem to be in much pain at this point, but it's hard to tell. At some point, we might consider surgery. But he also has cardiomyopathy, an enlarged heart. It's mild now, we'll keep an eye on it. We can put him on medication if necessary."

Tears filled Lena's eyes.

"I'm sorry," she said, waving the tears away. "Anything, these days."

Ralph put an enormous hand on her arm, but the touch was gentle.

"It's a wonder that he has survived this long," he said.

Lena stood, walked to the edge of the cement foundation, and stopped, as if the fence was not gone but invisible. She stared into the scrub woods behind the building.

"Sometimes I wish Nick had stuck to stuffed animals."

Ralph walked up behind her, blocking the sun and leaving her in shadow. Then he laughed once, a ponderous sound which seemed to emerge from a deep well. Ralph passed over the imaginary border of the cement and turned to look Lena in the eye.

"Nick isn't good with limits."

"Don't I know."

Alice stepped out of the building. Ralph looked up.

"Milly just threw up on Chester," she announced."

"Go," Lena said.

"I love my job," said Ralph.

*　　*　　*

The door to Nick's tiny room creaked as it slowly opened, waking him. The lights in the room were off and the illumination from the hallway was blinding. Nick held Sancho up to block the source of the light. He could make out only the outlines of a tall figure dressed all in white.

"Oscar?"

There was no answer.

"Lena?"

Again there was no answer.

"God?"

A deep voice echoed in the silence of the tiny room.

"It is the nature of Visions that they are not incremental."

Nick put Sancho down and relaxed back on the bed, rubbing his eyes.

"Hello, Leonard," he said.

Breath, Smiles, Tears

As she stepped into the elevator in the Wells Fargo building, Lena smiled, enjoying the aroma from the two large cups of coffee that she carried (Monday was her day). The weight of the overloaded briefcase slung over her left shoulder did not bother her, nor did the busy caseload for the week, nor even the thought of Nick unsupervised for the day. The weekend had been unusually, splendidly normal.

Nick had been released from GVPI somehow, she wasn't sure how. Both Preston and Doctor Richardson claimed no knowledge or responsibility.

But the weekend had been calm, even fun. She and Nick had actually done regular things. They went to a movie. Shopped for groceries. He raked the leaves in their tiny yard (leaving Sancho inside in case of allergies).

They even took a quick trip out to the zoo to check on the progress of the Crustacean exhibit that Nick had inspired. The construction was almost complete. Soon the lobsters Nick had rescued would be moved to their new home, and the exhibit would open to the public. Even the governor had promised to attend.

It reminded her of the first days of their marriage, when anything done together was a joy. The memories had many layers, but the essence remained. Imagination in reverse is

Memory, Nick liked to say. Maybe it was true, but true in his sense of the words.

Lena continued to smile as she traversed the long corridor of the forty-fifth floor. As she reached the offices of Ward and Grant, she noted with approval that the space across from her, vacant for some time, was now being renovated. There was no sign outside yet, and she wondered who the new neighbors were. She peeked through the missing double doors, found no clue. But the workers were making haste.

As she walked through the door of her own office, Sharon met her with a hug, not simply uncharacteristic, but unimaginable. Sharon did not hug.

"I'm going to miss you," Sharon said.

"Are you going to the Ladies Room?" Lena asked.

"No. I'm taking the job. I thought you knew."

"Job? Wait? What? What job? Why would you take a job? And why would I know about it?"

Sharon seemed genuinely surprised.

"I assumed Nick would tell you," she said.

Lena sat and closed her eyes, trying to will away the disaster. She knew it was coming. It always came. The nice weekend was just the perfect setup.

She opened her eyes.

"Nick, my husband Nick, offered you a job?"

"I thought he was your ex-husband?" she said.

"He is."

"So he's your husband and your ex-husband?"

"Apparently in some universes they are not mutually exclusive. I haven't worked it all out yet."

"Okay. Just trying to stay current."

"Aren't we all?"

Lena pulled Sharon into her office. She offered her one of the cups of coffee, then offloaded her briefcase onto the glass desk, something she never did.

Lena sat on one end of the sofa, edging in next to the six-foot-tall plush gorilla. Silently she tried to anticipate the extent of the current tectonic shift in her life. Sharon sat on the other end, adjacent to the pink winged unicorn and allowed Lena time to bring order to her questions, if nothing else.

After a moment, Lena opened her own coffee and drank.

"Hot!" she said.

Sharon got up and brought Lena a glass of water from the pitcher behind the desk, freeing it from the clutches of a fuzzy purple sloth. Lena alternated sips of coffee and water, until finally she had a breakthrough, and spoke.

"Nick offered you a job?"

"Yes."

She was silent again, evaluating the information. Then:

"Nick. Offered you a job?"

"Yes. Your ex-ex-husband offered me a job."

Lena raised both the water and coffee cup to her mouth, before Sharon put a hand out to prevent the impending collision.

"When?" Lena asked.

"Saturday."

Lena alternated sips of coffee and water again for a few moments. Sharon waited patiently.

"What does he want you to do?"

"It wasn't very clear. He said we would figure it out later."

Lena nodded.

"That sounds like Nick."

Sharon sensed that sufficient time has been allotted to Lena's emotional stabilization.

"Are you upset?" she asked. "I assumed you knew. He said you would be fine about it."

"I am upset. But not with you."

"Good."

Lena put down the water and concentrated on the coffee.

"I don't understand."

"I can see that."

"Are you unhappy here?"

"Of course not."

Lena stood and walked to the windows.

He's...Nick. The job, whatever it is, doesn't exist, except in his mind. He doesn't even have a job himself, unless you count working at the animal shelter. So how can he offer you one?"

"I know. I know."

She turned back to Sharon.

"Then why?"

Sharon shrugged.

"The money."

"The money?"

"Yes," Sharon said. "He's going to pay me a million dollars a year."

"A million dollars a year?"

"Plus benefits."

Lena moved unsteadily to the chair behind her desk, removing her briefcase from the glass surface and setting it on the floor to one side.

The elephants had migrated back to the shelves behind her. She swirled in the chair, set down her coffee cup, and carefully gathered the tiny red elephant. She held it out in front of her, balanced on her palm.

"Sharon. Sharon Sharon Sharon. Sharon."

"Is that a question?"

"So it seems."

"Five."

Lena swung around in her chair.

"Five what?" she asked.

"Five Sharons."

"That's not the question."

"Don't blame me. I didn't ask it."

Lena paused, spun in her chair one more time, then reached across the desk toward Sharon.

"Sharon, this is Nick. He has no money. He has no job. He has no job to offer you. It's a fantasy. He is delusional. You know that."

"I do."

"So?"

Sharon took a final swallow of coffee, calculated the precise angle, then tossed her empty coffee cup into the recycle bin, as she always did. She wasn't sure that paper coffee cups were recyclable. But she thought they should be, so she kept doing it.

"Look," she said. "Obviously if someone off the street came up to me and offered me a job making a million dollars a year, I would say it was too good to be true. But with Nick, if he says something is going to happen, no matter what it is, no matter how improbable and preposterous, you have to admit there is a decent possibility of it actually happening. Because it's Nick. At least that's what Oscar thinks."

Lena grabbed the edge of her desk.

"He's got Oscar involved too?"

"Yes."

Lena shook her head.

"So where is this job, where is whatever is supposed to happen supposed to happen? Lake of the Isles? Our house? Is that why he raked the leaves?"

"I thought you knew."

Lena brought her hands together in front of her, waved them in earnest supplication.

"Please stop saying that."

"He rented the offices across the hall."

Lena's head hit the desk.

"Would you excuse me?" Lena said. "I have to take care of someone."

Sharon rose.

"In what sense?"

Lena lifted her head.

Oh, Sharon thought.

*   *   *

Lena stormed across the hall, fought her way through the thick plastic tarps taped over the opening, only to find a jungle of hanging cables and missing ceiling tiles awaiting her.

The workers had evacuated. But alone in the middle of the jungle, Oscar was sitting on a solitary folding chair with blueprints spread out over the floor surrounding him. As Lena approached, Oscar looked relieved and asked:

"Can you read these?"

Lena ignored the question.

"Where is he?"

"I'm never sure how to answer that question," Oscar replied.

"He's not here?"

"No. He called this morning and asked me to stop by and see if I thought the space was big enough."

Oscar turned 360 degrees, carefully surveying the empty area. Lena never shifted her gaze from him.

"I don't think it's big enough. Do you?"

Lena was ordinarily very good at not being angry at the wrong person. It had helped her succeed in many areas of her life, including her current professional one. So now she tightly controlled her impulse to grab Oscar and shake him. But she could not entirely control the blend of fear and fury in her voice as she slowly whispered "Big enough for what?"

Oscar considered.

"It wasn't very clear. He said we would figure it out later."

Lena looked around the space. What would he be planning here? What could enter his mind that he would need this space for? She sighed. She would not have been surprised to find a circus here by next Monday. No not a circus. Nick would not allow animals to be used that way. A zoo? Possibly. Nick approved of zoos, good ones anyway. But he had a relationship with the Minnesota Zoo now. An indoor urban dog park?

Or.

A law firm?

She gave up. There was no end to the possibilities, and no predicting them either.

"Let me see the blueprints," she said.

Oscar handed one over and Lena scanned the plans. There were two very large corner offices. That was a bad sign. Half a dozen smaller offices of varying sizes were scattered among multiple conference rooms, work areas and open spaces. All very carefully planned, systematic, and hierarchical.

She concluded immediately that this was not Nick's work. She remembered the sessions they had had planning the office space for Ward and Grant. Nick had designed what he called hover desks, magnetically supported workstations that moved in any direction, which would be automatically reconfigured each night at based on a randomizing algorithm. He wanted corridors based on Escher drawings, and a reception area with Chagall-like stained glass windows.

She held the paper up high and close to see the date. Four weeks ago. Four weeks? That was long before he had mentioned the possibility of going back to work.

She handed the plans back to Oscar.

"You don't know where he is?"

"Sorry."

Lena turned to go, then turned back.

"What did he say he would pay you?"

"A million dollars a year."

"And you believed him?"

"Sure. It's Nick."

*   *   *

Lena, having taught the plastic tarps a sharp lesson earlier, won her way through them more easily this time and returned across the hall to her office. Sharon was packing the boxes she had unpacked earlier.

"Can you call Harvey?" Lena asked. "I need to find Nick. Fast."

Harvey, once the doorman at Lena's apartment building on Hennepin Island, now managed the property for her, in addition to various other tasks. He was especially good at finding Nick, and had a particular genius for convincing him to stop whatever he was doing and come home. Lena had never actually seen him perform this trick, so she didn't know what methods he employed. But his Marine counter-insurgency training probably came in handy.

Sharon nodded to the hallway leading to Lena's office.

"Harvey is here?" Lena asked. This was a very bad sign in a day already full of them. And it was still morning.

"What am I doing today?" Lena asked.

"An excellent if slightly existential question."

"And the answer is?"

"Whatever you need to. I cleared your schedule."

"Thanks." Lena said, dashing into her office. She reappeared after a minute.

"I thought you said Harvey was here?"

"Not Harvey."

"Not Harvey is here. I don't understand. Why don't I understand anything today?"

"Not Harvey," Sharon said, nodding to the hallway again.

"There is no one in my office."

Sharon pointed to the hallway. Lena turned to look, past her office, to the very end of the corridor. She had almost forgotten Nick's office was even there.

Lena took a slow step down the hallway. Then another. It was like an out-of-body experience, or watching herself in a horror movie: the victim walking down a dark hallway with a closed door at the end, cellos playing short ominous discordant phrases. Maybe this was the score to her life.

Lena reached the end of the hallway, placed her hand on the handle, slowly twisted, pushed open the door, and stepped through a time warp.

Nick was at his desk, dressed as he always dressed in his custom Italian blue pinstripe suit. The fear she had been feeling gave way to surge of strange and unexpected joy, as if she had been granted a wish, the opportunity to live the years again, with a man who was not ill, who was the partner she expected.

Images blasted through her mind of the way she had thought her life would be with the man she had thought Nick was.

She realized how much she missed him at work, how much she still wanted the partnership they had once had. And she could not deny that it felt right for him to be here, even after all the years. He belonged with the law. He belonged with her.

But despite the temporary thrill, she also knew that it could not work in the long run. They had tried it and it had almost ended them both, her emotionally and him completely. She had decided—there was one possible path in which they could remain together. It was narrow and treacherous, but she had committed to it. She thought Nick had too, but now he was here.

Sancho was in the corner seated in a tiny white wicker rocker. The color had once matched his fur so closely he almost disappeared into the background, except for the black button eyes and felt nose. Now the white had turned to grey, but he did not look aged or discolored to her, not anymore; it was the opposite somehow: burnished.

She turned to Nick. If Sancho had aged, Nick had reversed the process, and looked the man he had been when he last sat at that desk. It might even be the same suit, though he had many identical ones. He had worn the same tailored blue pinstripe suit every day for as long as she had known him. Maybe it was a genius thing. She had read somewhere that Albert Einstein and Steve Jobs always wore the same outfits. Not the same as each other. Or the same as Nick. But the same as themselves. To themselves. Of themselves.

Nick looked up at her and smiled, ending her train of thought (or bizarrely winding and eclectic trail of avoidance/desire for escape).

She laughed.

And he laughed.

"That was not the reaction I was expecting," he said.

"No? What were you expecting?"

"I don't know. Armed guards? Harvey leading a squadron of Marines?"

"He's on the way."

Nick leaned back in his chair, which squeaked from disuse.

"Call him off."

"Nick, I thought we settled this?"

"I never liked settling."

"Which is why your legal practice never made any money."

Nick smiled again.

"I know. You taught me that."

"Excuse me?"

"You taught me that settling is winning. One of the many things you taught me."

Lena picked up Sancho and sat in one of the chairs in front of the desk. She didn't remember sitting there before, had seldom been in this office, even when it was in use. Nick was restless, would always come to her office.

"Really? You never mentioned this before," she said.

"I mean it. Many things."

"Such as?"

He thought for a moment.

"You taught me how to ride a bike. Not why. But how."

Lena nodded.

"Go on."

"You taught me how to sculpt gelato with your tongue."

She nodded again.

"That is one of my special talents."

Nick leaned forward. Another squeak

"You taught me about entropy."

Lena paused.

"Entropy? That doesn't sound like my word."

Nick's hands folded together in front, a forgotten gesture she had seen many times with clients.

"You taught me that, in life, things that are broken can't be unbroken. They have to be mended."

Lena closed her eyes. He meant it. But what did it mean? Mended. Mended how? And what was he mending?

Nick leaned back and forth in the chair several times, making a squeaking sound, which to Lena sounded a lot like the discordant cellos.

"I've missed that sound," he said. "Though I think it's about a half tone deeper now. Either the chair is rusting or I've put on weight."

"You haven't put on weight. You haven't changed at all. You look just like you did when–"

She stopped.

"When I worked here?" he added. "Before you asked me to leave?"

"When we first moved in here," she finished.

Nick stood and looked out the windows. The dark blue suit was outlined by the almost turquoise sky.

"It was snowing that day," Nick said. "Do you remember? You were worried that the furniture would not get here and I said this was Minnesota and unless a glacier moved through it would get here. The furniture got here, but we didn't leave. We pushed the desks together—I knew we should have gone with those hover desks— piled the coats on them, and spent the night."

Lena waved away the remembering.

"Yes, yes, great night, romantic night, unforgettable night. Nick, what are you doing here? What are you doing in general?"

He turned. His turquoise eyes matched the sky.

"Mending."

*   *   *

Sharon posed silently outside the door to Nick's office, like a modern version of Themis, the Greek Goddess of Justice, except instead of scales she held a stapler and instead of a sword a staple puller. She knew that the loud alternating sounds and silence were outside the scope of her powers to influence. She had fought that battle at Lena's side for years, until she realized the real battle was inside. So she retired from the field, though she left room in her charter for occasional forays.

This, she knew, was not the time. Still, she watched the door to Nick's office. Lena's style of exit she would determine whether she should pack or unpack.

The door opened. Lena exited calmly, shut the door, and silently by-passed Sharon on the way into her office.

Sharon waited for any sign of Nick. When he did not appear, Sharon dropped both items onto her desk and followed Lena.

Lena was sitting calmly at her desk, hands folded in front of her, a gesture of Nick's she hadn't realized she had adopted.

"How do you feel about Switzerland?"

"I'm fairly neutral," Sharon replied without pausing.

Lena laughed without sound.

"That was good. That was good. Have to remember that," she said with almost no inflection.

Sharon examined Lena's face for a moment, then got up and walked back to Nick's office. It was empty.

Completely empty.

No Nick.

No furniture.

She returned to Lena's office.

"Did he jump?"

Lena did not exactly nod. Or exactly not nod. Her head moved both up and down and side to side, like a bobblehead dog.

"In a way," Lena replied.

"You pushed him? We have to get rid of the body."

Lena looked up at Sharon.

"Actually," she said, speaking very slowly, as if the words were being thought and spoken simultaneously. "I'm thinking of getting rid of mine."

Sharon crossed her arms. It wasn't quite as intimidating as Lena's classic motion, though she had been practicing.

"What does that mean?" Sharon asked.

Lena reached into her briefcase, pulled out an envelope with lots of brightly colored stamps, and handed it to Sharon.

"I've been offered a position heading up an international commission on animal rights. In Geneva."

Sharon opened the letter, scanned it, realized it was in French, and put it back in the envelope. She sat on the edge of the glass desk, which was sturdier than it looked.

"You can't take it."

Lena opened her mouth but no sound came out for a moment. Then:

"The timing seems appropriate."

"Why?"

Lena stood.

"Nick wants to come back to work. He wants to practice law again. I thought I had talked him out of it, but here he is. Honestly I don't know where else he could practice. He needs an environment that will protect him from himself, and people around him who will watch for signs."

"Of?"

Lena shrugged.

"The usual. Stress. Delusions. Ambulances. Fire departments. SWAT teams."

Sharon paused, looking out the window. Then she shook her head.

"It's not fair, to put you in that position for life."

Lena glanced at her wedding ring: the uncut red stone still looked as if it were welling out of her finger. She had not stopped wearing it, even when she and Nick were not together. But it didn't look like a traditional wedding ring anyway, something that probably should have tipped her off.

Lena took the ring off and held it out.

"Life is what I signed up for," Lena said.

"Not this life. This is not the life you signed up for."

Lena slipped the ring back on.

"I signed up for life with Nick. This is life with Nick."

"You are allowed some input in that life. You are allowed some happiness."

"That's what I have been trying to do. But..."

Lena paused.

"You know how to get rid of a body?" she asked finally.

*　　*　　*

The desk hit with a thud as Nick and Oscar set it down. The desk, two office chairs, a folding chair, and a tiny white wicker rocker were the only furniture in the entire space.

"That was heavy," Oscar said.

Nick wiped his hands with a white linen handkerchief.

"Hover desks. Nobody listens."

Oscar smiled.

"You just keep thinking Butch. That's what you're good at."

Nick smiled back.

"So you're Sundance now?"

Oscar shrugged.

'Just trying it on. I need a nickname."

"I'll think of one for you," Nick said.

Oscar shook his head.

"That's not how it works. It needs to be organic, to arise from the spontaneous recognition of the essence of my being."

"I see," Nick said. "Good luck with that."

"Thanks," Oscar replied. "I keep hoping."

Nick picked up the blueprint and spread it out on the desk. One long finger traced the lines over and across, outlining the multiplicity of confined spaces. He frowned.

"I don't think so."

He selected a blue marker from his jacket pocket and walked to an empty wall, where he drew an odd shape like a fist with the thumb extended.

He stepped back and nodded, then began marking dots here and there on the figure. He stepped back again, several steps this time, and looked to Oscar.

"Yes?"

Oscar nodded.

Nick leapt back in and drew a circle off to one side.

"This is the campfire."

Oscar glanced down at the mark.

"Campfire?"

Nick crossed his arms, careful to miss his suit with the marker's point.

"I know," he said. "Everyone always puts the campfire in the center. But really it needs to balance—" He drew some wavy lines. "The waterfall."

Oscar looked back and forth between the two marks. Nick seemed to be writing in hieroglyphics.

"There's a waterfall?" Oscar asked.

"Sure. Every office needs someplace where people can sit and feel just peaceful. Nothing I like better than a peaceful workplace. Really helps me concentrate."

"Me too," Oscar agreed. "The Institute is quiet mostly, when everyone is on their meds."

Nick concentrated, scanning the paper from various angles.

"You know maybe we shouldn't have a campfire," he said finally.

"I like the campfire."

"I do too. But we need a negative carbon footprint."

"How about a virtual campfire?"

"Perfect!"

Oscar smiled.

Nick put the marker in his mouth for a second, then drew straight lines over and below the circle for the campfire. He looked again, then nodded.

"I think a hologram, with the lasers here, here, and here," he said with assurance. "Now, where are we going to put the dog park?"

Oscar scanned the figure from various angles, just as Nick had done.

"Here?" he said, pointing.

Nick smiled and drew something like an infinity sign.

"Exactly."

"It definitely cuts off any straight lines," Oscar added.

Nick examined his handiwork.

"Small price to pay for beauty."

*　　*　　*

The Wells Fargo Center was constructed on the site of the old Norwest building, which had burned in 1982. When selecting the location of Ward and Grant, Lena had looked at several other sites that were more practical from a cost perspective. But Nick had liked the location near Nicollet Mall, and she liked the idea of a renovated site, especially one walking distance from the courthouse and government center, and a short distance to the river and its bike paths. At the time, there was no way to predict the requirements of their work; Nick's cases had been chosen primarily on the basis of, well, only Nick knew. If the issue interested him, he took the case. It was not a lucrative methodology.

"Lena! How are you?" asked the woman standing by the desk. Amy had been the building property manager for some years. Lena knew her well.

"Fine. Fine. Fine," Lena responded.

"How is Nick?"

"Fine. Fine. Fine."

"Coffee?"

"No."

Amy cleared the papers on her desk.

"It's not time to negotiate your lease, so I'm guessing you are here about the space opposite your office."

"Yes. I noticed it has been recently rented."

Amy pulled out a file.

"Actually that space was leased about a year and a half ago. The lease was prepaid for five years."

Lena frowned.

"What?"

Amy nodded.

"Yes, it's just been vacant. But the lease was recently transferred to a new organization called, let me see, yes: The Sancho Foundation."

She looked up.

"I don't have any details on them."

Lena tried to correlate the information. A year and a half ago would be just after the time of Lobstermania.

"Can you tell me who held the lease before that?"

"Sure. It was a company called Idiosyncratic Visions, LLC. No data on who owns it. A subsidiary of a subsidiary, that sort of thing."

Lena sighed. Nick was more than capable of that kind of insularity. And the name was certainly descriptive. But something about it didn't seem his style.

"Thanks, Amy," Lena said, gathering herself.

"Sure. I heard you and Nick were back together. How's it going?"

Len smiled.

"Smashingly."

*   *   *

Oscar told his jokes for the children assembled at the party, performed his balloon animal impressions, and even some magic tricks, with cards that flew through the air only to be discovered in someone's pocket, and knots that disappeared and flowers that appeared from nowhere.

Then it was Nick's turn. He settled himself with Sancho on a picnic table, and leaned forward, gesturing for his young audience to do the same.

"One day a young girl very far out to sea in a tiny boat is caught in a terrible storm and thrown overboard. She is a strong swimmer but try as she might she can find no sight of land.

"As she begins to sink into the cold water for the final time, commending her soul to the gods of Tide and Ocean, something comes up from the deep deep depths of the sea and swallows her whole.

"At first the girl isn't sure what has happened. She is in a large bluish mushy wet space with only a tiny opening above. But then she hears the sound, long and low, rising and falling, like a cello echoing the music of the sea itself. And she recognizes the sound immediately, as any girl of the sea would. She has been swallowed by a whale.

"Now inside a whale there is no sun or moon, no night or day. So for some long unknown time, the girl lives inside the whale, and all the however long the while, the whale sings to her. The whale sings her awake and sings her to sleep and sings the hunger out and sings the fear away.

"Soon the girl learns the songs and begins to sing along. After a while, they sing in harmony. Sometimes the whale sings the low part and the girl the high, and sometimes the reverse.

"Eventually the girl hears other voices, outside voices, dim at first but growing louder, voices singing along, other whales, in three parts then four, then more and more, uncountable voices in canon and counterpoint.

"The girl joins in as best she can, losing her sense of time and self, yearning to hear what is beyond her, notes too low for human senses, voices too far for human ears.

"Finally the whale opens his mouth and the girl sees an island before her, with an abundance of fruits and fresh water, beautiful flowers and perfect weather. The girl walks out of the mouth of the whale onto the beach and breathes the fresh air and stares into the blue sky. She turns to the whale, bows deeply, and says 'Thank you for saving me and bringing me to this paradise.'

"The whale replies 'you are most welcome.'"

"'You can speak!' exclaims the girl in deep surprise. 'I didn't know. In all the however long we traveled together, you never once said a word to me.'

"The whale sends a spout of water hurtling high in the air, which is how whales laugh.

"'I thought you understood,' says the whale.

"'Understood what?' asks the girl.

"'Why speak when you can sing?' the whale says as he dives under the waves and rejoins the deep sea chorus."

*   *   *

It was Nick's chair. Lena preferred the sofa, where she could sit cross-legged and align her papers around her, with her tablet and cell phone each resting on an arm and her laptop perched on the back.

Nick never sat cross-legged. He could get his long legs into the position, but he could not get out of it fast enough to suit him. If he was working, he liked to be able to move as and where the inspiration launched him.

From his chair, Nick moved the curtain aside and peeked out. Lena was still sitting outside on the front stoop, not moving. Nick let the curtain drop back into place, got up from the chair, walked quietly toward the front door, and opened it.

Lena looked up, almost but not quite surprised. Nick reached down, slid his long arms underneath her, and lifted her up.

"How do I love thee? Let me count the ways."

He stepped inside, set her gently down.

"I love thee to the depth and breadth and height my soul can reach, when feeling out of sight for the ends of Being and ideal Grace."

He shut the door, turned the inside lock, then the deadbolt.

"I love thee to the level of everyday's most quiet need, by sun and candle-light."

He took her briefcase, let it slide to the floor near the umbrella stand.

"I love thee freely, as men strive for right; I love thee purely, as they turn from Praise."

He took the keys from her hand, dropped them in the ceramic dish on the black lacquer table that she had inherited from her mother.

"I love thee with a passion put to use in my old griefs, and with my childhood's faith."

He grasped the lapels of her overcoat, slipped it down off one arm.

"I love thee with a love I seemed to lose with my lost saints"

He stepped behind around to her other side, pulled the sleeve from her other arm.

"I love thee with the breath, smiles, tears, of all my life!"

He moved in front of her, tossed the coat towards the coatrack; it missed but neither laughed.

"And, if God choose, I shall but love thee better after death."

He moved to kiss her but she put her hands on his chest, stopping him. Then she kissed him and pulled him down onto the coat.

*   *   *

"You need to talk to me," he said.

"Do I?" she asked, rearranging her blouse.

Nick nodded.

"In a minute'" she said. "I'm going to change."

"Please don't," Nick said smiling.

Lena smiled as well. An old routine.

She went upstairs, took a quick shower, put on her warmest PJs and thick pink socks, and returned downstairs. Nick had poured a glass of red wine for her, a glass of punch for himself. She sat cross-legged on the sofa and took a sip of the wine.

"So," she said. "How was your day?"

"Fine. Busy."

"I can imagine."

"Can you?"

"Not if I can help it."

"How was your day?"

"Fine. Busy."

Nick reached far out with his glass and touched hers.

"To being fine and busy."

They drank.

"Some furniture went missing at the office today."

"Really? Where was the last place you saw it?"

"Under you."

"I'll keep an eye out."

"That's okay. We don't really need it anymore."

"I see. Well, then. Just as well."

"Just as well."

Lena drained her glass and stood.

"I'm getting some more. Can I get you anything?"

"No. No. I'm fine."

"And busy."

Lena went into the kitchen, poured another glass, drained it. She returned to the living room.

"Let's take a walk," she said after a moment.

"It's cold outside."

"In Minnesota, this is not cold."

"You're in your pajamas."

"I'll wear a coat."

"Okay. Wolfram?"

Wolfram raised his head and dark eyes glittered in Nick's direction.

"Let's leave the entourage at home this time. Just you and me."

Nick shook his head and Wolfram lowered his, after a glance at Sancho. Lena slipped into her boots. Nick helped her on with her coat and slid into his jacket and topcoat.

On the stoop, Nick turned west toward the lake but Lena turned east toward Hennepin and Nick corrected his direction. She slid her arm into his and they walked in silence. At Hennepin Avenue, they turned north and continued without speaking.

When they reached the coffee shop, the line was short. Lena ordered a small vanilla latte. In a show of support (for Lena and the world), Nick ordered a large fair trade organic carbon-free certified brew. They took a seat in at a small table in the back. Lena sipped her latte.

"Nick."

"You're frothing at the mouth," he said.

"You've seen it before," she said, taking a napkin and wiping away the bubbles.

"Nick," she continued. "I know you were disappointed when I said I didn't want you back at work."

"I was. I want to work. With you."

"I know," Lena said, "I just. I can't do it. I need. I just can't."

He held his hands up.

"I know."

Lena took another sip.

"I'm glad you agree."

"I do. You should come work with me."

She slowly crumpled the napkin in her fist.

"That's not what I meant."

"I'll pay you a million dollars a year."

"Stop."

"Two million."

"Please."

"Three. Final offer."

She stared at him.

"Okay, four million," he said. "Four million is my absolute final offer until my next offer."

She shook her head, releasing the napkin. The wet folds clung together.

"You need to stop offering people money," she said. "For some reason they believe you."

"They should."

268 • STEPHEN EVANS

That stopped her. She knew that confidence. She took a sip of coffee to cover her surprise.

"Where are you going to get that kind of money?" she asked. "Or any money?"

"Leonard."

"Leonard?"

"Leonard."

"Leonard who?"

"Leonard Reed."

Lena crossed her arms. That was a name she hadn't heard in a long time. Nick had spoken of Leonard Reed before as if he had known him, a former student who had no talent for the law. His abilities lay elsewhere apparently, as he ended up one of the richest men in the country.

"I heard he was dead."

"Just a rumor."

"You're getting money from Leonard Reed," she said carefully, "the billionaire who disappeared ten years ago."

"He didn't disappear," Nick corrected her. "He just hasn't been seen."

Lena paused.

"Except by me of course," Nick clarified.

"Excuse me?"

"He has been seen by me," Nick said. "I wouldn't count on money from someone I couldn't see."

"I see."

"Unless they were Imaginary."

Lena covered her mouth with her hand, as the foam threatened to erupt again.

"I see."

"And Sancho saw him. I have a witness."

Lena released herself.

"Oh. Well then. Four million it is."

Nick reached over and took Lena's hand.

"You're skeptical."

Lena pulled away.

"Why should I be? If you say it, I believe it, like everyone else we know."

Lena started to remove her coat, then remembered she was in her pajamas, so she shrugged it back on.

"So?" she asked. "You and Leonard are starting a company? A law firm? What?"

Nick smiled.

"A private foundation."

"A foundation. Well, you could certainly use a new one of those."

"You're not being very supportive."

She feigned a laugh at the joke.

"Come on, let's go. I'm getting overheated."

She saw Nick smile.

"In this coat."

Nick refrained from the rejoinder, which surprised Lena. Too obvious, maybe, for his taste. Instead, he got up and dumped his coffee into the trash. They followed a circuitous path through the crowd and exited into the cold. The temperature had dropped considerably in just their few minutes inside. Lena looked up, couldn't see stars, but it didn't feel like snow.

They walked south on Hennepin, then turned up a side street towards the lake.

"I'm just worried," Lena said finally. "Look. A foundation is maybe shockingly possibly a good idea. You could do some good without actually practicing law."

"That was our thinking."

They walked a few more blocks in silence. The night air was still, which Lena was grateful for. Even a September wind off the lake would have been frigid. As it was, the chill was invigorating. As was the thought of Nick not working with her, she had to admit.

She nodded finally.

"Okay. I'll talk to some of our contacts in the nonprofit world and see if I can get you some seed money."

Nick smiled.

"I have money."

"How much?"

"A billion dollars."

Lena stopped and turned to Nick. She wanted to see his face when he answered.

"A billion?"

Nick nodded.

"One hundred million a year for ten years."

"From Leonard?"

"From Leonard through contributions from various corporate intermediaries. His name is not to be mentioned publicly."

"That I completely agree with," Lena said.

She looked carefully at Nick. In the pinkish light of the street lamp, his blue eyes seemed, what color, grey maybe? But clear.

She believed he believed it. And Sharon was right. It was Nick. You couldn't absolutely rule it out, not even something as fantastic as this. But even if it was a fantasy, challenging Nick's delusions was futile, Lena knew. He was just too smart, had too facile an imagination. She started walking again, a little faster.

"Well, just in case Leonard decides he needs a new imaginary island and doesn't come through, we should look for some other sources."

Nick took her hand, realized they were bare, reached into her pocket, pulled out her ruby-colored mittens, and handed them to her.

"I guess it wouldn't hurt," he said.

"Thank you," Lena said, pulling on her mittens, walking and talking faster as her thought process began to accelerate.

"And you need to stop promising people these million dollar salaries. Even if you had the money, the IRS would object."

"They'll be disappointed."

"The IRS?"

"No, the people."

She finished donning on her mittens, reached into his pocket, handed his gloves to him.

"The people know you and they will understand."

"Won't you be disappointed?

He stopped to put on his gloves. She waited for him.

"No." she said. "That's one thing I insist on. The foundation is yours. The firm is mine. You stay on your side of the hall and I'll stay on mine."

Nick flexed his gloved fingers.

"Tabled for future discussion."

Lena sighed, took his gloved hand with her mittened one, and started walking again.

"Why did you choose that location anyway? You promised me faithfully when we started living together again that you would never enter that building."

"I had to. My office was there."

She stopped and confronted him.

"Because you rented the space!"

"I had to."

"Why?"

"If I didn't, they weren't going to let me put my office there."

Lena sighed and started again.

Nick began swinging his arm, the one holding Lena's hand. Lena had a fleeting image of them as Dorothy and the Scarecrow off to see the Wizard of Minneapolis.

"It will be great," Nick said. "We'll set up a picnic table in the hallway and we can meet for lunch. Plus it's good for the environment. We can carpool to work."

"Fine. But I'm instructing Sharon to intercept you whenever she sees you."

"Sharon works for me now."

Lena started walking faster still. Nick's long legs were able to keep pace, but the arm swinging diminished.

"That's something else we have to discuss. You can have Sharon part-time. I will feel better if she's keeping an eye on things. We'll find out what the median salary is in a Minnesota nonprofit for her job type. What's her title?"

"Vice President for Keeping an Eye on Things."

"We'll call her the Chief Operating Officer. What is Oscar's title?"

"Vice President of Not Letting Me Forget Things."

"Okay. We'll call him the Director of Information Technology."

"He's also the Principal Balloonologist."

"We'll add twenty percent for that."

"You really should let me hire you."

"No. I really shouldn't."

"I can pay you more than you."

When they reached the end of the street, Lena pulled Nick across to a park bench and sat. They were almost at the crest of the lagoon on the northern end of the lake. It was dark by the shore, and still. Nick put his arm around Lena, and they sat for a while without speaking.

The park was deserted, no sign of life, not even wind to invigorate the fading plant life along the shore. Soon, the water would be frozen over, and the ice covered with snow. At some point, when the ice was thick enough, the City would clear a space on the surface, for the daytime skaters and hockey players, and bring portable lights out for the nights. Cold, ice, and snow, were part of life in Minnesota. You knew them, understood them, enjoyed them as you could, coped as you needed, and kept on living.

Lena lifted a crimson paw to either side of Nick's face and looked intently into his eyes.

"Nick, I need you to promise me one other thing. We need to keep our work, and our finances, separate. Otherwise I'll worry too much. Too much more."

Nick nodded.

"That's what you need?"

"That's what I really really need to the depth and breadth and height my soul can reach, when feeling out of sight for the ends of Being and ideal Grace."

Lena knelt on the chilly surface in front of Nick and enveloped one of his hands in both of hers.

"This is the tricky part, Nick. We can live together. We know in our hearts we're married. But we have to keep things legally separate, personally and professionally."

"I understand."

"Do you?"

Nick paused a long time, head down. Lena imagined him watching with his mind's eye as the Visions tumbled like dice. Then he lifted his head. He was smiling.

She had tried for years to immunize herself against his smile by understanding it, but in studying it she had done the opposite. She could now read it too clearly, could see beyond what he wanted her to see, to what he did not want her to see, and maybe beyond that, to what he didn't know himself.

Of course it was not beyond Nick to intentionally create these levels. He was a superb performer, and his nuanced expressions in the courtroom (and elsewhere) were masterful. But she didn't think he was acting.

Of all of Nick's superpowers, his energy, his memory, his Visions, this was maybe the most powerful: his honesty. The force of the truth he offered you, when he wanted to, was overwhelming.

Something in his countenance seemed woeful, and something underneath that, joyful, when he said "I do."

Passion Put to Use

All week, Lena walked briskly past the plastic screen draped over the door across from her office, trying to pay no attention to the man behind the curtain. She was physically successful, but reigning in her imagination proved much more difficult.

Nick had not returned to his office at Ward and Grant, which Sharon in a preemptive move was now occupying. Certainly Sharon could use the space, since her job long ago had grown beyond receptionist (if it had ever been just that).

At home, there was a conspiracy of silence. Neither Nick nor Lena mentioned Nick's daytime activities. They drove to the office together and in the evening Nick was waiting for her in the car. Otherwise both of them acted as if nothing had changed. Rituals resurfaced from times before the divorce: favorite restaurants, day trips to Stillwater and Northfield, planning vacations they would never take. It was so ordinary Lena found it disconcerting; normal was not normal.

One morning the plastic curtains were replaced by two Chagallesque stained glass doors with brass handles. An empty frame hung next to the doors. There was as yet no nameplate.

Lena pushed through the heavy doors. Inside there was no circus or zoo, not that she could see anyway. Three steps led up to a large open space, three or four times the size of her offices.

She walked cautiously up the steps and found herself at the edge of a pool of water. The pool was irregular, the edge winding in and out as it passed through the open space. Tree trunks, fake she assumed but seeming real, placed at odd intervals, appeared to be growing through the ceiling. She recognized various types common in Minnesota: American elm, Norwegian Pine, White Oak. At miscellaneous spots along the border of the pool, plain wooden benches were set.

She realized then that this was not a pool but a lake. It was fact, a replica of Lake of the Isles, with one exception: there were no islands.

There was not a straight line or right angle in the entire space. Walls surrounded the area, following the outline of Lake of the Isles Parkway, which circled the real thing, while allowing some space for park/office, covering even what might once have been windows. The walls were blank, but she suspected they would not remain so for long. The carpeting was an artificial turf; at least she hoped it was, because she didn't relish the sounds of lawn mowers in the office next door. But most of the space was taken up by the 'lake' itself.

On the far side of the office, the western 'shore' of the lagoon, Nick was sitting on a replica of his usual bench, staring out at the lake. He did not appear to notice her, but Sancho, next to him, appeared to be 'watching' for her. Lena had not been there two minutes and already felt herself running out of mental single quotes.

She strolled along the shore, up the eastern edge of the lagoon, and down the western edge, as she had in reality so many times. Lakeshores, Nick had explained to her once, were fractal in nature, patterns recurring again and again. He had launched into a long explanation involving someone named Mandelbrot and coastline paradoxes, and when he started on crystals, fluid turbulence, and galaxy formation, she had stopped paying attention. Apparently, that had been a mistake.

Another recurring pattern, she thought, as she neared the bench where Nick was sitting.

"Feels like something is missing," she said.

"I was just thinking the same thing," Nick replied. He picked up Sancho and patted the empty space on the bench. Lena sat next to him.

"I was referring to the islands."

"They're Imaginary."

Lena frowned.

"You keep using that word. I don't think it means what you think it means."

"It's conceivable," he replied.

Lena laughed.

"When I say imaginary," she continued, "I mean, what do I mean, I mean 'not there'. When you say it, it sounds like 'more there'."

"More or less."

"I don't understand."

"I understand."

"I know you do. That's why I'm asking."

"No. I mean, I understand that you don't understand."

"So can you explain it please?"

Nick paused, crossed his arms.

"Tolkien tells us–"

"See you did it again."

"What?"

"You say Tolkien like you're saying Tacitus."

"Well, he was a Professor of Medieval History.

"No that was C. S Lewis."

"Oh. I get them confused."

"Or was that T. H. White? I get them confused.

"I don't get them confused."

"Or D. H. Lawrence. Why don't Twentieth Century English writers have first names? I don't understand."

"I understand."

"You understand that I don't understand?"

"No I understand what you don't understand."

"Oh. You're very understanding."

"It's what I do."

Lena felt the need for reinforcements, reached across Nick, and pulled Sancho onto her lap.

"Just explain please."

"Then stop interrupting."

"Proceed, Counsellor."

"Thank you, your Honor. Tolkien tells us—"

"Oh, back to that are we?"

Nick glanced over at her. She shrugged. Sancho bounced. Nick continued.

"Tolkien tells us that elves live in two worlds at once, the Seen and the Unseen. It's like that with me."

Lena paused, evaluating the possibilities.

"Are you saying that you're an Elf?"

"No, I'm saying that Elves are Imaginary."

"Well obviously."

"So you understand."

"That elves are imaginary? Of course."

"Well, it's the same with me."

"You're imaginary? I'm beginning to like where this is going. You're imaginary and I'm the one who is delusional."

Nick stood and surveyed his domain.

"In the Imaginary realm, all the things that are and the things that should be exist together, and nothing ever passes away. In the Real realm, probabilities converge, existence narrows, and everything passes away. Living in both isn't easy. Hank calls it Imaginative Dissonance."

"Doctor Richardson knows you're imaginary?"

Lena looked at Sancho in surprise.

"You'd think he would have mentioned something like that," she said, whispering into floppy grey-white ears.

"Probably a doctor-patient confidentiality issue."

"Then shouldn't the confidentiality be imaginary?"

Nick reborrowed Sancho from Lena and held him up high.

"Take Sancho."

"Thank you I will."

Lena rereborrowed Sancho and held on to him tightly.

"Sancho," Nick said, raising an eyebrow, "is completely Imaginary. Wolfram is so Imaginary that he barely exists on this side any longer. You are Imaginary, though you struggle with it."

Lena paused, nodded.

"Yes, I definitely feel the Imaginative Dissonance."

Nick spread his arms wide, lifted them over his head, then crossed them, and Lena suddenly remembered the gesture from his classes; it was his I'm About To Begin A Long Complicated Discussion So You Should Pay Close Attention gesture. Nostalgic Dissonance, she thought.

"I think Ontological Dissonance is more correct really," Nick said. "But there is dissonance. Like music, sometimes it is joyful and sometimes it is painful. Sometimes the dissonance grows so great that it has to be resolved."

Lena frowned.

"What happens then?"

"Then you just make a wish and pass solely into the Imaginary Realm."

Lena gave him a wry look.

"Yeah, well, while you're married to me, this is a no passing zone."

"But we're not married."

"Don't say that."

"Okay. We are married."

"Don't say that either."

Nick paused.

"I do sense some dissonance. I'm not sure how Imaginative it is."

Lena looked out at the water. It seemed to change from blue-green to blue to green and back, probably something to do with the illumination. Then again wasn't everything?

"So this is your new office," Lena said. "Tell me you didn't order hover desks."

"Oddly enough, I could not find anyone who manufactures them. Some people just have no vision."

"Imagine that."

"Apparently I'm the only one that can."

"Imagine that."

"No, I ordered desks built into the ceiling that will rise and descend on cue. But I can't decide what the cue should be. Maybe a secret word that changes every day. "

"You always were a Groucho Marx aficionado."

Lena paused, then took Nick's hand.

"You didn't charge this to our credit cards, did you?"

"Of course not."

Lena sighed in relief.

"It wouldn't fit. I'd have had to mortgage the house."

Lena squeezed his hand very hard.

"But I didn't," he said quickly. "When I told the architects and the contractors about the new Foundation and all the good work we were going to do, they were happy to be a part of it."

"And the billion dollars," Lena added.

"That helped."

"And they believed you."

"Of course. Otherwise, why would I need an office like this?"

"Of course."

Lena paused again, framing her words carefully.

"So. Why would you need an office like this? I mean, trees, Imaginary islands, hover desks, if you could find them."

Nick stood and gazed out happily over his domain.

"If you are going to do something extraordinary, you need an extraordinary space."

Lena nodded, then stood up next to him

"So. Imaginary Islands."

"Just for now," Nick said. "They're on backorder."

*   *   *

As Lena exited, a man in white entered the room from a hidden door set in the northeast section of the wall.

"You always wear the same suit," Nick said.

"I learned from the Master," Leonard replied.

He took a seat on the bench next to Nick and Sancho. They sat silently for a while, looking over the water.

"This is peaceful," Leonard said after a few moments.

"It's a beginning," Nick replied.

The man in white nodded, then gestured toward the doors.

"How is it going?"

Nick shifted his head left then right, then said:

"She's adjusting."

Leonard thought for a bit.

"Well, as someone who has been dead for a decade, my perspective may be different. But what we are doing is necessary, don't you think?"

"I do."

The man in white nodded again, then his eyes narrowed.

"Are you having second thoughts about the plan?"

Nick sighed.

"I don't make plans. I have Visions."

*   *   *

Doctor Richardson pushed Volume 12 of the *Minnesota Journal of Alternative Psychiatry* towards Nick.

"Page 144," he announced.

Nick reached for the magazine, sat, opened to the page, quickly flipped a few pages, and closed the volume.

"I decided not to use your name, even though you gave me permission," Richardson said.

"I saw that."

Richardson waited.

"Are you going to tell me what you thought?"

"Do I ever?"

"Make an exception."

Nick picked thumbed through to the article.

"You want a personal appraisal, or a literary one?"

"Personal of course."

"Personally I thought it was very literary."

Richardson smiled but looked intently at Nick.

"You of all people are entitled to have an opinion. Required even."

Nick pushed the magazine back across the desk.

"We are just going to have to agree to disagree. I am not mentally ill. I am not delusional. I just have a unique vision of the world and I behave accordingly."

Richardson sat back.

"Having a unique vision of the world and behaving accordingly is a very good definition of delusion," he said.

Nick mirrored his position.

"From my perspective, it is you, most of you anyway, who are delusional. I mean that in the nicest way of course."

Richardson smiled.

"I did allow for that possibility in the article."

"That was thoughtful of you."

Richardson pulled his notebook out of his desk and opened it.

"So," he said. "Where is Sancho today?"

"In the hallway with Oscar and Wolfram. They don't like being separated anymore."

"Oscar and Sancho?"

"No. Sancho and Wolfram."

"I see. Your puppet, sorry, Imaginary American, doesn't like being separated from your Irish wolfhound. Well, that's understandable. They do share a certain consonance of objectives: wolves and all."

Nick smiled this time.

"You are being sincere, which I have learned is your deepest expression of irony. And I understand your point. But yes, there is a bond between them."

"How does that make you feel?"

"It's better than their arguing all the time."

Doctor Richardson nodded.

"You have a very strong bond with Sancho yourself. And Wolfram. You saved him."

"He would have done the same for me".

"Maybe he did," said Dr. Richardson.

"Lena called you, didn't she?" Nick said.

"Called. Emailed. Stopped by. I hear from her more than you."

Nick sighed.

"I'm glad," he said.

"You are?"

"Yes. I hope you can help her. She has a lot of problems."

"I'm not sure I'd use the plural there."

"Nice."

Richardson paused, not as if he was waiting but as if he were thinking about what had been said. It was the one technique that seldom failed with Nick. He was compelled to fill the silence. And what he would fill it with was usually revealing in some sense, if not necessarily apropos of the discussion at hand. This time however was almost never.

"Lena tells me that you have been seeing an old friend recently," the doctor continued.

"He's younger than I am."

Richardson waited again, hoping to coax something more out of Nick, to no avail.

"I'm wondering if maybe it is time to try medication again. You are entering into what sounds like a very stressful period. Medication may be beneficial."

"No."

Richardson nodded, made a note in his notebook.

"What should I tell Lena?' he asked. "She's worried."

"I know."

"Can you blame her?"

"I never blame her."

"I know."

*   *   *

Oscar, Sancho, and Wolfram glanced up in one motion as Nick exited Doctor Richardson's office.

"Are you ready for our meeting tonight?" Nick asked.

"I guess so," Oscar said. "I've never been on a board before. Are you ready?"

"I've been on many boards," Nick said. "But I think this one is going to be something special."

"Wonderful!"

"Shouldn't you be attending the ward, or something?" Nick asked.

Oscar looked up at him.

"I like to think of you as our resident alien," Oscar said, handing Sancho back to Nick.

Nick looked at Sancho and said:

"Funny. That's how I like to think of myself."

Oscar arranged the benches in a circle around the holographic campfire. As he pondered how long it would take the lasers to roast a marshmallow, Ralph and Alice came in and sat opposite him, followed soon after by Sharon, who sat next to him.

He looked at Ralph and Alice and wondered if some day he and Sharon would be together in the way they were together. Despite the fact that two people could hardly be less alike, Alice so tiny and Ralph so huge, Alice so outspoken and Ralph so quiet, no one ever said Ralph or Alice, or even Ralph and Alice, but always RalphandAlice. Oscar hoped for the day it would be OscarandSharon. SharonandOscar would be just fine too.

Then again, he thought, no one ever said NickandLena, always Nick and Lena, or Lena and Nick. Yet he did not doubt that they were as powerfully connected as Ralph and Alice. Maybe because in some ways Nick and Lena were outwardly more similar than Ralph and Alice, people took more trouble to separate them in their minds. They were both lawyers, both brilliant and accomplished. He resolved to be attentive to the nominal permutations of couplehood. There were many factors to be pondered, and he yearned for understanding, among other things.

Sharon nudged Oscar.

"Where is he?"

Oscar shrugged.

"He said to be here. That's all I know."

Sharon sniffed.

"Where is she?" Oscar asked.

"Not coming."

"Not surprised."

SharonandOscar nodded to RalphandAlice, and waited.

*   *   *

Lena emerged from her office, loaded down with briefcase, coat, and gloves. Nick and Sancho were waiting.

"Where's the third member of the triumvirate?"

"Home snoozing in the parlor. I didn't want to wake him."

"Parlor?"

"That's what they called them when he was young."

Lena put a hand on Nick's cheek, handed the briefcase to his Non-Sancho hand, laid her coat over his arm, and put on her gloves.

"I'll get him something to eat when I get home," she said. "Is Leonard joining you?"

"No. He hates meetings. He trusts me to handle things"

Lena reclaimed her burdens.

"Well, so do I."

Nick smiled, glanced at the double doors behind him.

"As long as Sharon is there to report back."

"Exactly," Lena said. "How long do you think you'll be?"

"This is our first meeting. Not long."

She checked the time on her phone.

"Okay. See you at home," she said, heading hastily down the hall.

*　　*　　*

Preston waved Lena over to the bar, where a glass of red wine awaited her, an Australian Grenache he knew she enjoyed but never thought to order for herself. The bar was crowded with attorneys mingling after work, talking about everything but law. Preston was a regular, as Lena had been during the years Nick was absent with leave. It was where their attachment had formed, and where it now remained formless.

Preston was patient. He knew that he was better for Lena than Nick. He also knew that Lena's attachment to Nick was far deeper than mere guilt, but that guilt was the first barrier to be eliminated. Preston knew that in the end she might not choose him. But he was determined that she should not choose Nick. Preston felt sorry for Nick, and even a sort of kinship. He knew neither of them could ever let her go.

Lena sat and downed the glass of wine Preston had ordered for her. Preston signaled for two more.

"So," he said. "I can tell we're not here to catch up."

"Not exactly. Though it is always good to see you. Truly."

"Thanks."

The bartender brought them two more glasses. This time she sipped, recognized the vintage, and signaled her appreciation. Then she moved to an empty table in a quieter section of the bar. Preston downed the rest of his first glass, picked up the second glass, and joined her.

Lena settled herself in, shut off her phone, and savored another sip.

"It's been a while since I've been here," she said.

"You were missed," Preston said. Lena glanced around, waived at familiar faces, some of whom looked surprised to see her. Or maybe surprised to see her with Preston.

The atmosphere in the bar brought something back that she had forgotten. The sense of relief, even somewhere far away, hope. Hope for what? Not love. No hope there. Hope for something undefined, and maybe the undefined nature of it was itself the hope.

"Thank you for the wine," she said. "How did you remember?"

"It's in your file," he said.

She looked at him to be sure he was kidding, which he was. She took another sip.

"Do you remember the name Leonard Reed?" she asked.

"The finance guy?"

Preston's hands smoothed his hair, then joined behind his head as he looked toward the ceiling. "Ran a hedge fund. Owned lots of real estate around the city. I think I had just joined the Attorney General's office when he disappeared."

"That's the guy. Was there an investigation?"

Preston paused, trying to remember.

"They started one. Didn't get very far. No evidence of anything criminal, of anything really. He was just gone."

Lena reached for the bowl of pretzels on the table, then thought better of it.

"And no one has seen him since?"

"Not that I know of."

"Can you look into it?"

"Sure. Why?"

Lena sat back, rolling the wine glass between her hands.

"He's Nick's new business partner."

Preston laughed hard.

"Perfect!"

Lena didn't laugh, so he said:

"You're joking."

Lena shook her head.

"I wish," she said, then took a sip. "Nick says he is starting a private foundation, and that Leonard Reed is funding it."

Preston leaned in, concerned.

"You think he is having hallucinations now?"

Lena shook her head, then shrugged. "Maybe. Probably."

A drop of Grenache leapt over the rim of the glass onto the table and spread rapidly to pink on the white tablecloth.

"Has he ever had them before?"

"Not that I know of."

Lena paused, regretting the stain, then took a paper napkin, folded it twice, and carefully blotted. As the stain spread to the napkin, the shape reminded her of Lake of the Isles, and she had that fractal feeling again. The stain expanded, and she breathed easier.

"I know it's not fair," Lena said, reaching into her briefcase and taking out a kit containing a microfiber blotting cloth, a small soft-bristled brush, and a travel-sized spray bottle of stain remover, "to ask you to help me with Nick."

Preston looked down, ran his hands through his hair again.

"It's not fair for you to be with Nick. That's the issue."

"Preston," she said, firmly but with understanding, then plunged valiantly into the task of removing the stain.

Preston cocked his head slightly and paused. He thought back to the few times he had seen her over the last few months. She gave the impression that she was suspended, like someone who had wandered unknowingly onto a tightrope.

Was she unknowing? How could she be? Maybe it was the depth of the drop that was unknown. If there was a bottom to that particular pit, neither she nor he could see it. But Preston had finally realized that the best he could do, all he could do, was stay close, and be there when whatever happened happened.

"You don't think it could be the real Leonard Reed?" he asked.

Lena laughed.

"As I've been told more than once recently: It's Nick. Anything is possible."

Preston nodded.

"Does he have any money?"

"Nick? I don't know. He is spending money, that's for sure. You should see the office he set up. He says the space and construction costs were donated. I hope so."

"I'll see what I can find out," he said.

Preston reached across the table and covered her hand with his.

"Are you sure you are safe?"

Lena gripped his hand, held it for a moment, then released it.

"Nick would never hurt me. I'm sure of that."

Preston stopped his reaction. He was too good a prosecutor to make an argument he could not win. But he noted for the record:

"He has hurt you."

"Preston."

"Sorry."

"No. I mean, thank you. I don't want to hurt you either. Should I not call you?"

He smiled and shrugged.

"I'd just call you."

*   *   *

Nick took his place at the campfire, holding Sancho at attention on his knee.

"Welcome. Thank you for being here, and for agreeing to be a part of this venture. You were all carefully chosen for your expertise in being able to put up with me."

Sharon raised her hand.

"Exception noted," Nick said.

Sharon lowered her hand.

"We here," Nick continued, "duly constitute the Board of Trustees for our newly formed organization: The Sancho Foundation."

Oscar stood.

"I second the motion."

"Not yet," Sharon whispered, pulling him down next to her, not letting go of his hand. Oscar gazed at his hand in hers as if a miracle had occurred.

"Lena isn't coming?" Alice asked.

Nick shook his head.

"Lena has declined participation at this time."

A worried look crossed Alice's face.

Sancho looked around the circle at each one individually. Then he nodded to Nick.

"For now, the responsibility falls to us."

"Responsibility for what?" Ralph asked.

Nick stood, almost spilling into the holographic blaze in his excitement.

"Our generous anonymous benefactor, my old friend Leonard Reed, is donating 100 million dollars a year for the next ten years to our private operating foundation and charitable trust. Under the terms of that trust agreement, and unlike most foundations, we will not spend a small percentage of our income on multiple projects. Instead, we will spend all of it every year on one project."

They waited.

"And that project is?" Alice asked finally.

"That is what the Board of Trustees will decide," Nick declared, sitting back down.

"The BOT," Oscar said, "Sounds very RUR."

Sharon squeezed his hand, which Oscar interpreted as affection.

"The BOT. I like that," Nick said. "We have only one guiding principle from our founder: do what no one else has thought of."

"He picked the right person for that," Oscar said.

"Everybody says that," Nick replied, stretching his legs out into the campfire, making sure to avoid the beam of the laser directly overhead, reserved for the marshmallows.

"I have been thinking hard about what our first project should be," he continued. "Obviously there are many worthy causes out there and selecting one will be difficult. I suggest three parameters: something not too far out of the box to start, yet something that will make a statement, and obviously something that can be accomplished in a year."

There was no response. Everyone seemed mesmerized by Nick's boots in the holographic flame. Nick interrupted the silence.

"So," he asked, pulling his feet back and reaching for the telescoping roasters, "who brought the marshmallows?"

*   *   *

"You're out of everything."

Oscar jumped. He was still not used to having anyone else in his apartment.

"How can you be out of everything?" Sharon asked.

"Because you use everything," Oscar replied.

Oscar had discovered early on that Sharon didn't like it when he agreed with her too easily. Conflict was not something that came naturally to him. But he had been studying Nick and Lena, observing carefully their rapid and pointed banter. At first they went so fast, and in such perfect rhythm, that he was intimidated. But now he was getting pretty good at it, if he did say so. There was a trick to it, something in the words that said you are completely and utterly wrong but I will love you forever anyway. He hadn't quite mastered that, but he was aware of it, and thought it was slowly seeping in.

"What are you doing?" Sharon asked.

"Just jotting down some ideas."

"Ideas for what?"

Oscar turned to see that Sharon was wearing his robe and found himself unable to remember the question.

Sharon, for her part, was mystified by her own attraction to Oscar. Nothing in her experience had prepared her for the feelings. Oscar's naturally sweet and gentle nature would in the past have ensured polite disregard. Now they spurred her in directions she did not entirely recognize.

Sharon peered over Oscar's shoulder, and he hastily covered the paper. But the thought of writing, or anything else, was quickly eclipsed by the smell of her hair, and the wetness of it brushing against his neck, the sound her hand made sliding along the strands as she pulled it back to keep from dripping on his work. Every day there was some new sensation.

"I can't see?" Sharon asked.

Oscar moved his hands, revealing the blank paper.

"I'm trying to think like Nick," he said. "It's not working."

"Thank you," Sharon said to the heavens.

*   *   *

The piano bench had been specially built, four inches higher than normal with steel-reinforced legs. The piano itself rested on a six-inch platform, which gave the instrument a distinctive resonance.

Ralph's hands rested on the piano, but did not invoke the keys. Ordinarily his hands decided what to play, which left his mind free to listen. But today even his hands seemed frozen in place.

"What do you think he means by Board of Trustees?" Ralph asked without turning.

Alice, though she was sitting in her chair in the living room not five feet from the piano, had not noticed that there was no music forthcoming. The copy of Animal Shelter magazine in her hands was upside down.

"You know what a board is," Alice replied. "We have one for the shelter."

One large hand dropped on the keyboard, which issued nothing close to music.

"I know. But what do you think he means? I have a feeling it's not attend a meeting once a month."

Alice noticed her magazine was upside down and quickly set it on the table beside her.

"I'm sure you're right about that."

Ralph nodded, then shook his head. His hands began to move over the keys, finding their way chord to chord.

It was an essential element of their partnership, these joint examinations of topics large or small. Twenty years before, they had moved their family from Alabama to Minnesota for the chance to work together at something they were passionate about: caring for animals. Ralph had never regretted the change, though he still thought of Alabama as home. They had built a wonderful life in Minnesota, raised their girls, dedicated themselves to work they believed was important.

But he wondered sometimes if it had been the right move for Alice. Look at the way she had jumped into this shelter redesign program, managing every detail, coming up with suggestions that he could never have thought of. She was so smart and capable in so many areas, she might have accomplished much more if she had gone her own way professionally. She might be the head of a national animal welfare organization by now. Or international.

Working with Nick had changed them both in a way. As wild and grandiose and yes crazy as his ideas were, the scope of them had altered their view of the world, and their place in it. Revealed new horizons. Whether they existed or not was an open question. But the revelation was real enough.

It was not something Ralph aspired to. And Alice had given no sign that she was not content. In fact, she had started to talk about retirement. But looking at her now, Ralph couldn't see it. Not for him. He would be fine with retirement. For her.

He stopped playing and turned back.

"When I asked him what we would be doing, he said 'anything is possible'."

Alice got up and moved behind Ralph, putting a hand on each shoulder, which even with him sitting she had to reach up to do.

"This is what I'm thinking," Ralph said. "Nick is a friend and he wants our help. And this may be a chance to do something extraordinary."

"And if the money is real," Alice continued his thought, "it would be a big help. The girls' education cost more than we planned for. But," she said, moving to the side and smiling up at him, "Our life is good. Our work is good. Maybe that's enough."

Ralph leaned down to kiss the top of her head.

"I hate when you do that," Alice said.

"No you don't," Ralph said.

He turned on the bench, encircling her with gigantic arms.

"No. I don't," she said, patting his cheek.

*   *   *

Lena turned ninety degrees and rested her head on Nick's stomach, curling her legs in so they didn't dangle off the bed. Wolfram lifted his head as she stirred, noted the odd juxtaposition, then relaxed back to sleep in his corner. They had not found a dog bed large enough for him, so they had placed a futon over the hardwood floor, which he seemed to like, since he no longer tried to get up on their bed during the night.

Lena shifted her weight to make sure Nick was awake.

"So," she said, "how was the inaugural meeting?"

Nick reached down, liberated her hair from beneath her head, and wound his hand in the red-golden tresses.

"Good," Nick said. "We had marshmallows."

"You need to look out for them, you know."

"I know. I made sure the trust agreement protects them."

"I saw. I don't mean just legally."

"I know. I will. We will."

"You mean you and Leonard."

"Sure."

They lay quiet for a few moments. Nick tried to wind a few wispy strands into braids but Lena stopped him, knowing what she would have to undo in the morning.

"It's not the same," Nick said.

"No?"

He clasped her hair in his fist, hard, not pulling, just holding tight.

"Without you. It's not the same without you."

Lena reached up and smoothed again, then uncurled and returned to the pillow, facing away from Nick.

"It wouldn't be the same with me," she answered.

*   *   *

The car crawled slowly around the crowded semi-circular drive in front of the Lindbergh Terminal at Minneapolis-St. Paul International Airport, then nudged in to the curb. Despite the sluggish pace, Lena felt as if she were flying already, watching from detached vantage the goings-on far beneath: Normal people leading normal lives going normal places.

The car stopped. Lena drew her gaze away from the many to the one.

"Thanks, Harvey," she said. "I expect to be back from the conference on Thursday, but it's possible I may extend. I'll text you if my schedule changes."

By the time Lena gathered her things and got out of the car, Harvey was already unloading her suitcase (only one this time) and signaling the curbside porter. Lena gave the porter her flight information (KLM, Minneapolis to Geneva), hoisted her laptop and briefcase.

"Which conference is this?" Harvey asked.

"International conference on animal rights and welfare," she said. "It's something Nick was involved in a long time ago, and when things fell apart I took over. It's once a year."

"Ah."

"This year it's about animals in war zones."

Harvey looked up.

"A lot of guys in Iraq adopted pets when they were on a tour. Not easy to bring them back. Do good."

Lena promised herself that one day she and Harvey were going to have a long chat. Though Harvey was not known for long chats. Or any chats.

Harvey turned to go, but Lena grabbed his sleeve.

"Look in on Nick and let me know if... you know, the usual."

"Will do," Harvey said, giving her a pat on the shoulder that reminded her of her father.

As the car pulled away, Lena felt the usual warfare starting between dread and anticipation. She knew the futility of worry, because whatever actually went wrong was going to be different than whatever she had imagined was going to go wrong. It was like having a child with magical powers. Or maybe just like having a child.

No, definitely not a place to go before a nine-hour flight. It was still an empty place, and the most serious cost of her marriage, the decision not have a child with Nick. It was an undercurrent to every day of their lives.

Lena bumped into a tall man in a grey suit before realizing it was Preston. She smiled.

"Thanks for meeting me here," she said.

"Sure."

"Let's get a drink."

"Sure."

They walked in silence down the concourse until they reached the Sky club and ducked inside. The waitress brought a glass of Chardonnay for Lena and scotch on the rocks for Preston, along with a tray of snacks.

"Everything okay?"

"Sure." Lena answered. "I'm just preoccupied with the conference. What did you find out?"

Preston sipped his scotch, then pulled a small brown notebook out of his jacket pocket.

"Nothing, or nothing conclusive," he said. "Leonard Reed has not been seen in a decade, but his business interests, including Reed International, are very active. So probably he is alive and well and very very private, and if I had had his money I would be too."

"So if Nick is having a hallucination," Lena concluded, "at least he found one that is plausible."

Preston exhaled hard, then consulted his notes again.

"I also confirmed that they did know each other, or at least that Reed was a law student and took one of Nick's classes. He never passed the bar or practiced law. But it doesn't seem to have held him back. He is still included in most lists of the richest Americans."

"Thank you," Lena replied.

Preston sighed.

"Well, you are probably boarding soon."

Lena looked around as if searching, then looked back at Preston, then down at the table.

"Can we just sit and drink until they call my flight. I would really appreciate that."

Preston nodded.

"Sure," he said, signaling the waitress.

*   *   *

The campfire flashed phantom flames as the Board of Trustees gathered. The marshmallows had been a success last time, though a touch underdone, so this time Nick brought doughnuts and coffee.

"Welcome," Nick said to the four friends sitting in front of him, and Sancho, who was in his lap. "Thank you for meeting again so soon. I know we are all anxious to get to work. In the future, we'll hire a staff to handle as much of the busywork as we like, but for now we will need to shoulder the tasks that will get us going on our first project."

"Which is?" Sharon asked.

"That is what this council will decide."

Nick looked around.

"Anyone have a project to suggest?" he asked.

No one spoke.

"Anyone? Anyone?"

Sharon nudged Oscar, who shook his head. Then everyone turned to Nick, including Sancho.

"Okay. I'll go first. Here is my proposal: we are going save the whales."

Blanks stares and silence all round.

"Shouldn't we do something closer to home?" asked Ralph. "I can think of a lot of good we could do right here in Minnesota."

"Excellent point. Clarification: we are going to save the whales of Minnesota."

Blanks stares and silence all round.

"There are no whales in Minnesota," Ralph said after a moment.

"Another excellent point. Clarification: we are going to save the whales of Lake Superior."

Ralph was ready this time.

"There are no whales in Lake Superior."

"That should make it easy," Nick replied.

Ralph nodded.

"Can't argue with that."

Nick waved his hand like a magician pulling a card out of the air and the hologram of the campfire turned into a map of Lake Superior.

"Anyway," Nick continued, "There are no whales in Lake Superior–yet. We are going to provide them."

Alice stirred.

"Lake Superior is fresh water," she announced. "Whales live in salt water."

"Yet another excellent point. I knew you were the right group for this. Obviously, we are not going to put any animals in danger. We will do this only in the safest possible way for all concerned. Based on my research..."

Nick waved his hand again and a list of articles on cetacean biology appeared.

"Whales can live in fresh water," he continued. "In fact, whales have been seen fairly frequently far up the St Lawrence Seaway. But in any event, we will provide them with whatever environment and care they need to flourish in Lake Superior."

There was general silence again. Nick waited.

"Where are you going to get whales?" Sharon asked finally. "You can't beam them up to your starship."

"We watched Star Trek Four last week," Oscar clarified.

"So did I—that's my favorite," Nick said. "The sea contains the hottest blood of all."

"They're going to need it," Sharon said. "Even Lake Superior freezes over in winter. How are they going to breathe?"

"The way the climate is changing, that may not be an issue for much longer," Nick noted. "Anyway, you are correct, all of these concerns have to be dealt with. As I see it, to start, we need four things:"

He waved his hand once more and a ghostly list appeared.

"First, we need whales, obviously. Second, we need a maritime research facility, I'm thinking maybe in Duluth. Third, we need a Cetacean biologist who will move to Duluth. Fourth, since Lake Superior extends across the border with Canada, we will need someone who can negotiate an international convention to protect the whales."

Nick waved the image away and waited.

No one spoke for a long time. Then Ralph raised a massive hand, which caused the holograph to flicker.

"Alice and I have contacts at regional animal facilities all over the US." he said, glancing at Alice for support. "We could, maybe, look for some whales."

Alice pulled his hand down into both of hers.

"I don't. I don't. Maybe. I could make some calls," she got out finally.

Ralph started to bend to her, but she gave him a look that said not here.

"Wonderful. Perfect," Nick said. "Let's start with something small, belugas maybe. They shouldn't have buoyancy problems in the fresh water, and they eat fish, which should be plentiful in Lake Superior."

"Yes," said Alice. "Let's start with small whales."

Ralph chuckled.

"Okay. Okay. Here we go," Nick said with excitement. "We're off and running."

"We should be running," Sharon said. "That is exactly what I don't know why we are not doing."

Oscar gave her a perplexed look.

"Never mind," Sharon said.

"Okay, then," Nick said. "I will take on the second task. I will have a chat with our esteemed Governor about requirement number two. We'll form a State-Private partnership to build a research facility in Duluth. I haven't been there in a while. Maybe there is some place on the water in need of renovation. So, what's next?"

He looked over at Oscar.

"I can check out biologists," Oscar volunteered.

"Perfect!" Nick said. "Try and find one with a specialization in cetacean neurobiology, someone who has done research in whale communication. We have a responsibility to communicate in a way they will understand."

"Great—we're going to talk to the animals," Sharon said.

"We haven't watched that one yet," Oscar noted.

Nick reached for a doughnut.

"So," he said after munching a bit," that leaves requirement number four. Who do we know who can negotiate an international convention on animal rights?"

"You should ask Lena," Oscar said.

"Where is Lena?" asked Alice.

Sharon glared at Nick with malevolent admiration.

"She's in Geneva negotiating an international convention on animal rights," she said.

Nick smiled.

"Well then," he said.

"I'll take this one," Sharon said. "Leave number four to me."

*　　*　　*

Harvey ordinarily took the long way home from the airport, winding along Minnehaha Parkway through the neighborhoods of south Minneapolis, past Lake Nokomis and Lake Hiawatha, then up past Lakes Harriet and Bde Maka Ska to Lake of the Isles. He didn't mind that Lena rode in the back seat, understanding that the time in the car was her transition time. If she was heading to the office, the back seat was usually covered with documents. If she was heading home, she usually sat quietly and watched out the window.

This time, Harvey sensed, was different. She asked him to take Route 62 to 35W, which would cut off maybe fifteen minutes from their usual leisurely route. He put on some music, but she didn't seem to notice.

When they reached her house, she retrieved her luggage herself and turned away with only a thank you. She usually invited him in, which he usually declined. She did not this time, and he was glad. Something was up. Both Nick and Lena were friends, and he did not like to get between them at times like this.

When Lena reached the stoop, she halted to listen, then changed her mind, opening the door quickly, and shutting it quickly. Without taking off her coat or dropping her luggage or keys, she charged into the living room to find Nick.

Nick was at the piano, studying the black and white layout of the keys as though it were an ancient language. Sancho was balanced on the top, at the point where the edge of the piano curved inward, like a torch singer heading into a ballad.

Lena dropped everything–luggage, briefcase, keys–on the floor, resisting the urge to hurl one or all.

"We had a deal," she said.

"Welcome back."

"You promised."

"Good flight?"

Lena sat stiffly on the sofa, then realized she was still wearing her coat and sloughed it off.

"I got Sharon's message at the airport."

"Which one?" Nick asked.

"Which message?"

"Which airport?"

Lena had to think.

"Amsterdam. Layover."

"Ah."

"Why?"

Nick closed the cover over the keyboard.

"Just wanted to set the timing in my mind."

Lena pulled out her ticket and held it up like a gauntlet about to be tossed.

"Nine hours. I have been in the air for nine hours. They almost turned the plane around, I was so upset."

"So?"

"So, so what?"

"Do you know anyone who could negotiate an international convention on animal rights?"

Lena threw the ticket at him. It was not a very effective weapon but it was all she had.

"How long have you been planning this?"

"I don't make plans. I have Visions."

She started forward, stopped, turned away, then rotated back, hands raised.

"What is marriage for you, Nick? I know what it is for me. What is it for you?"

Nick did not pause to ponder.

"I can't imagine my life without you," he said. "So I have to Imagine it with you."

Lena nodded, sighed, nodded, sighed. She turned and collapsed into the sofa.

"I won't do this again Nick. I can't. I have told you that over and over. And I mean it. But."

"But?"

She beckoned him over. He walked to her and sat.

"This is what I thought about for the last nine hours, or nine years, maybe. I'll give you a choice."

"A choice?"

"Yes. And I want you to take your time and think carefully, because there is no turning back from this."

Nick got up, and went to his chair, sat looking at her.

"Okay. Shoot," he said.

She did not take the bait.

"Here it is: We can be together here or we can be together at work. We can't do both. I can't. You have to choose."

Nick paused.

Lena waited.

"So," he said, drawing the word out. "You are telling me that I have to choose between our marriage and our partnership at work."

Leno paused. Hearing it her head was one thing. Hearing it out loud was different. Then she nodded.

"Yes. Yes. That is exactly what I'm saying."

Wolfram lifted his head and looked at Nick, then Lena. He elevated his frame carefully, sidled to the sofa and lay down at Lena's feet.

"Hey," Nick complained, "No taking sides."

"Nick. Choose."

"What if I don't?"

Lena pulled out another plane ticket.

"Then I am getting on a plane back to Geneva tonight. I have been offered a job there. I will take it. Unless you choose."

"One or the other."

"Yes."

"Marriage or work."

"Yes."

Nick closed his eyes.

"If I have to choose—"

Lena went to him, knelt by the chair, and took his hands.

"Please."

Nick looked into her eyes and said:

"I choose work."

Lena didn't move for a moment, as if she could not comprehend what he said. The she pushed away from him and stood.

"Work?"

Nick nodded.

"I choose work."

Lena could not speak for a moment.

"Over our marriage?"

Nick nodded.

"Yes."

"After you pleaded with me, begged me to get back together, told me you loved me, couldn't live without me."

"All true. I would prefer both. But if I have to choose, I choose work."

Lena stumbled back to the sofa and collapsed on it, unable to speak. How was it possible she had never imagined this?

Everything became clear now. She had asked him once if he had married her so she would be his partner, and basically he had said yes. She had not believed him at the time, but of course it was true. Her whole life revolved and settled in a configuration she had never expected. Nick was her partner. That was his vision. And always had been.

"Okay. Okay. If that's the way you want it," she said at last.

Nick slipped off the chair, arms around her.

"It's for the best," he said. "This is who we are. It's what we do. It's what you do, what you have always done, for others, and for me."

Lena pushed away and glared at him.

"I can't believe you are choosing whales over me."

"In a way, I'm choosing you over you."

Lena put her hands to her head.

"What does that mean?"

Nick took her hands.

"On average how many hours a day do you spend at work?"

"I have no idea."

"I do. You have always put in twelve-hour days. In the last few months, it has been more like fourteen or sixteen. Some nights lately you don't come home at all."

"It's just work. You can't think..."

"I don't. But let's say you work just twelve hours a day. You sleep six. An hour at the gym. An hour for food or errands. That leaves four hours a day for us. So my choice is twelve or four."

Lena shook her head.

"Time is not a marriage."

Nick smiled.

"Marriage is Imaginary."

Lena shut her eyes. When she opened them she knew the world would not be the same. There was sadness in that, and deep down, relief, and deeper still and rising, grief.

She finally opened her eyes and looked at Nick. He was watching her, smiling. He was actually smiling. But she read his smile, or thought she did, and knew he was feeling the same. They had crossed a line.

"Okay," she said, "When we have some time, I'll look around for a place. You can stay here, near the lake."

"No," he said firmly. "This is your home. I'll move out."

Lena was too much in shock to argue.

"Fine," she said.

Nick sat next to her on the sofa, not touching.

"I can't believe this," Lena said in a whisper. "I feel like just we decided to get divorced again."

"We don't have to. We are."

She turned to look at him.

"Are you sure?" she asked.

"I am," he said.

She leaned against him then. His arms looped around her and held her for a moment. She looked up at him, then slid away.

"So. Let's get to work."

Depth and Breadth and Height

Minnesota Governor (and former mayor of Minneapolis) Monica Ryland stepped to the podium to announce the opening of the new Crustacean exhibit at the Minnesota Zoo. The crowd was small, maybe 500 or so. But she noted the presence of more than one national media outlet, those who had covered the original Lobstergate, as it was now widely called. The publicity from that one episode had given her national prominence, and a helping hand from the Mayor's Mansion to the Governor's Mansion. Now there were rumors the President would ask her to join the cabinet, possibly as Secretary of the Interior. But she liked her job and planned to stay for a while.

After her typically brief speech, the Governor thanked Nick for the initial donation to fund the new exhibit, and then commended representatives of the other major donors, some of the largest corporations in the state, including several of the grocery chains who had 'donated' the lobsters initially.

The Governor resisted the temptation to glance at Lena, who was also sitting on the platform, to see her reaction. She knew Lena well from her time as Mayor. She had also come to know Nick, both from the adventures that had occasionally reached the Mayor's desk, and the due diligence prior to suggesting (through the Attorney General's office) his release from psychiatric confinement.

Nick stood and waved, but declined to speak. One by one, the Governor introduced the members of the Board of Trustees of The Sancho Foundation. She then invited Lena to step forward and announced that Lena would be joining Nick as co-executive director.

Lena glanced a moment toward Nick, then stepped to the microphone.

"We are not here to celebrate lobsters, or zoos, or ourselves for being enlightened enough to celebrate lobsters or zoos. We are here to celebrate the fact that our relationship to the world is a choice, one that we all make every day. That choice matters. Thank you for making this choice with us. But there are more to come. I hope we can make those together, as well."

*　　*　　*

After the speeches, Nick wanted to spend some time at the exhibit, so the group had agreed to split up, then meet back at the parking lot.

The Minnesota Zoo is almost an island, surrounded by lakes in each direction. A vaguely circular path wanders around the 'shoreline'. Nick stayed to commune with his lobsters. Alice and Ralph borrowed Wolfram and Sancho and headed for the southern circuit. Oscar, Sharon, and Lena wandered north for a while, until Lena took a seat on a bench in front of the moose enclosure.

Lena was fond of moose. They were the elephants of the new world.

Calm.

Stately.

Intelligent.

Calm.

She found them relaxing. The wild moose population in Minnesota was declining rapidly, she had heard. Calm was an endangered species thereabouts.

The weather had finally turned, dropping into the twenties during the day, and teens overnight. That was Lena's annual cue to switch from coffee to tea, and she held a paper cup in her hands. Lena sometimes indulged in a yerba mate, or a jasmine-infused white tea. But in general she preferred and Irish breakfast team or Constant Comment, unsweetened, with a splash and a half of milk. Soothing tea. Comfort tea. Normal tea. She couldn't identify the tea she was currently drinking; it was whatever the vendor sold. But on this chilly day it was fine.

Sharon shifted uncomfortably on the hard bench.

"He really said that?" Sharon asked.

"He did," Lena said.

"Nick said he would rather work with you than be married to you?"

"He did. I couldn't believe it. But he did."

Sharon paused.

"You're sure?" she asked again.

"There was no possibility of misinterpretation. When I got your message at the airport, I was furious. Then somewhere over Greenland, I had this moment of clarity. It shocked me. But I knew what I had to do. Or what I had to ask him to do. So when I got home, I confronted him. And I said you have to choose: marriage partner or work partner. And he chose work."

"He didn't."

"He did. And my moment of clarity became very obscure."

Sharon pretended to sip her tea. She liked tea, but was uncomfortable with the connotations. She would never have survived in a Jane Austen novel. Mr. Darcy would have fled in horror. The thought made her laugh, which made Lena look up.

"What?" Lena asked.

Sharon shook her head.

"Something completely different," she said.

"That describes every day of my life."

"Some people would think that's a good thing."

"The road of excess leads to the palace of wisdom."

"Did Nick say that?"

"No. He just lives it."

Sharon took another pretend sip.

'Who said that? Somebody said that."

"William Blake."

"No. Not him."

"It's a quote by William Blake from The Marriage of Heaven and Hell. Which is apt."

Sharon sighed.

"Susan Sarandon. That's who said it."

"Her too," Lena agreed.

She lifted the cup to her nostrils and inhaled until the orange spices transported her for a breath or two. Tea is my madeleine, she thought.

"He didn't mean it," Sharon said.

"William Blake?"

"No. I don't know. No. Nick didn't mean it."

"I think he did."

"He can't mean it. He is, pardon the expression, crazy about you."

Sharon paused. Being Lena's friend required a delicate balancing of perspectives.

"I have no doubt that Nick loves you," she concluded.

"Some of the Nicks love me," she said. "I'm just not sure it's a majority anymore."

"Maybe there's been a coup d'état."

Lena weighed her own multiplicity of perspectives.

"Or maybe he loves me but not enough. Not enough to give me what I need to love him back. And maybe I don't love him enough to put aside what I need and just love him as he is. What is need anyway? Do emotional needs really exist? Are we really that fragile? Am I?"

"Those were rhetorical questions, right?" Sharon said after a moment. She set the teacup down on the bench, watching it carefully to make sure it didn't tumble off the uneven surface. She didn't want it but she knew that if it spilled Lena would give her hers, which she also wouldn't want, but more so.

"Maybe," Sharon said, "this is a chance for both of you to set yourselves on a new path, a more stable sustainable path, a path that will allow you some peace, and maybe even a chance at happiness."

Lena looked closely at Sharon, then smiled.

"How are you and Oscar?"

Sharon raised an eyebrow.

"You're changing the subject."

Lena's smile expanded.

"Actually," she said, "I think you changed it. You started out talking about me, but you ended up talking about you."

Sharon turned away, since she didn't want Lena to see her smiling. In doing so, she saw Oscar, who was nearby talking with a balloon vendor, trading professional secrets no doubt.

"I know you're smiling," Lena said, smiling.

"Stop," Sharon said, grinning.

"Oh my," Lena said. "I ought not to have mentioned the subject."

"This will never do," Sharon concluded.

*   *   *

The crowds had dispersed, thinning out to a few families strolling through the exhibit. Nick sat on a bench, watching the children watch the lobsters.

The exhibit space was designed to look like an underground cave. A tunnel opened up in the center of the exhibit, allowing 360-degree viewing of four crustacean environments: Northern Atlantic, Caribbean, Pacific, and Australian. The Northern Atlantic area was in front of him, and the lobsters he had rescued were scattered throughout.

The lobsters, all Homarus Americanus, likely from Maine waters, crawled in slowest motion across the craggy chill surfaces of the enclosure. It was difficult to distinguish their dark green color from the grey rock underneath. Once in a while, one of them would propel backwards a few feet, a sudden explosion of motion then a return to stillness.

Governor Ryland gestured for her State Police escort to stay put, then approached Nick. He stood. She sat. He did too.

They did not speak for a while.

"I'm a little surprised," she said finally, "at your attitude toward zoos. You don't think even the good ones are exploiting animals?"

"Did you know that lobsters can be different colors: there are blue, orange, albino, even two-toned lobsters?"

"I didn't know that."

"Zoos aren't perfect, obviously," Nick explained, "even the best ones. The thing about saving anything is that it doesn't end there. You have to keep on saving them. And you have to save them for something. Life is just like that. The world is just like that."

"But they don't have a choice."

"I know. But we have to. That is the burden of action. We don't make those choices in a perfect world."

"True enough. Have to remember that, don't we?" she said.

Nick nodded.

"We do."

"You did a good thing. Odd but good."

"We did."

The Governor laughed.

"I didn't have a choice."

"No, I guess not."

"I would prefer not to be in that position again. Next time talk to me first."

Nick nodded.

"I promise."

The governor frowned.

"You asked to see me."

Nick nodded.

"I did. I haven't had the opportunity to thank you for getting me released from psychiatric care."

The Governor replied in her best pure-vowelled drawl.

"Since you helped get me elected, I thought I should do what I could. But honestly, it wasn't much. I just requested that the Attorney General's office review the case. They took it from there."

"Really? The Attorney General's Office. Well, whatever you did, I appreciate it."

Nick held out his hand. The Governor shook it.

"Is that it?" she asked.

Nick smiled.

"No. I'm sure you and especially your staff have some concerns about our new organization and attaching your name and reputation to it. I just wanted to assure you that we are legitimate in every way, and we are going to do some very good things for the State of Minnesota."

The Governor released his hand.

"I'm glad to hear that. I also have to say that if I had not heard your wife, if I can I call her that, your wife say the exact same thing, we would not be having this conversation."

Nick laughed.

"I'm not surprised," Nick said.

The Governor smiled then herself.

"Can I ask you a question? It is something I have wondered about."

"Sure?"

"You were an inpatient in that psychiatric facility for, what, six months?"

"About that."

"Why?"

"I was committed by a judge."

"I know. But you can't tell me you couldn't have talked your way out of there in thirty days at most. Why did you stay? Why did you wait for me to act?"

Nick coughed, then said:

"I think you and I are going to be good friends. No one else has asked me that."

"So what is the answer?"

Nick smiled.

"Time is Imaginary. And I am Imaginative."

"I see. Are you sure that somewhere deep inside, maybe some place you don't acknowledge, you didn't feel the slightest need for help yourself?"

"I know I need help. I can't save the world by myself."

Nick stood and walked up to the window in front of him. He pointed to the lobsters in the tank, careful not to smudge the surface of the glass.

"I released 144 lobsters in that pool at the mansion. About a hundred have survived. One hundred saved, out of millions each year."

The trooper nearby pointed to the imaginary watch on his wrist. The Governor nodded to the trooper and walked up to the window next to Nick. He didn't turn, but she could see his frowning face reflected in the window, lobsters in the tank seeming to crawl through his head. She frowned herself, then brightened.

"It's a beginning," the Governor said. "When I ran for mayor, I thought we were going to turn the city into a Utopia. No crime. Plenty of jobs. You learn to accept that you can only do what you can do in the time you have."

"Utopia," Nick repeated, and nodded. "It's a beginning."

*   *   *

Oscar stood by the railing of the caribou exhibit, directly opposite the moose, holding a raft of balloons. The balloons were different from the ones Oscar normally used at parties. His were standard rubber balloons. These were Mylar, shiny, strong (except around the edges where they were bonded together), but not malleable. These balloons were cut in the shapes of animals. Some of the balloons were the complete animal, but others were just the head. Oscar found these disconcerting. He preferred his own creations.

Sharon left Lena on the bench, walked up behind Oscar and kissed his neck. Normally they were about the same height, but in her heeled boots she was a couple inches taller.

"So you found a new herd," she said, nodding at the balloons.

"Change is good."

"What are you doing with those balloons?"

"The regular guy went on break," Oscar replied. "I volunteered to stand in for him."

Sharon put her arms around him.

"Can I have one?"

"No," Oscar said.

Sharon paused.

"I can't have one?"

"No."

She paused again.

"Why?"

Oscar looked around to see if anyone was watching. Lena was lost in her thoughts. Some of the caribou across the way looked intrigued. But he decided to risk it. He leaned in and whispered.

"I can't give you one," he said. "I have to give you all of them."

Sharon whispered back.

"Oh Oz."

And there it was: Oscar's nickname, perfect and simple, and obvious once discovered, as most perfect things were.

Oz.

Of course.

Oz offered the raft of balloons to Sharon. She hesitated, then bowed to the moment and the disconcerting destiny of her baffling affections.

*   *   *

"Alice, you're the greatest."

"Don't start with me, Ralph."

Ralph and Alice strolled along the broad path circling the various outdoor exhibits. The southern route led past the bears and the tigers, and they were just approaching the prairie dogs.

Alice carried Sancho nestled inside her coat, button eyes and grey ears exposed, while Ralph held Wolfram's leash. Ralph was large enough to make Wolfram appear almost normal size.

"We should get back," she continued. "We have our own zoo to mind."

"I know," Ralph said, stopping and turning toward her. "I know how important our work is to you. And to me. I am so proud of what we have done together. We have cared for our animals. We have educated the public. We have saved lives."

Alice waited, then said:

"But?"

Ralph couldn't help laughing.

"It's hard to have a serious conversation with a woman who has a puppet in her cleavage."

Alice glanced down.

"There's plenty of room."

"Don't I know it."

Alice walked up to the railing. The domes of the prairie dog dens dotted the enclosure like a miniature moonscape. But there were no dogs to be seen; they were all sensibly indoors.

"You know what really worries me?" she said.

Ralph loomed beside her, blocking the wind. Wolfram looped around the other side of her, and settled in for a nap.

"What?"

She looked up. Thin clouds diffused the sunlight, which formed a blurry halo around Ralph's head. But she was used to the sight and didn't remark on it. Some things don't need to be said.

"I'm starting," she said, "to get excited about this."

"I know."

Alice leaned back against the railing, her head just topping the highest bar.

"Things are good," she said finally. "Is this really the right path for us, at this point in our lives?"

"Nick wants our help."

"I know."

"He trusts us."

"I know! I love him. You know I do. I am even starting to enjoy him."

Ralph leaned back against the railing as well, then stood straight. Leaning for him was sometimes a perilous exercise. The world wasn't built for someone his size. It was something he shared with Wolfram. And in a way, Alice. And in another, Nick.

"But you don't trust him," he completed.

"I trust his heart. But not his head."

Ralph raised his arms and crossed them, and the shadow seemed to swoop in over them, as if an eagle had escaped its cage. No wonder the prairie dogs were hiding. Even Wolfram woke at the motion.

"Maybe, he doesn't either," Ralph said. "Maybe that's why he needs us."

"Maybe," Alice echoed. "But whales? I don't get whales in Minnesota."

"I don't either. But."

"I know. It's Nick."

"Maybe he's crazy, or maybe he knows what he's doing. Probably both."

She pulled Sancho out of his warm enclosure.

"Tell us what you know!" she pleaded. Sancho's glittering eyes were gay.

They turned and walked in silence towards the wild horses.

*   *   *

Lena was alone standing by her car when Nick arrived. Alice and Ralph had taken the rest of the group back to town in the shelter van. Nick had wanted to rent a limo for the occasion, but they weren't sure Wolfram would fit.

"Have you looked for a new place to live yet?" Lena asked.

"Yes."

Lena had not expected that answer.

"Oh. I was thinking maybe that we could go looking together. I don't have anything planned this afternoon."

Nick was silent.

"Have you found a place?" Lena asked.

"Yes."

Another unexpected answer.

"Where?"

Nick waved vaguely.

"The movers will have picked things up by now. I thought it would be easier this way."

Calm.

Nonchalant.

Cold.

This was a strange new Nick, Lena thought. One more to add to the pantheon.

*   *   *

Briefcase in hand, listening to nothing, Lena sat on her stoop.

He was not there.

He would not be there.

Why was she sitting there?

There was nothing to listen to.

Nothing to listen for.

Even the sparrows were silent.

The bushes next to her still had a covering of snow that the steady wind had not blown away. Maybe the snow provided some protection. The wind chill was the real danger now.

Lena imagined them in the dark, feathers fluffed out against the cold. She worried about them, so small and frail. But she figured they were fine, their down probably warmer than hers. Every year, they survived whatever came their way. How? Lena did not know. Nick would know. She would have to remember to ask him. Next time she saw him. Or maybe, they were gone too, gone with Nick to wherever he had gone. The movers had taken them, taken all the life. And the silence was not silence really. It was the sound of being alone.

Maybe this was now the soundtrack to her life.

Lena stood, fished her keys from her briefcase, grateful for even the noise of rummage and clink, and opened the door.

The lights were off.

She let her briefcase slide to the floor, dropped her keys, heard the loud clunk as they hit the tiled floor.

She turned on the lights.

The ceramic dish was gone. And black lacquer table she inherited from her mother. And the umbrella stand and the coat rack.

She looked into the living room. Then the kitchen. Then the bedroom. Everything was gone. Even the washer and dryer.

Lena stood for a moment in silence. Then she laughed, a brief burst that cut itself short.

He said he was moving out.

It hadn't occurred to her that he would take everything with him.

She floated more than sank to the floor, gazed around, unable to focus. But then, there was nothing to focus on but bare walls.

She closed her eyes to the tears. They came anyway. She had asked for this moment years before, when she made the decision to file for divorce. But it hurt more this time. Maybe because it was his choice. Or maybe the years had dimmed the recollection. Imagination in reverse is memory.

Then it had never really felt like he was gone. But now the emptiness was different. Absolute. There was no sense left of him, of them, even of her. Just empty space.

She laughed abruptly once more and stood. Then she noticed an envelope taped to the front door. She opened it (it was not sealed) and read:

Lena,

Dante wrote of L'amor che move il sole e l'altre stele. I know my love cannot bridge the space between us or reclaim the years we have lost. But I also know that time and space have no claim on the love that I feel, always and everywhere, for you.

Nick

PS—Sancho misses you.

Lena folded the letter and inserted it back in the envelope. Then she opened it again, read it again, then refolded the letter the opposite way, as a charm or spell or prayer, and once more placed it carefully in the envelope.

By Sun and Candle-Light

When the elevator stops on the forty-fifth floor of the Wells Fargo Building in downtown Minneapolis, Lena puts out her hand to hold the door. After a moment, an alarm blares. She steps out, releasing, and the door shuts behind her. Shifting her load, she walks steadily down the empty corridor.

At the end of the hallway, she stops and performs her ritual invocation, running her fingers across the raised letters of the sign, and then again, backwards. She opens the door, walks into her office.

A man is sitting in one of the side chairs, dressed all in white.

"Either you're not imaginary or I'm now delusional too," she says.

"Actually, those are not exclusive," Leonard responds.

She sighs.

"You're definitely Nick's student."

"I'm trying."

"Where is he?"

"I never know how to answer that question."

Lena eyes narrow slightly and she returns to the hallway, notices the newly installed sign for The Sancho Foundation, pulls open one of the double doors, enters, and almost trips over a black lacquer table.

Her table.

Lena looks around the space. Her dining room is nearby, the table set for two. Her living room is set up in the southwest corner, near the channel that leads to the Imaginary Cedar Lake. The furniture from her den, including her bookcases and all her books, are settled along the eastern shore, with a reading nook sheltered by some probably fake Norway pines. Even the washer and dryer stand in the far section near the waterfall. Her bedroom set floats on the nearest of the islands, which have apparently arrived from backorder. Nick is in bed, dressed in full blue pinstripe regalia, reading a book.

Lena lets her briefcase slide to the floor near her umbrella stand, drops her keys in her ceramic dish on her black lacquer table, then tosses her coat onto her wooden coat rack.

It misses.

She laughs.

Nick does not look up.

"So it occurred to me, as the deeply compassionate being that I am, that since we're now going to be working together twelve or fifteen or twenty or even twenty-four hours a day, you should be as comfortable as possible."

"Very thoughtful."

"The happiness of others is itself my satisfaction; I do not expect another recompense," he reads aloud. The sound echoes strangely in the open space, as if the dimensions are far larger than they seem. Or Nick has added sound effects.

Lena meanders around the shoreline, which gives her time to sort through the events of the last few months, and envision the next few minutes. As usual, she wonders how far ahead Nick has foreseen the events, and what is left to be discovered.

She arrives at the spot closest to the island, sits on the bench, and places her hand on Wolfram's frame. He rises, slowly crosses to the island, and settles in by Nick. His eyes gleam like water.

"Tell me why," she says.

Lena crosses her arms and waits. Nick closes the book, lays it on a large rock beside the bed. He spreads his arms.

"I can't imagine my life without you," he says, "so I have to Imagine it with you."

Lena kneels down by the water's edge and, seeing her reflection in the calm, shiny surface, dips her right hand through the image. She lifts the water up in her palm, then casts the glittering droplets at Nick.

"Tell me why," she says again.

"L'amor che move il sole e l'altre stele."

She waits at the edge. The waterfall rushes down, flowing across and into the lake, white noise softening other sounds in the space. She slips off her shoes, steps in the water, finds it surprisingly warm.

"Oh, wait, wait," Nick says.

He stands and waves his hand. A holographic rainbow appears over the surface. Lena takes three quick watery steps, then one more up onto the island, which rocks slightly. The surface under her feet is slightly yielding, grainy, more a skin than a floor.

She slips both hands around his neck, pauses, pulls him forward, kisses him.

"Tell me why," she says a final time.

He lifts Sancho into the air and slips inside. His eyes glow with vision. Wolfram curls around her feet as Sancho takes her damp hand between his soft fuzzy paws.

"On this island, there is no time. No day. No night. No past. No future. There isn't even any Now. There is only Always. If you are ever here, you are always here."

And then she has a vision of her own. And with that vision comes a certainty that the choice she must make has already been made, and that he knows it, has known it, and that it is the same for him. The elemental forces have aligned. A word of resistance would alter their course. But no resistance is possible or even at that moment conceivable for either of them.

She pulls Sancho to her.

"Then I won't say good-bye."

The Ends of Being

Imagination is a keyhole.
You can peer through it.
Or you can unlock the door.
Imagine.

Acknowledgements

Many thanks to the generous and talented people who have helped with this book, including Liv Blumer, Izzy Ballard, Amanda Larson, and the good folks at Unbridled Books, who originally published *The Marriage of True Minds*.

Finally, this story would not have been written if not for the inspiration and encouragement of my aunt, Margaret Norris. The book is dedicated to her memory.

About the Author

Stephen Evans is a playwright and the author of *The Marriage of True Minds* and *A Transcendental Journey*.